BLAKE

AN EIDOLON BLACK OPS NOVEL: BOOK 2

MADDIE WADE

INTRODUCTION

Blake
An Eidolon Ghost Ops Novel: Book 2
Calvin Blake and Grace Paxton

Blake
An Eidolon Ghost Ops Novel: Book 2

Calvin Blake and Grace Paxton

Published by Maddie Wade
Copyright © July 2019 Maddie Wade

Cover: Envy Designs
Editing: https://www.blackoediting.com
Formatting: https://www.blackopalediting.com

COPYRIGHT

ACKNOWLEDGMENTS

As always there are so many amazing people who helped bring this book to life. My wonderful beta team, Greta and Deanna and you read my books in such a rough draft and are always so encouraging and supportive. You kick my ass when I need it and don't sugar coat shit. I love you for that. Your feedback is so critical to a good book and I hope I do you proud.

My editing and proofing team—Linda and Pam. Thank you for making my rough opal shine.

Thank you to my fabulous reader group Maddie's Minxes, your continued support means the world to me, you are all so much more than people who read my books, to me, you are friends. You keep me going and help me out of a funk when I have no idea which way is up. Tracey, Carolyn, Kellie, Maria, Greta, Deanna, Becky, Rihaneh and Linda L for making the group such a friendly and welcoming place to be.

My ARC Team for not keeping me on edge too long while I wait for feedback.

A big thank you to all the bloggers, authors, and friends who promote my books and help others to find my books. Without you I would not be able to do this.

Lastly and most importantly thank you to my readers who have embraced me wholeheartedly and shown a love for the stories in my head. To hear you say that you see my characters as 'family' makes me so humble and proud. I hope you enjoy this new series as much as I do.

A huge thank you to Sensei Dave Flaherty MBE for your help with the fight scene. You are a gentleman, a fabulous role model, and advocate for Jujitsu and all the youth coming through.

This book is dedicated to Military Veterans who fought and still fight every day for us. You are all heroes without you we would not have the freedom we do or know the safety we take for granted every day. Thank you.

PROLOGUE

THREE YEARS Ago

Blake slammed his hand down on the desk, anger making his fist shake as he tried to control it. He glared at the woman across from him who had given the order that had nearly got his principal killed. "This was a fucking shit show, and you know it. I should never have been moved at such late notice and swapped out for some fucking green kid." Blake paced then, his hands threading through his short blonde hair in frustration at the situation.

The woman opposite looked at him calmly, barely a hair out of place, her suit wrinkle free as if she was ready for church. Nothing like a woman who had nearly gotten the Queen murdered with her incompetence. "I understand you're upset."

Blake spun on his heel to face her. "Upset? Are you fucking with me right now? I'm fucking livid. Whose idea was it to swap me out for that FNG?"

"I am not aware what FNG means," replied Commander Helen Pope with a dangerous edge to her tone that made Blake stop.

Blake leaned into the desk making the woman stand and face him, not backing down an inch. "It means fucking new guy!"

"Yes, well, to answer your question it was not my idea. The order came directly from the Deputy Commissioner." She sighed and sat back in her chair. "Listen, Blake, you're a good officer, the best we have. So no, I don't know what's going on, but I intend to find out." She looked at him sternly then. "But if you raise your voice to me again, I'll have you demoted back down to Police Constable before you can even blink."

Her tone made Blake sit down opposite her, his anger at her leaving him and his next words were sincere. "Fine. I apologise."

He had a lot of respect for Helen Pope. She had worked her way up the ladder in a very male dominated job. Not only had she done well for herself, but she had done a lot of good within the police force and especially with Protection Command.

"Is she okay?" he asked knowing that she may not tell him.

Blake took his job as PPO very seriously. These people relied on him to keep them safe while they went about their jobs and lives. The only way to do that was to build a rapport with them, gain some trust, and he had done that. Now the new Deputy Commissioner had come in and decided that the PPOs would work on a rota system. Each officer would take turns protecting different people.

"Yes. She is resting comfortably in her suite at Balmoral. It wasn't your fault, Blake. This rests with me."

"No, it doesn't and you and I both know it. This new system is dangerous and it's going to get someone killed." He took in a breath. "I'm not sure I can watch that happen." He leaned back in his chair; his hands crossed in front of him as he delivered the words.

"What are you saying, Blake?" Commander Pope asked directly.

"That I'm tendering my resignation with immediate effect."

He watched as a flicker of emotion flew across the Commander's face. She was an attractive woman, and at fifty was still in prime fitness. She had even been known to take one of her men down to the mat in practice. She wore her greyish blonde hair pinned back in a tight bun at the back of her neck and never gave in to female fripperies like make-up. She was a hardass, but he respected her and enjoyed working for her, but he couldn't work under the new commissioner and the new guidelines which all but guaranteed he would be attending a state funeral at some point.

"That seems rather hasty," she said slowly her hands resting on the desk, her fingers peaked.

"It might be, but I've given it careful consideration. I can't in good conscience do this job if I feel I'm compromising the safety of those around me, most especially the principal. I either do this properly or not at all."

Pope nodded. "I see. We'll be very sorry to lose you, Blake. It goes without saying that your commitment and drive on the force will be sorely missed. That said, I do understand and if you ever change your mind, you know where I am."

"Thank you, Commander, it has been an honour to serve under you," he said with genuine feeling.

"I'll have your papers drawn up, but I need your shield and firearm."

Blake produced both and with only the slightest feeling of reverence placed them down on her desk. He raised his hand as she stood and saluted her which she returned. "Ma'am," He dropped his hand and turned to leave.

"Blake."

He turned back to her. "Yes, Ma'am?"

"Do you know what you will do now?"

He shook his head. "Not a clue," he said with a grin that had turned many a woman to mush.

She nodded but seemed unaffected by his charm. She went to her desk and jotted down a number on a piece of paper and handed it to him. "Give this guy a call. He's putting together a team, and I have a feeling you would be a good fit. He's a bit of a stubborn hardass but a good man with good morals. Tell him I sent you."

"Thank you, Ma'am," Blake replied and looked down at the card in his hand.

In her elegant, feminine handwriting she had written *Jack Granger* 07892 778 923.

Blake left the Scotland Yard building for the final time and shoved the card in the back pocket of his black trousers. He would give him a call, maybe. But first, he wanted to check for himself that the Monarch, Queen Lydia II, was in fact okay.

Taking his phone from his pocket, he dialled the number he knew by heart and waited.

"Hello?"

"It's me. Is she okay?" he asked not beating around the bush.

"Yes, she will be. She's a bit shaken, but the Duke is on his way home and should be here in due course."

"Good. Listen, tell her to take care and if you need anything just ask."

"I'll tell her," the man on the other end of the phone said.

Blake hung up and sighed. He felt like he was abandoning a good woman and her family, leaving them to fend for themselves, but he couldn't be part of cost-cutting that put people in danger. Pulling at the tie around his neck he headed to the tube. He needed a week off, a willing woman, and a large bottle of Vodka. Then he would see what his future held.

CHAPTER ONE

TODAY

The pounding of his feet was the only sound he could hear apart from the ones he associated with nature and he loved it. Blake had taken to having his morning run at five am since he had settled in this beautiful part of the country.

The river Wye flowed beside him as he ran, the sound of birds singing in the trees. Just him and the ground in front of him as he ate up the miles. His muscles beginning the warm burn at the eighth mile, his breathing unaffected by the strenuous pace he kept up. His knee was another matter though, but he dismissed the pain.

This time allowed him to think, his mind was clear, no white noise from Liam or Gunner prattling on like old women. No barking orders from Jack, no woman screaming he hadn't called her. Blake had a lot on his mind, not least the fact that the last two missions they had gone on—not including the one with Alex and Evelyn—had been huge clusterfucks and resulted in at least one of the team injured every time.

The last one Mitch had just missed having his head taken off by a stray bullet that still couldn't be accounted for. The time before that, he himself had almost stepped on an IED. A fucking IED that had been set on a private piece of land in the Cotswolds for fuck sake. It was only by the sheer grace of God that Liam had spotted it and pulled him out of harm's way or he would have more than a torn ligament to worry about. He would have had bits of his body missing at best and would be dead at worst. Not something he wanted to think about.

Something was up. Jack and Alex were staying tight-lipped about it and he didn't fucking like that. They had always operated as an open team and he had liked that about them, but now closed-door discussions were going on and it made him feel vulnerable and Blake didn't like to feel vulnerable.

He was still on sick leave until he could prove to Jack and Waggs —the team medic—that his leg was up to scratch. That meeting was later today, and he was going to do everything he could to get back on the rota. He wanted answers and he wasn't going to get them doing physio in the gym. He was lost in thought, but he knew that for the last mile he'd had a tail and wondered what that was about.

She had been running behind him for a few minutes now and while Blake was a lot of things, an idiot wasn't one of them. Blake grinned at the image that popped into his head—tight lycra shorts and sports bra, luscious rich red hair pulled back into a ponytail, sexy curves bouncing as she ran. It made his dick twitch thinking about the controlled, smartass redhead being all sweaty after a run. Pulling to a sudden and deliberate halt he spun, allowing her to collide into him. Grabbing her upper arms to stop her from going over on her sexy derriere, the oomph that slid from her mouth as her tits collided with his chest was the hottest thing he had heard in months. And considering he'd left the bed of a sexy blonde this morning too exhausted to move let alone nag him for his number, that was saying a lot.

"Pax, what can I do for you?" he said running his eye suggestively over her fucking knockout body.

Her eyebrow raised at his blatant perusal, but her nipples hardened delightfully almost making him forget where they were and who she was. He let go abruptly and stepped back causing her to stumble forward an inch.

"What makes you think I want anything?" she asked tilting her head making the hair from her ponytail skim the porcelain perfection of her skin. He watched her raise her hands to her hips and followed the movement before mirroring it.

"So, you want me to believe you just happened to be out running at five-thirty in the morning on the same route as I was using?" he asked with a note of disbelief in his voice.

"Well aren't we Mr Conceited today. What's the matter, Blake, not fucked anyone yet today and it's making you grumpy?" Her voice held a touch of disdain and something else. Pique if he wasn't mistaken. Heat mottled the skin of her chest as her anger rose.

"Not conceited. Just know what I know." He moved an inch into her personal space, his head tilting down at her, a ghost of a grin on his face.

"Oh my God, you already fucked someone today! You are disgusting!"

"What's the matter, Pax?" He raised his hand and followed a droplet of sweat as it ran down her cheek and neck and then disappeared into the top of her sports bra. His finger just grazing the curve of her breast. He felt her shiver and knew it wasn't from the cold. "You still pissed I wouldn't fuck you in Monaco?"

He saw the second his crass comment broke the desire in her heavy-lidded hazel eyes.

"You jerk," she hissed stepping forward and shoving him back on his heel making him grin further. "As if I would let you anywhere near me."

They both knew she was lying. They had come very close to fucking on that mission, leftover adrenalin and an attraction that would burn hotter than the sun but also burn out. He had put the brakes on that one in an uncharacteristic move that still made him wonder if he had lost his mind.

Pax was fucking stunning in every way—tall, slender, perfect

English rose complexion, even though she was from California. Thick red hair he wanted to wrap his hand around as he fucked her from behind. Curves to die for, sexy curvy ass, beautiful tits he could get lost in, and a cool composure that made a man want to break through it. Made him want to find the soft middle and make it his.

Make it mine? No, that was wrong. He just wanted a taste, but he hadn't. She was Evelyn's friend and he didn't fuck over his friend's friends. No matter how often he dreamt of them together or jerked off to their image. Goading her was fun though.

He blatantly looked at her nipples. "You sure, sweetheart? Because your body is saying one thing and your sexy mouth another."

"You know what, just forget it," she said and turned to storm off, but he grabbed her arm and stopped her.

Blake knew he was acting like a dick. He had pushed it too far and that wasn't like him. He was a flirt, but he wasn't a dickhead like some men, and he didn't disrespect women and let go of her arm. "Listen, sweetheart, I'm sorry. I was a dick. Can we start over?"

She crossed her arms over her chest, and he fought the groan as the movement pushed more skin into view.

"Why are you such a dick to me?" She seemed to genuinely want to know.

"All that hair, those curves, and that attitude. It's like kryptonite to a man like me. I see it, I want it, but I don't hurt or screw around with people that might have to have my back one day. And that makes it hard for me to be around you. You have a mirror in your house?"

She frowned at him seeming perplexed. "Of course."

"Then you know what you look like. You have to know the effect you have on red-blooded men."

"Are you saying you're a dick to me because you want to fuck me and can't?"

"I'm saying I'm a dick for that, and definitely a dick for starting this conversation." He heard the sweet sound of her laugh. "That sounds good, Pax. You should do it more often instead of the cool, ice queen thing."

She immediately stopped at his words. "Ice Queens don't get burned," she replied softly, and it made him sad that she thought that way.

"How about we go and grab a coffee and you tell me why you were stalking me." He held up a hand as she began to deny it. "Don't lie or it will piss me off."

Pax looked him dead in the eye as if assessing him and deciding what to do. She seemed to decide it was worth a shot and nodded. "Fine. Know anywhere open at this time of the morning?" she asked as they walked back towards town.

"Yes, I know the perfect place." He winked, not able to resist flirting with her. *It's only flirting. What harm could that cause?*

A FEW MINUTES LATER, Blake led her up to the front door of his flat and stopped to insert the key.

"This is your place!" she stated rather than asked making him wonder what else she knew about him.

He turned to her, key still in the lock. "Worried you won't be able to keep your hands off me?" he asked with a grin.

Pax rolled her eyes and sighed making her chest heave in a very distracting way. "Child," she admonished as she waved him to get on with it.

She acted like she was unaffected by him, but he knew she wasn't. Blake knew for a fact that if he kissed her, she would go up in flames for him and that wasn't him being a conceited ass as she put it. That was, in fact, the chemistry between them. The chemistry that had been there from day one. It was how he knew it would burn hot and fast, and things that burned too hot either burned out quickly or consumed you. He didn't want either of those things to happen with Pax. Plus, he liked her. She was fun to flirt with, intelligent, and smart. He didn't want things to be awkward between them.

Pushing open the door for his flat, he threw his keys in a bowl that sat on a table by the door and walked straight to the coffee pot, flipping the switch and grabbing two cups down from the cupboard overhead. He saw Pax discreetly checking out his place and wondered what she thought of it. He turned as she ran her hands over the back of the sofa and the soft wool blanket that was draped there.

"This is not what I expected." She looked down her straight nose at him, her hazel eyes twinkling with delight and just a touch of mischief.

He swept his hand out to encompass the open plan living space. "Yeah, well, I have two sisters and a mother who love to decorate so blame them. I just paid the bill."

The kitchen was white gloss cabinets with a black tile floor and dark aubergine splashbacks. An island unit separated the kitchen from the living area. Pale wood covered the floor with two deep cream fabric couches covered in cushions of cream, purple, and damson sitting opposite each other. A black and glass coffee table sat in the middle with a natural wicker footstool beside it. The double floor-to-ceiling windows were bay in style and had a cushioned seat where he could sit and watch the world go by or just think. Heavy mushroom coloured curtains hung there held back by black hooks.

"I like it!" She walked around then let out a squeak when she almost tripped over something on the floor. Pax bent and picked it up, holding out the small, pink toy guitar for him, one perfectly arched brow raised. "I didn't know you played." A smile played at the edges of her lips.

"Oh yeah, I'm just waiting for a call from my music producer and then we're taking this thing global." He smirked as he took the guitar from her hand and played 'Twinkle, Twinkle Little Star' on it.

"Very impressive," she said nodding her head. "I can see how you will become a huge rock star with that talent."

He placed the guitar on the coffee table with a grin and walked back towards the kitchen to pour coffee into two mugs. "Coffee and one sugar, right?"

"Yes, please," she answered stepping towards him to take the coffee.

Blake moved to the couch and plopped down on the end while she sat in the one opposite him and gave her a cheeky grin. "So tell me why you were stalking me in the park this morning apart from the obvious of wanting to check out my form?"

"I need your help."

"I guessed that bit, Pax. But how exactly do you need my help and why me?"

Pax placed her coffee on the low table and leaned forward, giving him a perfect view of her cleavage which he really didn't need right now. Pulling his mind from the gutter he concentrated on her face and for the first time since he had met her, he saw a vulnerability that he'd always suspected was there, but she'd never lowered her guard enough to show him.

Blake waited, knowing that his silence would help her to open up and tell him what she needed. The room was silent as he watched her wrestle with whatever it was that was going on in that beautiful head of hers. He sipped his coffee and watched as she stood and paced to the window, looking out at the world that was starting to emerge and start the working day.

He kept his eyes off her long legs, and instead watched the curve of her neck as she dropped her head and then seemed to straighten, pulling herself together. Her body language suggested she had come to a decision. She glanced back at him and found his eyes. Hers were focused and determined—a look he liked on her just as much as the soft looks she gave her friends. He hoped to earn one of those himself one day.

"I need you to help me put my father behind bars."

CHAPTER TWO

GRACE PAXTON WATCHED as Blake's eyes flared wide for a second before he got control of himself and locked his reaction down tight. Slowly, he placed his mug on the table and walked towards her. She tried not to let her eyes trail down the perfect form of his body. Muscular and tall without being bulky, he prowled like a big cat; his movements controlled and powerful.

It made her breath hitch as she watched him. Blake was cover model handsome, golden blond hair, and sexy, almost electric blue eyes that always seemed to twinkle as if he had a hidden secret and would share it with you if you let him in. He was precisely Pax's type on paper and that was exactly why she couldn't let herself be drawn into his sphere.

She had dated her fair share of blond, blue-eyed hunks and every single one of them had let her down. Either in the bedroom, where their looks was all they had going for them, and she discovered the hard way they were 'two pump chumps' who were finished before she even got started, or they had commitment issues. Then, it wasn't her, it was them. So she had sworn off good looking men. She would find herself an average guy with a boring job who would worship her.

She almost laughed out loud at that, realising as Blake came to stand almost in front of her that she would eat a regular, average guy for breakfast and be bored within a month. Blake though, posed too much threat to her. Not physically. No, he would never lay a finger on a woman in anger. Blake loved women and she knew from the file and background check she had done that he was protective of his younger sister and his four-year-old niece.

No, Blake would break her heart if she let him in because he wanted to fuck and run, and she wanted a family one day. All his cheeky cocky attitude and his cute sweetness were dangerous though because it made her forget who he was, and that was a manwhore.

"I'm sorry, Pax. I must be losing my hearing because I thought you said you wanted to put your father in jail."

He was standing too close, the scent of manly sweat mixed with his deodorant making her head spin. Stepping around him and moving back to the couch and picking up her coffee she took a sip using it as a shield to hide how he made her feel. "Yes, that's what I said."

Blake leaned against the window frame and she saw him take the weight off his left knee and wondered what had happened. "Why?"

She dragged her eyes from his powerful legs up past his folded arms to his face which had just the smallest of frowns on it. "Because he's a criminal and he killed my best friend and now he's a threat to another child. I won't stand by and let him do it again."

Pax felt the familiar ache in her chest as she thought about Benny. He had been her best friend in school and later her first boyfriend. Then he was gone. Taken by the other man she adored— her father, her hero, and now her enemy.

"Okay, back up. Your dad killed your best friend and now he plans to kill again, and you want to stop him. Is that correct?"

"Yes, but it's complicated." He had no idea just how fucking complicated it was.

"I bet it fucking is." He raised an eyebrow which suggested he wanted more details.

Pax sighed. "My father is Robert Paxton. He owns Sana Pharmaceuticals. He and I are *estranged* shall we say."

"Go on," Blake said.

His full attention on her made her uncomfortable and Pax hated asking for help especially his. "You have to understand; I was a complete daddy's girl growing up. He was my hero. I'm an only child and he and my mother doted on me, gave me anything I wanted. I was naive and stupid."

"You were young and innocent and trusted your parents. No shame in that, Pax," he said sweetly.

She looked up at him and saw nothing but understanding in his eyes. Blake was a good guy despite his man slut ways and good looks, and that was the problem. It was easy to keep the simmering sexual tension at bay when the guy was an asshole but when he was sweet; yeah so much harder. "Yeah, maybe. Anyway to cut this long story short, when I was seventeen my best friend and high school boyfriend, Benny was diagnosed with a brain tumour. He went through rounds of chemo and radiation as the tumour was inoperable. My father offered him a trial of a new drug they had been developing for cancer patients and Benny jumped at it."

"I'm hearing something you're not saying here, Pax."

"The drug killed him. I know he was going to die anyway, but the side effects of the drug caused kidney failure which led to pressure on his heart. He died a horrible death, but my father covered it up, deleted all evidence of the drug trial, and paid his parents off. I confronted him about it, and we had a terrible fight." Pax looked up clearing her throat of the emotion that had come from nowhere. "Needless to say my father and I don't speak. I go back once a year for Thanksgiving for my mom, who has no idea or pretends not to know, and that is the extent of our relationship now."

"And why now? Why do you want him locked up now and not then?" Blake's tone wasn't judgemental, but more someone trying to understand.

"When I left, I said I wouldn't come after him because I loved him if he promised not to do it again." She gave a humourless laugh and shrugged. "Again, naive and honestly, I didn't have the skills or knowledge to bring a company or man of his magnitude down."

"Come on, Pax. Enough with the half-answers. If you want me to help, I need everything from you."

Blake moved to sit beside her. Pax couldn't help the feeling he meant more than just information. A shiver worked its way through her which he noticed as his eyes moved over her skin. "You're cold. Let me get you a hoodie." He stood abruptly and left the room.

Pax rose too and rubbed her arms. The sweat from the run had cooled and the cooler air in the flat made her feel cold.

Blake walked out of what she assumed was the bedroom with a dark blue hoodie in his hands and shoved it towards her. "Here take this."

The material was soft and worn and clearly a favourite of his. She murmured her thanks and slipped it over her head taking in his familiar scent and fighting the urge to bury her nose in it or rub her cheek in the soft fabric. She was tall but it fell to her thighs, leaving her looking half naked and slightly daft.

"Right, let's have the rest," he said pouring them both fresh coffees adding milk and sugar to hers without a reminder.

"My father is doing a trial on a very high profile child and I know for a fact that he doesn't have it going through the MHRA and the FDA turned it down based on the high number of negative side effects and their frequency."

"What drug?"

"It's called RXA 1 and it's used for patients with hypertrophic cardiomyopathy. It's used to make the thickened heart contract more, allowing the heart not to have to work so hard."

"Okay. I don't see an issue so far."

"RXA 1 is around half the price of other similar drugs to produce and get to market so it has huge profit margins. The scope to make billions is extraordinary."

"Yes, but that's part of drugs companies. They make money and we get what we need."

"Not when then the drug causes kidney and liver failure in over half its patients and the results are being fudged." She was disgusted and hardly able to believe what her father was willing to do to people to make money.

"Wow. So, I have two questions. One, how do you know all this because it certainly isn't in the public domain and two, who is the high profile child?"

Pax looked away knowing that this might be the killer. "I know because I have someone inside my father's company. It may have escaped your notice, but I'm not the same naive child that left my father's home. I have skills now and contacts, and when I got wind of this a few years ago, I contacted a friend in the USA who was happy to do some digging for me."

"And this friend," he said not sounding entirely happy with her response, "are they still providing information?"

"No. I lost contact about three months ago." That was also another worry she had to get answers too.

"I see. And the child?"

She took a deep breath knowing it was now or never. "It's Princess Louisa."

The room went silent as she watched a tiny nerve tick in Blake's cheek. The only sign that her words had any impact on him at all.

"Why me?" His voice had dropped to a frosty level that made her glad she had the hoodie on. He was not the sweet, flirty, sexy guy now. He was cold, controlled, and lethal and that was what she needed.

"Because you have an association with the Palace, know their ways. I plan to go undercover as a nanny and get as much information as I can. Time is tight and I need to start working this as soon as I can."

She didn't add that she had been receiving death threats. No need for him to know about that just yet, plus, she was sure it was a ploy. Her father was an ass, but he wouldn't hurt her.

He watched her then shook his head. "No. I'm sorry, Pax, I can't help you."

He moved towards the door and Pax followed, her heart sinking as she realised her last hope was fading and she would have to do this alone. Zenobi was spread out on jobs all over the world. The only reason Roz allowed her to work this was as the face of the Athena Art Gallery, she was in the office the most and had time.

Pax had skills, but she was not an operative like the others were. She had some training in hand to hand and weapons, but she wasn't like Mustique or Bebe. Her skill lay in her organisation and information capabilities. She made sure the girls had what they needed to run a successful op including contacts, safe houses, and equipment. She handled the contingencies, the travel, she was instrumental in the success of things, and she could handle some undercover work but not deep cover like Siren or Lili.

Moving slowly to the door she stopped, and made him look at her, locking her disappointment down tight so he could never see how much his saying no had cost her. "I thought more of you than that, Blake. I saw a good man, a man that cared under all that bravado. I guess I was wrong. I won't make that mistake again." She stepped into the hall stopping suddenly to whip the hoodie over her head and throw it at him. "Goodbye, Blake."

As she walked away, and knowing he was watching, she put extra sway into her hips. He wouldn't know how much it hurt to ask for help when that was something she never did, and have it kicked back in her face. That was another lesson she learned this morning—not to ask anyone for anything. Then she never had to say thank you or be disappointed when the answer was no.

CHAPTER THREE

BLAKE LEANED against the door frame with his arms crossed over his chest watching as Pax proudly walked away. He could see she was trying to hide the disappointment he knew she felt at his refusal to help her. He waited until she was out of sight and then moved inside, the hoodie hanging from his hand. He slammed the door and tried to figure out exactly what it was he was feeling.

His chest felt heavy and his gut churned—he felt suffocated and he didn't like it one bit because he realised it was guilt. He felt guilty for not helping her. But he couldn't go back into that world. A world where lies were the norm and people would stab their own brother to get ahead. He had been reminded of it working Evelyn's case and he didn't want to get any closer to the royal family than he had to.

It had been the only stipulation he'd had when he'd signed on with Jack and Eidolon and discovered the Palace would be a big contract for them. He didn't directly have anything to do with that side of Eidolon. Nobody knew why and nobody could ever know. It would destroy so many lives and for nothing. That part of his life was over, and he wouldn't go back.

He couldn't help the niggle in the back of his head that told him he was making a big mistake though. Pax didn't seem the type to ask for help and yet she had. Not from her friends but from him. It made no sense to him and that was another reason he wouldn't get involved —she was hiding something from him. That both pissed him off and intrigued him equally.

He moved towards his bedroom, which unlike the rest of the flat was completely his design and style. Dark grey walls, pale distressed wood floor, black bedding, and black and white prints on the wall with an orange chair in the corner near the window. It suited him. Masculine, clean, and understated.

Tossing the hoodie in his hand on the bed, he shed his shorts and t-shirt and threw them in the general direction of the laundry basket as he stepped into the glass shower stall in his en-suite and turned the dial on the shower. The cold spray hit him like needles of ice as he waited for it to heat a little, enjoying the cooling water on his heated skin.

It was going to be another hot day and he knew that he would be back in here by nightfall. Quickly he squeezed some shower gel into his hand and washed his body and hair trying to ignore his hard cock, but his mind kept skipping back to Pax in that damn running outfit. The image of her hot and sweaty filled his mind, her long thick hair wrapped around his fist as he fucked her mouth while he watched her swallow his length.

A droplet of pre-cum on the head of his cock had him taking it in his hand and jerking off. He felt the tingle of his impending climax along the base of his spine before it moved up his balls and he released all over his hand in a powerful orgasm that had him panting way more than his morning run had.

Blake cleaned off and feeling slightly less frustrated, but definitely more like an asshole, he wrapped a towel around his waist and moved to the kitchen to grab a fresh coffee. It was his third already this morning—none of which he'd actually managed to finish. Taking it back to his room, he sat down on the end of the bed to get dressed—pulling on jeans and white polo shirt before adding socks and cool grey and blue retro Adidas trainers.

Standing, he snagged his wallet off the dresser and slid it into his back pocket, tucking his phone into the front one, and a knife onto the sheath on his leg. Lifting the mug he downed the almost too hot coffee, nearly burning his throat in the process and glanced at the hoodie on his bed.

Without thinking, he picked it up and brought it to his face burying his nose in it and inhaling like some testosterone filled fifteen-year-old with a crush, not a grown man who could get pussy whenever he wanted it.

The scent was a mixture of his deodorant and something that was all Pax. He had recognised the smell as hers straight away. It was sweet and delicate, slightly citrus but with floral hints to it. The scents mingled together made his stomach tighten and his dick harden. He liked the smell of her on his clothes and a strange part of him wished she had kept the top. He liked the idea of her wearing his clothes.

Coming to his senses he tossed the top in the laundry and made his way to the door ignoring the half-empty mugs on the coffee table. He had shit to do today and answers to find. He didn't have time to spend thinking about Pax and her problems, or her sweet body. He needed to know what was going on with his team.

ARRIVING at Eidolon he used his ID code to get past the new gatehouse Jack had added a few weeks ago. It was an added measure of security for the grounds and the people inside. Frank Drake was the new guard on the gate and was a highly decorated former soldier in the US military. He was also their friend Zack Cunningham's father in law. Frank and his wife had followed their only daughter to the UK when she'd married Zack, but Frank wasn't enjoying retirement and wanted a little action. Blake wasn't convinced this was it, but he was a good guy.

"Hey, Frank, another hot one today."

"Gonna be a scorcher," he said.

Blake could tell by his grin that he was happy to be useful again. "Make sure you get Jack to sort you out a fan or something."

"Boy, I've spent many a day in the desert. I don't need no fan, and I certainly don't need no coddling."

"Yes, sir." Blake grinned back at Frank and offered him a quick salute.

Blake drove through the gate and around the back where the team parked. Blake parked his Audi A8 Sportback in the almost full space and looked over his teammate's cars. Alex had a BMW M5 which perfectly suited him, Reid a Harley, Jack drove a 4 litre Range Rover that looked like it could run over all their cars without moving from second gear, while Decker had opted for the Mercedes E-class. Finally there was Mitch's Ford Ranger truck that needed to be fucking cleaned.

He stepped out and moved to the rear entrance stepping through using his thumbprint and then waiting for the biometric scanner to let him into the central hub of the compound. And that was what it was, with a gym, a training room, weapons and shooting area, three conference rooms, and a barracks-style bunk room with kitchen, showers, and chill out area for when they had short periods of down-time but needed to be at the base.

He walked down the hallway past the conference rooms and through another set of secure doors passing the fully equipped medical room complete with surgical table, and towards Jack and Alex's offices. Behind their office space were the weapons rooms and even a tiny panic room for any high-profile clients to use if needed.

He rapped on the door and waited for Jack to call him in. He was a few minutes early, but Jack expected that. He wouldn't tolerate his men being late for anything, it showed tardiness and he wouldn't excuse it.

"Come in," Jack called, and Blake pushed down the handle and moved into the room closing the door behind him.

"You wanted to see me?"

Blake looked around the office. It was a clean space with no windows and only a few certificates on the wall. A large desk and two chairs on his side and Jack had a black leather office chair that reclined. Jack spent a ridiculous amount of time at work so that made sense to Blake. A large side unit housed a permanently full coffee pot and a stack of mugs.

"Yes, Blake, take a seat," he said indicating the chair. Jack sat back, his hands lose in his lap, posture relaxed as he studied Blake for a second. Blake got the distinct impression Jack was looking for something, only he didn't know what it was.

"How's the leg?"

"Good. I have another round of physiotherapy later and I'm hoping Waggs will sign me off so I can get back to work."

Jack nodded his blue eyes piercing. "That's excellent news." Jack leaned forward suddenly, his arms leaning on the empty desk, fingers linked.

"Yeah. I hate being injured."

"Don't we all. What about the others?"

At his question, Blake got the feeling in his gut that perhaps he was missing something. "They seem fine." He crossed his foot over his opposite knee and placed his hands on his belly as he leaned back in his chair. "You going to tell me what's really going on or are we going to play cat and mouse?"

Jack chuckled but there was no humour in it, just a hint of exhaustion. "We have a mission coming up. It's dangerous and there are a lot of moving parts that could go wrong. It's one I need to handle personally but I need someone here to have Alex's back while I'm gone," Jack said thoughtfully.

"Why me?"

"Because you're the only one I trust right now that can do the job apart from Alex."

Shit Blake knew it was bad, but he didn't think it was this bad.

"What is going on, Jack?" Blake was annoyed with everyone giving him partial answers today—first Pax and now Jack.

"We have reason to believe there's a traitor inside Eidolon."

"*Bullshit.* Not one of these guys would sell out." Blake stood, angry now and moved around the room needing to pace.

"I thought that too, but there have been a number of mission failures and leaks that can only have come from inside. I've narrowed it down, but I don't want to say anything until I know for sure who it is and their reason for betraying us."

"Fuck. This is shitty fucking bollocks." Blake felt the ache in his knee from pushing himself too hard this morning as he paced.

"Yes, it is, but I need you to keep a lid on it. We can't have the men distrusting each other and pulling this team into the grave. It's bad enough Alex and I feel that way."

"Alex knows?"

"Yes. Him and Gunner. Gunner overheard a phone conversation I had with Alex when they were in Monaco. Alex noticed it first on the case with Evelyn. There's no way Michaela Kirk should have known where to find him in Paris. That's classified information. Only members of the team know we did that job."

"I did wonder at the time but honestly, I forgot about it. So you going to tell me what you want me to do?"

"Just keep vigilant. Act normal and keep an eye on these three men."

Jack handed Blake a sheet of paper containing three of his teammate's names. He looked up suddenly with shock on his face. "No fucking way."

"I know. It's an absolute clusterfuck to even think it let alone say it, but we've narrowed it down to those three. Everyone else checks out, and believe me, we checked thoroughly. I know what laundry tablets you use, what porn you like, how much you spend on clothes... fucking everything. If there's one thing my brother does well it's cyber snooping."

He was right. Will was not only a hacker but a gifted inventor of all things technical. He was the silent partner in Eidolon and therefore wasn't around much, but he was a good guy and always the go-to for this sort of thing. Lopez was their NSA analyst and he was good on computers and with data, but Will was the dog's bollocks.

"Has Decker given you a profile?" Blake asked not seeing his name on the list.

Jack shook his head. "No, as I said it is only me, Alex, Gunner, and now you at the moment. I want to try and keep this on the down low. It isn't exactly good for business or moral."

"Yeah, understandable. So, I go about my business as usual and look into things discreetly?" He would need to flex his investigator's muscles as police work was a slightly different skill to busting asses on missions or guarding targets for the government or Royalty.

"Yes. Just stay off one more week on the," he paused to do the air quote sign then, "sick, and cover Alex while I'm away. Use Pax's case for cover if you need it," Jack said making it clear that he knew about that. Blake didn't bother asking how, Will more than likely.

"I'm not going undercover at the Palace." That was the one thing Blake wasn't willing to give an inch on.

"I don't care what you do, just keep me updated on this."

"I can work the US angle, but I'll need to go out of the country for a few days. When do you leave?"

"Five days, six at most and I'll be gone for four or five days."

"Is anyone going with you?" Concern for Jack and his friends filled him, and he wasn't able to stop the bitter taste of betrayal that one of the three men on the sheet were responsible.

"Yes. Mitch, Waggs, Liam, and Reid." Jack held Blake's eyes at the declaration.

Blake watched him, not sure of his response because he didn't know what to think. "Is it wise taking men you know may have betrayed us?"

"Maybe not, but like I said, we can't let doubt bring this team down and even while we investigate, we have to believe in innocent until proven guilty. It's the only way."

Blake and Jack were similar that way. Both believed in the black and white of innocent or guilty, friend or foe, which was why he left the Met. He hadn't known whose side he was on in the end.

"Okay. I'll look into it and let you know. If I decide to help Pax, I'll let you know too." Blake stood, knowing the meeting was over.

Jack stood and walked him to the door. "I'm sure I don't need to say it, but nobody must know about this."

"Of course."

"Now get your lazy ass to physio. There isn't room for slackers on this team," Jack bellowed as Blake walked away chuckling.

Physio was a fucking bitch and Waggs pushed him hard. The ex-Green Beret didn't seem to know anything other than full speed. Sweat was pouring off Blake by the time he did the last set of reps on the rowing machine. His legs felt like jelly when he stood to do the cooldown.

"You trying to kill me?" Blake gasped as he bent over trying to catch his breath.

"If I were trying you wouldn't be talking," Aiden Wagner aka Waggs said.

Blake sank to his ass before lying on his back and stretching his leg out above him. "You think I can go back on duty yet?" He knew the medic wouldn't pass him unless he was absolutely sure.

"Probably another week of light duty then we can get you back on the rota."

Reid and Mitch walked in then bullshitting about who had the best shot. Both had buckets of experience with firearms. Mitch was ex-SO16 swat, and Reid was Hostage Rescue. Blake wasn't sure who he would put his money on in a straight-out competition. The two men made their way to the boxing ring gloves on, ready to spar. He couldn't wait to get back to that. He missed sparring, it gave him a release much like fucking did with the adrenalin and endorphin rush.

"Hey, Reid, you fancy a pint later?" Blake shouted.

Reid looked over at Blake, his hands already up guarding his face. As an ex-FBI hostage rescue member, Reid was well rounded as an operator, and he also had that Southern USA accent that had women fighting to drag him into bed. The fact that he was a complete gentleman and charming with it meant that he was the perfect wing-man. The muscle and tattoos didn't seem to hurt either. "Sure. See you around eight-ish?"

"Waggs, you fancy it?" Blake asked.

"Na, not me."

Not one to go out socially a lot, nobody really knew what Waggs did with his time. His family were in the States and he only seemed to go out with the team occasionally.

"If you change your mind, you know where we'll be," Blake said as he headed to the showers.

"Yeah, thanks, man."

Blake showered and dressed in clean clothes consisting of dark wash jeans and a navy polo. He was combing his hair when Alex walked past the door. Slamming his locker door closed he jogged to catch up with Alex. "Alex," he called. "You coming out tonight?"

Alex turned. "Not sure. I'll see what Evelyn's wants to do."

"Come on, man, bring her out. Reid's coming and I'm gonna give Gunner and Decker a call. Liam is away for the weekend, but I'll see if Jack wants to come." Blake had an ulterior motive for trying to get the team together. He wanted to see as many of the potential traitors in a relaxed setting.

"Yeah, sure. Why not? See you later." Alex turned again and walked away towards his office, probably to call Evelyn. That man was so pussy whipped it wasn't funny, but Alex was happier than Blake had ever seen him, so it was all good.

AT 8:15 that evening he took the tray of drinks from the bar and walked out to the beer garden of the Vault. It was a traditional British pub complete with a dark wood bar, brass pumps, and glass optics with cardboard beer mats on the wooden picnic tables. It was also their favourite haunt and he reckoned they probably put about eighty per cent of the takings in the till every weekend.

Placing the tray down he handed out drinks to everyone. "Evelyn, my favourite woman in the entire world." His words got him an eye roll from Alex and smirk from her.

"Dry spell, Blake?" He could see the laughter in her eyes.

"Of course not. You know I only have eyes for you." He watched Alex frown at his joke and laughed at him.

"Dick." Alex threw a bag of peanuts at his head in retaliation.

The night progressed. Everyone was relaxed and nobody seemed the slightest bit tense. Whoever the traitor was, he was a fucking good actor because Blake couldn't detect anything. This was going to be harder than he'd thought.

As Blake lay in bed around midnight his mind went to the three men on the list. He had played the situation with Eidolon over and over in his head and couldn't find a tell of any kind.

He felt dirty investigating his friends. It seemed disloyal. He remembered how every single member of the force had hated it when the IPCC started sniffing around. Kicking the sheet off, he turned on his side trying to get comfortable. It was hot and muggy and while he loved the sun, he hated the night heat.

Heat led his mind straight to Pax and how she'd looked that morning. She was fucking beautiful, but it was more than that. Beautiful women were ten a penny. She had something unique—a fight, a spirit, and sexy sassiness that made his dick hard. He tossed onto his other side as he replayed their interaction and realised it wasn't just that he wanted to fuck her. He did but it was more than that. He fucking liked her—talking with her, teasing her, making her smile.

Blake groaned. When was the last time he'd really liked a woman and wanted to spend time with her? It hit him like a punch as he remembered the previous woman that made him feel this way. Immediately, he locked those thoughts away not willing to go down that path again. That part of his life was over, and he wouldn't go there.

Pax had asked for his help though and he couldn't shake the heavy feeling of guilt he felt every time he thought of her. Maybe there was a way he could help her look into her father without involving himself in the Palace bullshit. Satisfied with the decision to help her he made a mental note to wake up early and go see her before his morning run.

CHAPTER FOUR

PAX HUNG up the phone resisting the urge to scream in frustration. Everything had gone wrong today starting with her disastrous decision to ask Calvin Blake for help. What had she been thinking of, asking that playboy for help? He was conceited, arrogant, entirely too sure of himself, and though she didn't like to admit it, played havoc with her libido.

Pax was a normal woman with normal sexual needs, and when faced with a pretty face and hot body, she responded to it in a completely normal way. That did *not* mean she had to act on it, and she'd had no intention of doing so. But now, now she wanted to kick and scream at the unfairness of it all.

She wasn't a woman to feel sorry for herself—she had a good life, an excellent job and friends, and her upbringing had been to all intents and purposes, idyllic. That fact she'd been blind for most of that, to who her father was, didn't distract from the fact she'd had it easy. So now fate, the miserable fucker, had found her and was going to play games.

Make her want a man she shouldn't. Make her need his help because he was the most viable option. Then when she'd finally swallowed her pride and asked, have him turn her down. *Well, fuck you, fate, and the horse you rode in on.*

"Hey, Pax, you closing up soon?" Bebe walked from the back office towards her. Bebe was one of the Zenobi girls who regularly took on undercover work. Her background was sketchy and one she didn't share with anyone.

"I have a client coming in twenty minutes to view the Renoir then I'm out. This day can go to hell."

She sighed and Bebe laughed, the deep rich sound matching the deeply seductive mystery of the woman with her dark brown, almost rich chocolate, coloured hair and her big brown, almost black eyes, their slight almond shape showing her heritage. "Want me to stick around and keep you company?"

Pax could see she needed about three days of sleep and wasn't going to keep her from her bed. "No. You look exhausted and this is hardly a high crime area."

Hereford was on the border between England and Wales and while definitely still in England and the locals would gut you if you called them Welsh, it was still relatively safe.

"Okay. If you're sure, I'll head out. I have a large glass of wine and a hot bath with my name on it waiting for me." Bebe smiled as she waved and slipped out the door.

Pax went back to the pick list in front of her. She had three girls out of the country that needed go bags put in safe places before midday tomorrow. She still couldn't get hold of the new supplier for the discreet weapons she needed, and her feet were hurting. She wanted to go home, pour herself a gin and tonic, slip into shorts and a vest top, and read the new thriller on her kindle.

She knew that wasn't going to happen though. She would go home and start researching a way into the Palace, study the skills she would need to get the nannies job for Princess Louisa without Blake's help.

Pax looked at her watch and cursed. The client was late, not that it was unusual. People with money often thought they could come

and go as they pleased without a thought for anyone else. Unfortunately for them, Athena Art Gallery didn't work that way. She would
give them ten minutes and then she would close up. Packing the
paperwork away and locking the computer down, she moved to the
gallery area and double checked the security on the paintings.

If there was one thing Zenobi did well, it was security. Nobody
would get past and it was why they didn't have security guards. That
and the girls, which for all her lack in that area included her, were
better trained than any security guard.

Checking her watch she noticed the ten minutes were up and
with a shrug flipped the lights off in the gallery, leaving only the lights
that illuminated the paintings themselves on.

She moved towards the desk to collect her bag when she heard a
sound a split second before someone shoved her violently forward.
Her face hit the edge of her desk, the pain sending her vision blurry
for a second as warm blood trickled down her face. Grabbing the
edge of the desk she used it to balance herself as she kicked back with
her leg, catching her attacker on the side of his knee. He yelped in
pain and Pax was surprised at how quickly he seemed to recover as
she felt her hair being grabbed from behind. Twisting, Pax realised
she was facing two men rather than just one, and it was the second
that had her hair in his grip. She fought harder, fear mixing with
adrenalin as the man holding her hair released it and grabbed her
around her arms, securing her against his massive body. Pax tried to
stay alert, to clamp down the fear that threatened to make her weak.
Both men had ski masks on, and were big, well over six feet tall and
muscular.

She struggled to try to loosen the grip the man had on her as the
one she had kicked moved in closer. His hands balled into fists as she
tried to get free, but she didn't have the same skills as the others. A
blow to the ribs made her lose her breath as pain radiated outwards.
Another to the other side made her cry out and she saw the man
smile.

A thousand thoughts went through her head as punch after

punch landed on her body and face until she felt numb. Her left eye was closing, and she could barely breathe such was the pain throughout her body.

Finally the man holding her spoke. "Enough. It's only a warning. We weren't meant to kill her." Pax immediately recognised his Boston accent.

"Let her go."

The other man's accent was less pronounced but still unmistakably American. She felt arms let her go and she fell to her knees as the man who had beat her caught her around the throat with his meaty hands.

Her hands flew to her neck, clawing at his hands as he squeezed. She felt her eyes go wide in terror as he began to choke her. Her vision started to go black as small dots danced in front of her. Seconds before she passed out, he released her, shoving her to the ground as she coughed and gasped, trying to get oxygen into her burning lungs which hurt like a bitch because of her damaged ribs.

"Stay away from things that don't concern you, bitch. Daddy can't protect you this time." The man spat the words at her before he hauled back and kicked her in the stomach, making her lose her much-needed air.

She watched from the floor as the two men left, letting the door slam shut behind them. Pax absently heard the sound of a car as it screamed away from the curb. She lay on the floor letting the pain radiate through her as she caught her breath. She knew the cameras would have captured it all and felt humiliation bubble under her skin. None of the others would have allowed that to happen. She needed to delete the footage before they saw it. Dragging herself upright took longer than she anticipated, sweat beading her brow as she struggled through the pain her ribs and abdomen.

She would have horrendous bruises tomorrow and she didn't even want to think what her face looked like. After what felt like a lifetime, she got to the door, closing and locking it behind her before slowly making her way to the back office, copying and then deleting the footage.

She didn't want anyone else to see it, but she wasn't stupid—she knew it was evidence and could hold clues. Once she had finished what felt like a herculean task, she considered how she would drive in such a state. But her options were limited. She would never walk it and a taxi driver would ask a thousand questions before demanding she go to the hospital. Driving was the only option.

Bending to nab her bag from the floor, she hissed in pain at the movement. Walking slowly to the exit, she bowed her head and avoided the camera as she locked up and went to her car. Pax drove home slowly thanking all the gods that she drove an automatic and had no need to keep changing gears. Even that minuscule movement hurt. Parking on the drive of her two-bedroom house, she cut the ignition and took a moment before hauling her body out of the car and ducking her head again so none of her neighbours would see her. The sky was dusky as the summer day gave way to the anonymity of night. Placing the key in the lock she let herself in and felt an instant sense of peace.

Her home was her sanctuary against everything that went on in her life. She had bought and paid for it with her inheritance from her grandmother on her mom's side. Every item in the house was hers, earned with hard work and tears. The money her father tried to put in her bank account was refused every month. Eventually she's started sending it straight to a charity she chose at random.

Pax moved forward, down the sleek wide hallway with cream walls and a blue-grey gloss on the woodwork, the floors a dark oak colour with a blue abstract patterned runner up the middle. That room led to the large kitchen diner with double doors out onto the lawn and deck area.

The kitchen had pale grey shaker-style units with white marble countertops in a U-shape separating the areas in the kitchen diner. Pale grey tile on the floor was repeated in the dining area that held a round, glass table. Grabbing a glass from the cabinet above the sink,

Pax filled it with water and knocked back two ibuprofens for the pain. They wouldn't kill it but they would take the edge off so she could at least undress.

Turning back the way she came, she moved slowly up the stairs wincing in pain with every step until she reached her bedroom. This was her favourite room in the house with its pale blush walls, thick cream carpet, and her king-sized bed with a floral pink and cream comforter and six toss pillows.

Pax took a minute and sat on the edge of the bed gingerly. She needed to get cleaned up, wash the blood from her face, and assess the damage to her body. Then she had to figure out a way to stop Roz from finding out one of her girls had let someone get the drop on them.

Feeling the painkillers finally start to offer some relief, Pax moved into the bathroom and looked in the mirror. It was as she feared—her cheek was cut but not deep enough to need stitches. Her eyes were black with the left one slightly closed, the finger marks on her throat were clear as crystal. She lifted her top and there was a bruise on her abdomen, and both her ribs were a marble of black and purple.

Never in her life had Pax been more thankful for the person that invented shirt dresses. She was going to write them a personal thank you just as soon as she felt like holding a pen. Slipping the buttons through the pale green silk buttonholes she let the fabric pool at her feet before she stepped into the hot shower allowing the hot spray to hit the cuts on her face and clean the blood away. Not bothering to wash her hair because she knew lifting her arms would be more pain than she could cope with right now, she stepped out and wrapped a towel around her.

After letting her body dry naturally, she slipped on the sleep shorts and vest by pulling it up from the bottom and climbed into bed. Pax thought sleep would be impossible and she'd spend all night going over it in her head, but blessedly she slept.

CHAPTER FIVE

Blake woke early as was his way. His head was clear despite the nine pints the night before and he knew he needed to drag his ass for a run. Crawling out of bed he dressed in shorts and a t-shirt he then necked a pint of water. Dehydration was a kicker at the best of times but in this heat, and with a hangover, it was a double whammy.

Hitting the street, he ran towards the park eager to see if he would run into Pax again though he thought the odds were slim. When she was knocked back, she didn't strike him as the type to ask twice. In fact, he half expected her to make him work for it when he said he would help her. He smiled looking forward to it.

After five miles he called it a day and went to shower and change. He was out the door by five past eight and driving towards Pax's home. He knew where she lived, he'd made it a point to find out when they came back from Monaco. Her home in the small village of Bartestree to the North of the city centre. It was a beautiful area and her house was on a small and exclusive estate with only five other homes. All 'new builds' with extensive gardens and private driveways and he wondered why she'd chosen there. He pictured her in a large apartment on the river not in a small detached house.

Parking, his smile grew as he prepared for the mental battle of wills he was about to face with Pax. If he were lucky, he would catch her still in bed all rumpled and mussed from sleep. The thought made his body respond as he banged on the door and waited for her to answer.

He looked up at what he assumed was a bedroom window and then banged again when she didn't answer. She was definitely there —her car was in the drive and he could see her bag on the floor in the kitchen as he looked through the window.

"Come on, Pax, open up. I know you're in there."

He saw movement at the upstairs window and grinned. She had been in bed. He waited for her to come downstairs wondering what was taking so long and then guessing she was probably making him wait on purpose. He heard the lock turn on the other side and grinned as she pulled the door open.

The smile died on his face when he got his first glimpse of her. His gut twisted and bile fury made his blood burn and his hands shake. "What the *fuck* happened?"

He pushed past her careful not to jostle her as he did. Her face was a mass of purple bruises from her eyes—one of which was closed —to her nose. His eyes moved down her throat and he had to physically restrain himself from going nuclear and scaring her when he saw the bruises on her neck.

Some motherfucker had put his hands on her perfect peach skin. Had dared to hurt a woman he cared about. A lot, if his need to hunt down the man or woman who had done this and break every bone in their body was any indication. He cared about this woman who hid behind her armour of designer clothes—more than he had even realised.

The way she moved towards him, her hand wrapped around her middle as she walked gingerly past him, made him realise the damage was worse than what he could see. Bile crawled up his throat at the thought.

Blake followed her keeping a tiny bit of distance between them.

"Pax." He called her name softly as they reached her immaculate and unused kitchen if the pile of takeaway menus were anything to go by. He moved in front of her as she dropped her face, not looking at him. He lifted her chin with his forefinger. "Honey, talk to me, please. Tell me who did this."

Her eyes met his and he saw shame, pain, and a hint of stubbornness that made him breathe a little easier. "Don't know. Just know I was warned to keep my nose out of things that don't concern me and that my dad couldn't protect me this time."

He would deal with that in a second, but he needed to know how serious her injuries were. "Did you go to the hospital?" She shook her head. "Call Roz?" Again she shook her head. "Where did this happen, Pax?"

"At the Gallery. I was just closing."

"They left you on your own?" He felt anger bubble in his blood at the thought of her facing someone on her own.

"Yes," she snapped. "The other girls would never have let this happen to them. It was my own fault. I should have been more vigilant."

"Bullshit," he roared and watched her wince. He instantly felt bad for shouting. "I'm sorry, Pax, but this is not your fault. It could happen to anyone. Fuck, it's happened to most of us at some time or another. You don't do dangerous jobs without taking a hit now and then."

He moved closer. She was looking at him like she didn't recognise him, and it frightened him. He wanted her smart mouth and witty comebacks. He wanted his Pax back—*his Pax*. Was she his? He didn't know but suddenly he realised he wanted her to be.

"They only beat me," she said.

"They? Only?" he asked confused for a second and stunned at the realisation there was more than one attacker.

"I mean they didn't rape me or assault me sexually. This was a warning."

Blake nodded not fully understanding but he would. He would

get answers just as soon as he made sure she was okay and not bleeding internally. He rested his hand gently on her hip bone and stroked his thumb over her cheek with whisper-soft tenderness. "You gonna let me check you over or am I driving you to the hospital?"

"You can do it." Her voice was husky, either from being strangled. Or maybe, just maybe, if the beating pulse in her neck was any give-away—it was him.

"Do you want to do it in here or the bedroom?" He watched her eyes dilate and she leaned into him slightly not even realising she was doing it.

"What?"

He wondered how hard she'd hit her head. "Get your mind out of the gutter, honey. When I fuck you it won't be when you're too busted up to enjoy it." His grin seemed to snap her out of her fog.

"Pig," she responded but with little heat.

"Let's go into the living room and I can check your ribs."

Blake pulled her gently with him to what he assumed was the living room. He wasn't convinced he could keep it professional if he got her upstairs. Reaching the door to the living room he pushed through and took in the cream carpet, cream couches, and pale dusky purple walls. A large television dominated the wall above the fireplace where a log burner sat below a heavy oak mantle. He was tempted to lecture her about having a tv on the wall above a fire-place but curbed it, deciding the timing was most definitely wrong. Vases of fresh flowers sat on end tables beside the sofa and a deep cuddle chair with an open book placed face down was on the back wall.

He realised that he had made a mistake when he'd thought this didn't suit Pax. It did suit her, just not the Pax she showed the world. The Pax that was starting to worm her way under his skin was a different thing, and this suited that Pax perfectly.

Blake led her towards the sofa facing away from the window and stopped. "You're going to need to lift your top."

He looked down and for the first time really took in the long legs, the shapely thighs, and the thin vest top that barely covered her tits. He sucked in a silent breath and said a prayer for patience.

Pax looked at him a beat before she slowly lifted the top until it was just beneath her tits, their curve teasing him. Blake instantly forgot about her sexy curves when the black and blue of her ribs came in to view. The desire to punch something made his body vibrate with suppressed anger.

Whoever had given this so-called warning had really gone to town on her. Her ribs were a marble of bruises in differing shades of blue and purple. His eyes shot to hers and saw she was watching him.

"I need to touch you, make sure they aren't broken." Blake's words were half request and half apology. He knew this would hurt and the thought of causing her any more pain than she was already in filled him with horror.

"It's okay, just do it."

Blake gently checked her ribs noticing the inhale as he did and offering her an apologetic look. "Sorry, honey."

He dropped his hands a few minutes later when he was satisfied her ribs were only bruised and not broken. It wouldn't feel like much of a comfort to her at that moment, but it made him give a sigh of relief. "Bruised not broken. You need to keep on top of the painkillers." He took a step back and moved towards the kitchen.

Pax followed him at a much slower rate than usual. He could feel her watching him as he walked to her freezer and started hunting through.

"What are you doing?"

He lifted his head and grinned. "Ice." He held up some frozen sweetcorn. "You need to ice them regularly to keep the swelling down."

"Oh, yeah, I guess." She shrugged then winced at the movement. "Fuck that hurts. Tell me this heals quickly?" she implored; her face worried.

Blake wrapped the sweetcorn in a dishcloth and turned her back towards the living room. "Yeah, it will hurt bad for about a week. You need to rest, ice them, and keep on top of the pain relief and breathe normally. You need to make sure your lungs inflate and clear properly or you'll get an infection that can quickly turn to pneumonia if you're not careful, and that shit is serious."

"Speaking from experience?" She sat slowly and took the makeshift ice pack he handed her.

Blake looked up and nodded as he pushed a footstool towards her and lifted her ankles so she was slumped and could lay back easier. "Yes. I've had busted ribs a time or two." He saw the twitch in her lips and knew she wanted to ask. "Rugby," he said with a lip twitch of his own at her stubbornness.

"Awe, I see."

"Where are the painkillers?"

"On the cabinet beside my bed." Her words came slowly, as if she wasn't sure she wanted him in her bedroom.

"Don't worry, Pax. I promise not to go through your underwear." Blake grinned at her before he loped away and took the stairs two at a time.

He found her room and Pax's scent hit him like a two-tonne truck when he walked in. He let the fragrance of her wind its way around him as he stood stock still and surveyed her very feminine room. He had the overwhelming desire to lie on her bed to hold her while she slept. Feel her curves and listen to her breathing go deep as she rested.

Shaking it off, he spotted the paracetamol and ibuprofen by the bed and snagged them before leaving the room and the fanciful notions it had put in his head.

He walked into the lounge to see she was watching the door for him, the tiniest bit of relief showing on her face when she saw him. He knew why she felt vulnerable and she would hate that, but it also gave him a ridiculous sense of achievement. She trusted him when she was exposed. He liked that and let the feeling settle in him.

"Here you go." He handed her the tablets before rushing to get her some water to take them with. He watched her swallow and then took the frozen sweetcorn away and pushed a cushion towards her.

"Every hour I need you to give ten big deep breaths to make sure your lungs open fully. Use the cushion in case it makes you cough," he said as he sat on the edge of the couch.

"Why are you helping me all of a sudden?"

He didn't know how to answer her question. Would he do this for anyone else? Maybe, but then perhaps not. Pax had woken a protective feeling the minute he saw her bruised and battered.

"Because someone hurt you and that shit won't stand." He cupped her chin with his hand and closed the distance. He saw her breathing hitch slightly and knew she wouldn't stop him if he kissed her, but she wouldn't forgive him for taking advantage of her vulnerability either. So he kissed her forehead and then stood. "I'm going to go check your cupboards and then go shopping. We need to eat and then we'll talk." The firm tone he used brooked no argument. He was also going to call Jack and give him a heads up, but Pax didn't need to know that.

He was a little perturbed when she didn't argue, but after looking at her relaxed face and closed eyes, he realised she had fallen asleep. He leaned over and stroked her face, anger burning through him that someone had done this to her, and he swore they would pay for touching her.

CHAPTER SIX

Pax woke to the sound of her front door closing and sat forward too fast making her cry out in pain. Blake was beside her in a second as he dropped the bags he was carrying at his feet.

"Hey, steady on. You shouldn't move so fast." Pax shot him a furious look. "There she is." His grin was wide. She'd obviously amused him with her displeasure.

Pax glanced at the bags and realised he had been shopping. "What's that?"

"Now, Pax, I know the subject of groceries is a bit foreign to you if your kitchen cupboards are anything to go by..."

"Hardy ha ha," she snapped fighting the warm feeling that he had been shopping for her.

His face went serious for a moment. "We both need to eat, and I figured you wouldn't want word getting around about this." He circled his finger in front of her face indicating her bruises. Her hand came up as she remembered her face. "This way we can eat and talk and decide the next step." He collected the bags and moved towards her kitchen as she followed slowly behind him.

"It is very nice of you and all, but this isn't your concern."

The pain of being turned down still festered. Pax leaned against the counter knowing that getting her ass on a bar stool would require more wiggling and couldn't face it.

Blake, who was in the process of unpacking eggs, bacon, bread, salad stuff, cereal, milk, and God knew what else, stilled. He turned to her slowly and she almost stepped back at the predatory look in his eyes. He moved until they were almost touching hip to chest. "It is my concern."

Pax fought the shiver his closeness instilled and looked up at him. "No, Blake, it isn't." Her voice was whisper soft and she wondered where the strong woman she normally was had gone.

Blake ran a finger down her throat, the movement so soft it was like a ghost touched her. "I made it my concern when you opened the door looking like you had done ten rounds with Anthony Joshua. Nobody puts their hands on you in violence. Not ever. So although I had come over to say I had changed my mind and was going to help you if you still wanted it. I'm now telling you I *am* going to help, and you don't get to say no."

Pax's mouth fell open at the intensity of his words, and she couldn't think of anything to say in response. His eyes fell to her mouth and she flicked her tongue to her suddenly dry lips. Blake's eyes darkened and she felt the electricity in the room fizzle with sexual tension.

"You can't just boss me around, Calvin Blake," she said using his full name.

"You like it when I boss you around, Grace Paxton," he replied also using her real name.

She found she liked the way her name sounded on his lips and despite the hot denial she was about to utter, there was something decidedly sexy about a man when he took charge and Blake was all man.

"Do not." She didn't care if she sounded like a five-year-old.

Blake ran his eyes over her body slowly before his eyes came back to her face. "Tell that to your body, honey," he replied and turned to start pulling pans from the drawers.

Face aflame, Pax looked down and saw her nipples were poking through the thin fabric of her top begging for attention. "Pig."

She turned and moved towards the stairs to try and find something more substantial to put between her and Blake. She heard his low, deep chuckle as she made her way upstairs and bit back the scream of frustration. Part sexual and part just annoying man-induced.

"Brunch will be in twenty minutes."

Pax slammed the door and swore she heard him laugh although that was improbable. Moving to the bathroom she surveyed her face and decided that there really was nothing to be done about it and opted for a quick wash before she braided her long hair down the side and let it hang across her left breast. She grabbed a white floaty skirt that came to just above her knees and a short navy camisole with a hidden shelf bra already in it. It wouldn't offer much of a barrier between her and Blake, but it was cool, and it was clothing not nightwear. It made her feel better at least.

Pax bit her lip as pain assailed her when she lifted her arm to pull the top on. Although she wasn't a seasoned warrior like the other girls, she wasn't a wimp either. That made her think of Roz and the bullshit she had fed her this morning about a tummy bug.

She felt a frisson of guilt but shoved it away. Roz didn't handle sickness well and since becoming a mom to two girls she'd had more sickness than she'd bargained for and she tried to minimise it as best she could. It only bought her a few days though and then she would have to come up with another excuse.

The smell that was coming from her kitchen made her belly grumble and she remembered she hadn't eaten since lunchtime yesterday, and then only a chicken salad with no carbs in it at all.

Making her way carefully down the stairs she found Blake setting her table with knives and forks and filling two glasses with orange juice. She smiled despite herself—he looked good in her kitchen. Pax stamped that thought out before it could take root and made her way towards him as he looked around and saw her.

"Perfect timing. The eggs are done," he said as he moved past her, putting his hand to her belly and running it along the gap where her waistband and top met in a completely natural move that made her feel warm inside.

Sitting at the table she felt her mouth water as he placed a plate with soft fluffy scrambled eggs, crispy bacon, fried tomatoes, toast, and hash browns in front of her. "Wow you *can* cook!"

"Yeah, as I said, I have sisters and those sisters learned to cook from my mum and so did I. My mum was adamant that no son of hers was going to rely on his woman to cook for him, so yeah, I can cook. Eat up. Give me the verdict." He dug into his own plate.

Pax placed a fork with the eggs in her mouth and groaned in pleasure. They were the best eggs she'd ever had and considering her family had chefs when she was growing up, that said a lot.

"Good?"

She opened her eyes that had closed in culinary ecstasy. He was watching her, his own heavy with desire. "Very good. Please pass my thanks to your mother," she said without thinking.

"You my woman, Pax?"

Pax had the unsettling feeling she'd trapped herself and given her growing feelings towards Blake away. "No, of course not." She laughed and waved her hand. "I'm thanking her on behalf of womankind in general for teaching you to cook for your... um... future woman."

"You're my woman." After that muttered pronouncement, Blake carried on eating his food while she stayed silent not knowing what to say for a second. She knew if she argued he would think she was protesting too much, but if she didn't, she was accepting it. She went with a dismissal instead.

"Pig."

He threw back his head and laughed at what was fast becoming her standard response to him.

The rest of the meal was eaten in a relatively comfortable silence until she whimpered when the bacon caught her throat which was sore from being strangled.

Blake's face went stony as she pushed the plate away and drank the fresh juice instead. "Go rest. I'll clean up and then we can talk."

Pax had the unsettling feeling that he would talk, and she would be expected to listen. "Fine."

Standing, she made her way to the living room that was cool and faced away from the heat of the midday sun. It was so unusual for the UK to have such high temperatures but to her it was normal, although she missed air conditioning more than she thought possible having taken it for granted all her life. She turned the fan on and opened the window that faced the back garden to circulate some air in the room and sat on the sofa.

Blake joined her a few minutes later and instead of taking the seat opposite, he sat beside her. "You want me to go first?" he asked as he twisted to face her.

Pax turned her head to look at him not wanting her body all twisted. "Well, you seem to have more to say than I do so go ahead."

Blake nodded. "I came here this morning because I'd changed my mind about wanting to help. I have my reasons for saying no and I won't go into those, but I do want to help you. That being said, this," he waved a finger at her, "changes things. I won't let anyone get away with putting their dirty hands on a woman and especially one that means something to me."

Pax felt her heart jump and her abdomen get heavy at his declaration. She wanted to ask him what he meant about her meaning something to him but didn't want to look weak and needy. It wasn't her style, at least not anymore. "So what is the plan?" she asked, ignoring his words.

"Right now, we get you healed up and then we travel to the US and confront your father head-on. There's no way to go in undercover now. They know you're on to them."

"My father wouldn't have done this." The need to defend the

father she still loved even as she fought to bring him down was not lost on her.

"Maybe not, but he needs to see what's going on and I need to get a read on things."

"But I don't need you for that," she said back peddling suddenly as she realised that being in her home country with Blake would feel too intimate. They would be away from the issues of working for opposing companies and him being a playboy with the power to hurt her. Everything would get muddied away from the UK and she knew it was a danger to her heart.

"You may not need me, but you have me." He took her hand rubbing the soft skin of her palm. "I want to help, Gracie. Let me, please? I wasn't bullshitting when I said I care about you. I do. Do I want to fuck you five ways from Sunday? Yes, I do. Will I hurt you intentionally? Absolutely not. I care, but if you want this to be strictly platonic, I'll pretend you're not hot as fuck and be your friend."

Pax had no idea what to say to that because he'd said all the right things. The problem was she didn't know if she wanted him to fuck her five ways from Sunday or be her friend. She very much feared it was the first and she couldn't bring herself to feel sorry about that. The delicious shiver in her body and the tingle in her clit as he'd said the word fuck made her want to climb in his lap and have him start now but she controlled herself.

"Deal." She stuck out her right hand for him to shake.

Blake took it and kissed the inside of her wrist. "You didn't say which it would be."

Pax could see the light dancing in his eyes and had the feeling she had bitten off more than she could chew this time. "All right, Romeo, tone it down a little." She smirked at him to cover the way his words and touch affected her.

"Fair point. Now, what have you told Zenobi about your absence?"

She watched him lean into the couch, the breeze from the fan making his hair move like a lover was running her hands through it. "I told Roz I have a stomach bug."

"And she believes you?" Blake asked looking slightly incredulous.

"Yes. Why?"

"Did you not leave any evidence of the beating you took?"

Pax thought back to the previous night and tried to figure out if she had removed all the evidence. She thought she had but he had her doubting it now. "No. I was pretty careful about cleaning everything up." she replied her brow furrowed.

"Impressive. Not many would think to clear away all the evidence."

"Yeah, well, attention to detail is my thing." She knew her voice was filled with pride.

Blake ran his eyes over her and nodded. "Yeah I know," he said somewhat cryptically. "So, tell me everything you can remember about the men who attacked you. Every little detail might help."

She told him everything from just before Bebe left to her getting home and falling into bed.

"Will Jack be okay with you leaving to go to the US on some mercy mission with me?"

"It's hardly a mercy mission. But I'm on leave still with this knee injury. He only has me doing torture physiotherapy with Waggs anyway. As long as I keep that up in some way while I'm away, he'll be fine with it."

"Okay," she said trying to hide a yawn. It was mid-afternoon already and after only getting a couple of hours of fitful sleep last night she felt exhaustion pulling at her.

"You should get some rest," he said softly, a look of tenderness in his eyes.

"I need to get a shower." She wanted to be clean but didn't have the energy for that either.

"How about you get a few hours' sleep and I'll help you shower afterwards?" Pax raised an eyebrow at his suggestion. "All in the name of getting you clean and comfortable. I won't look I promise." She could see the slightest twinkle in his eyes.

"Hmm, we'll see?"

Blake stood and moved away, and she had a sudden desire to ask him to stay. She didn't want to be alone. It was silly and weak, and she almost bit her tongue off trying to stop the words from spilling out.

He got to the door and turned to her. "You a heavy sleeper?"

"Mostly, why?"

"I'm going to go and cut your lawn. It's like a jungle out there."

He pointed to her front and back garden that she hadn't had a chance to cut yet. She had planned to do it one evening this week, the grass grew so fast in this heat she had to do it weekly. Pax had actually found she enjoyed it but had been so busy she hadn't had time.

"Oh, okay. Then, yes, I can sleep through that." She didn't add the sense of relief she felt knowing he was sticking around would help her sleep. No need to act like a complete wet fish.

"Get some sleep, Pax. Shout if you need me." He wiggled his eyebrows suggestively and gave her a grin that practically melted her clothes off it was so hot.

She grinned to herself as he walked away and then settled as best she could with her arms around a cushion and fell into a dreamless sleep knowing she was safe.

CHAPTER SEVEN

BLAKE STRIPPED his shirt and threw it on the rattan chair which made up part of Pax's impressive garden furniture set. It was nearly thirty degrees Celsius and he was sweating like a whore in church. He wiped his brow and pushed the mower towards the front of the house to do the front lawn.

He had checked on Pax a few minutes earlier, and she was out for the count. He had been planning to go into the office and talk to Jack but had seen the hesitancy on her face when he'd stood and knew she felt vulnerable. So he'd decided to stay and mow her lawn. He could have chatted with her all day. He found her interesting, funny, and witty. She also had an air of vulnerability that intrigued him.

Pax was outwardly confident, composed, take charge, and full of attitude, but he now saw a side he hadn't noticed before and he found he liked that almost as much. He wasn't sure how helping her shower was going to work out later though. He was entirely in control of his own mind and body, but he'd never achieve sainthood was never in the cards for him.

Pax intrigued him in a way that went beyond the sexual desire he felt for her. Yes, he wanted her with a need he had never felt before.

He had fought it in Monaco, had tried to hide the need he felt, but now he was loath to do that. Was it love? No, it wasn't love but it was something more profound than attraction. He wanted more from her.

Blake wanted to wake up and make her breakfast and mow her lawns. He wanted to sit for hours as they talked about life, then strip her naked and make her scream his name until she had no voice left. The timing sucked. The shit with Eidolon and the crap with her father all made it the wrong time, but he felt unable to stop the forward momentum between them—he didn't want to.

He plugged the mower in and tipped a wave at the older couple opposite who watched him with suspicion, making them smile and wave back somewhat awkwardly at being caught looking. He didn't mind. In his book nosy neighbours were a good thing—they kept women living alone safer.

He was on his second turn of the lawn, his mind swimming with everything, when he saw a car pull into the small cul-de-sac. His muscles tensed as he stopped what he was doing and watched it come closer until it pulled to a stop behind his car. He was silent as Alex and Evelyn got out. Alex looked mildly apologetic and Evelyn slightly confused at seeing him there.

"Sorry, man, I tried to talk her out of it." Alex shrugged as Evelyn turned and gave him a withering look which made Alex smile more.

"Blake, what are you doing here?" He could hear the suspicion in her voice.

"Mowing a lawn." He knew he was being deliberately obtuse with his answer and didn't care.

Evelyn moved to go past him. "Fine. I'll ask Pax."

Blake's hand shot out as he stepped forward to stop her. "Pax isn't feeling well." He made it clear she wasn't getting past him.

Alex moved in behind Evelyn but didn't comment. Blake figured that Jack had told him the score and Alex was in an awkward position.

Evelyn turned and glared at Alex. "Is this why you kept

distracting me this morning?" Blake could hear the accusation evident in her voice.

"No, mi nena, I just can't keep my hands off you. Distracting you was a bonus."

Evelyn shook her head but the smirk on her lips told Blake she wasn't really angry with Alex. "I want to see her!" Evelyn's demand made Blake realise she wasn't an ordinary woman. Evelyn was an operative and she wouldn't back down.

"Sorry, Evelyn. No can do." He wasn't willing to back down either and make Pax feel like he had betrayed her. He and Evelyn stood facing each other for a second until he heard the door open behind him and spun to see Pax.

"Pax." Evelyn gasped pushing past him.

As he went to move to stop her, he felt Alex put a hand on his shoulder. "It's done."

Yeah, it was done and now he had to try and help Pax minimise the damage. Leaving the lawn mower in the middle of the lawn he followed Alex in and shut the door behind him.

He watched as Evelyn sat Pax at the dining table and then sat down beside her looking worried and accusing when her eyes came to his.

"Why the fuck are you looking at me like that?" Blake could feel fury at the unspoken accusation waltz through him.

"Calm down, Blake. She knows it wasn't you," Pax said the sleep still evident in her voice, along with pain.

He saw it though, even as she fought to put the wall up between her and the outside world. He hated seeing the shutters come down as she tried to shrug the persona of Perfect and Capable Pax into place.

"What happened?" Evelyn asked taking Pax's hand in hers.

"It's a long story," Pax deflected, and he saw Evelyn look at Alex.

"Why don't we go outside? I have a few things I need to discuss with you in private," Alex said turning to Blake.

Blake turned towards her to make sure she was okay with it. "Pax?"

She waved him off. "Yeah sure."

Blake walked towards the back sliding doors and pulled them open before stepping out as Alex followed. Blake checked his watch and knew Pax was due for some more pain relief soon but would give her and Evelyn a little time. He didn't go far though, wanting to be close in case she needed him.

"You and Pax, huh." Alex had no accusation or question in his voice just a plain statement.

Blake ran his hand over his head as he went to sit in the shade on the rattan sofa. Alex followed and sat opposite him letting the sun hit his face. Being from Cuba and growing up in Florida, Alex loved the heat and the sun.

"It's complicated."

Alex laughed. "It always is my friend. Tell me what happened to her."

Alex's demand sobered Blake and he was unsure for a second on how to answer him, torn between his loyalties to Pax and Eidolon. He figured Eidolon deserved his loyalty first, so he told Alex everything he knew but left out the bit about seeing two sides to her.

"Why did she wipe the cameras at Zenobi?"

"I don't know for sure, but I think she feels embarrassed that she let them get the drop on her."

Alex nodded as if he agreed. "Evelyn said she's been different since Mònaco but not in any specific way. I guess this would be why. I tried to stop her coming over, but I don't think Evelyn knowing is a bad thing. Pax needs to see how much Zenobi values her and maybe that can start with her opening up to Evelyn."

"Maybe." He heard a laugh come from inside and knew it belonged to Evelyn. Blake took that as a good sign.

Alex studied Blake across the coffee table. "Jack told you then?"

Blake knew what he meant. "Yeah, what a complete clusterfuck. Do you have any thoughts on it that would help?"

Alex sat forward and leaned his arms on his legs that were encased in cargo shorts. "I keep thinking I do and then something happens, and I change my mind. I've been absolutely sure it was all of them at one time or another. Which is shit because they're all good men, or I thought they were..."

"Has Will looked into their backgrounds?" Blake knew as he asked the answer was probably yes.

"Yeah, he ran all that. They all came up exactly as we expected with nothing of any consequence to be found."

"What about family or close friends? None of these three would betray Eidolon without good reason and I don't believe it's simply for money. We make a fuck load more than most men in our position. Have him look into their families along with friends from way back. I think the link is there, and we need surveillance on all three of them."

"Backgrounds we can do," Alex shot off a text most likely to Will, "but surveillance is going to be almost impossible without A them knowing and B who the fuck would we ask? We can't ask our guys because we don't want that kind of poison leaking through the team. We can't ask Fortis as they have enough of their own shit going on."

"What about Zenobi?"

"No. Jack won't hear of it. If he can't trust his own men, there's no way he'll trust outsiders."

Blake sat back and thought for a minute, there had to be a way to figure this out. "What about we give each of them intel that nobody else knows except us? If it gets out, we have our answer."

"We could do that." Alex swiped a hand over his chin. "Give me three scenarios and I'll see if we have enough to make it believable."

"Fine, give me tonight to put something together." Blake was relieved that at least he was getting somewhere. "I have to go to the US at the end of the week with Pax to try and sort this shit with her father out. There's more to that than I think she realises."

"No problem. Keep in touch daily though. With things as they are and targets on our backs, we don't want anyone off the grid. The men know to keep their trackers on at all times. Jack put that in place after the last mission went south."

Blake had been there when Jack had made the announcement that all time off was cancelled and trackers were to be left on until he knew they all had their heads in the game.

He had been pissed at the time. He'd felt Jack was blaming them for things that weren't their fault but now he understood. Jack was trying to keep a close eye on the three suspects.

"The trackers are on watches though, so aren't foolproof."

"Jack had some planted in their vehicles too and on the new weapons holsters they wear. They may take the watch off and maybe even find the trackers, but the holsters usually stay on them and can't be detected on a usual scanner unless they go through an airport scanner. As no leave has been granted, it shouldn't happen."

Blake looked at the door as it slid open and Pax and Evelyn walked outside. Blake felt his eyes move over Pax as she walked towards them behind Evelyn. Her gait was slightly lopsided, and he knew she was in pain. He waited until she got to him and sat down, her body leaning into his slightly but not touching.

"Pax told me everything. Thank you for taking care of her when we should have been doing so." Evelyn's tone conveyed her upset and anger. He instinctively knew most of it was aimed inwardly. "I have agreed with not saying anything to Roz, but Pax has also agreed that when this is over, she'll tell Roz herself."

"You don't have to thank me, Evelyn." Blake dropped an arm behind Pax and pulled her into his side kissing her head. He felt her tense and then she seemed to relax into him as she let whatever misgivings she had, go.

"No, I see that," Evelyn said with a smirk, "but you have them anyway."

"Will you lot please stop treating me like I'm a sick child?"

Blake chuckled at her pout. He leaned forward and whispered in her ear, feeling her shiver. "Want some more pain killers, honey?"

"Yes. Please," she said waspishly as if the manners that were natural to her forced themselves past her pain.

"Sure thing." He chuckled again before kissing her hair and standing.

She swatted him away. "Don't kiss my greasy sweaty hair, you freak."

"And on that note, it's time we left." Alex's grin was filled with sympathy.

He walked Alex and Evelyn to the door to see them out.

"Anything you need from us before we go?" Alex asked.

"No, not right now. I'll call you later with those things we discussed though."

Alex nodded. "Cool. Good luck with the patient. If she's anything like Evelyn, she'll have you pulling your hair out in a week."

Evelyn punched Alex in the gut at hearing his words which he took as he wrapped her in his big arms laughing and kissing her cheek.

He watched them walk away and thought he had never seen a couple more in love. They lit up for each other. They were the people others wrote or sang about. They completed each other in a way he'd never thought he would have, and he'd been okay with that. But now he wondered if he wanted it and if maybe Pax could be that person for him.

He laughed off the idea of him and Pax having that kind of love. She wanted him yes, but she was in no way catching feelings for him. She was too guarded and prickly but perversely, it made him want to peel back the layers until he got past the prickle and found the soft and sweet peach inside. They would either be mind-blowing together or kill each other. He was eager to find out which one it would be.

CHAPTER EIGHT

THE LAST TWO DAYS, much to her continued surprise, had been uneventful and somewhat relaxed—even pleasant if she didn't count the continued nagging pain in her ribs. Blake had spent them pottering around her house, fixing things she hadn't asked him to fix but none the less needed to be done, and she hadn't gotten around to it. Their evenings had been spent either watching boxsets. One about a gang of outlaw bikers, the leader of which had a strong resemblance to Blake, the other had been a series about nerd scientists who shared an apartment.

Pax had never really watched anything like them but she found herself hooked and eagerly waited for Blake to join her so they could watch a couple of episodes together before he crashed on the sofa and she went to bed alone.

Going to bed alone was something she had done most of her life, but it was getting harder and harder not to invite the sexy man who was intent on looking after her into her bed. Blake was a shock to her system in some ways.

After their talk where he'd said he'd cared and wanted to help her, and the subsequent kiss to her hand where he'd made it clear he would pursue her—he hadn't. Despite thinking she would find it annoying and she'd be trying to fight him off, he wasn't even trying. It made her wonder if he had changed his mind about wanting her.

After Alex and Evelyn had left the other day with Evelyn promising not to tell Roz, Blake had handed her two ibuprofen and informed her he was going to help her wash her hair and shower. Despite her initial protestations she had given in.

Blake had told her to kneel on the bathroom floor while he bent her head over the bath and proceeded to wet her hair with the shower head and then massage the shampoo into her scalp until she felt a groan of pleasure slip from her lips.

"You enjoying yourself?" he asked with a chuckle.

"This is like a religious experience," she returned. "Where the hell did you learn to do this?"

"I spent a summer working a Saturday job at a hair salon when I was sixteen," he replied as he rinsed the suds away and then worked the conditioner through her long hair right to the very tips.

"You did?" She was thrown by the vision of Blake in a hair-dressing salon.

"Yep. One of my buddies worked there. He said that on week-ends it was a flood of teenage girls. He was gay so it wasn't his thing, but I saw the opportunity to pull lots of girls and applied. I got the job and spent a delightful summer washing hair and pulling girls. It was a good summer."

Pax laughed at the wistfulness of his tone but inwardly felt jealous knowing he probably did this for all the women he had ever been with.

"I haven't done this in years, probably not since I left the salon," he said as if reading her mind.

"Yeah, well, anytime you feel the urge..."

"Oh, I know where to come when I feel the urge, Pax. Don't you worry."

His chuckle made her blood heat. It had been sensual and inti-mate, and she had thought he would take things further but after helping her wrap her hair in a towel, he had run her a cool bath and left her alone, telling her to shout if she needed help.

She hadn't and every day her ribs felt a little better and although her bruises were now turning a sickly green colour, they also felt a lot better. But Blake hadn't touched her or been in any way flirtatious with her and she found she was disappointed.

"You want anything before I sit down?" he asked as he walked in the room fresh from his shower with his hair still wet, wearing gym shorts and a wife beater top that made his arm muscles look huge.

"Do we have any of that birthday cake ice-cream left?"

He nodded and went to fetch it. Returning with the tub and two spoons he settled beside her and handed her a spoon as he grabbed the remote. "What do you want to watch?"

"The biker one please."

There was no way she was telling him she had an unhealthy attraction to the main character because he reminded her of him. Blake grinned and hit play on the last episode of this season. Pax was relieved to hear there were eight more for her to binge on when she was ready.

She sat through the first episode noticing that Blake was leaving all the big cakey bits for her to eat and smiled.

He motioned to the near-empty tub. "You done?"

"Yeah, I'm fit to burst." She patted her belly as she leaned back on the sofa.

"Ready for season two?"

"I need to get another drink first."

Standing, she felt happy that she had managed to go longer without the pain killers. She got herself a cold glass of water and grabbed him a beer from the fridge before moving to sit back down. She felt Blake's eyes on her and turned to look at him. "What?" she asked with a raised eyebrow.

"Just impressed with how you're recovering from such a nasty attack," he said as he studied her.

"Yeah, well, I can't take credit for that. I guess I just heal quickly," she replied with a shrug.

"I meant mentally. You seem to have taken it in stride."

She felt him slide his arm along the back of the sofa and became acutely aware that he would only need to move his hand an inch and he would be touching her. Her instinct was to tell him that she was unaffected by the attack and that she didn't think about it and relive it but that would be a lie. The truth was, she was affected. She did relive it, but she wasn't afraid and that was because of him. Because Blake hadn't left her side since he'd arrived two days ago.

She slept easy knowing that Blake stood between her and anyone who wished to harm her. He had become her protector, her constant.

"I'm stronger than I look but mostly it's because it's hard to feel afraid when you have someone willing to stand between you and those that want to harm you." She knew he deserved her honesty.

"I think it has more to do with you than me. You're much stronger than you realise. I don't think that it's training either. I think you have an inner strength."

"Roz has taught me a lot. I owe her more than I can ever thank her for."

"How did you end up with her and Zenobi?" His finger began to trace a line from her shoulder down her arm. It was an innocent touch, in no way meant to be sexual, but it was driving her insane.

She tried to ignore it and answer his question. "When I left my parent's home, I had five hundred dollars in my checking account and a suitcase full of big dreams and not much else. I was determined to prove to my father I didn't need or want his money. Within two days I'd had my suitcase stolen and was staying in a pay by the hour motel off the highway. I ran out of money pretty quickly and was down to my last cent when I heard shouting outside my motel room door. I was terrified but I've always been one of those people that was too curious for her own good."

Blake lifted a brow and she laughed softly. "Well, you can guess what happened next. I opened the door. I shouldn't have, I know it was foolish. I cringe every time I think about what could have happened."

"What did happen?"

"I found Roz slumped by my door barely conscious. She was bleeding from a knife wound to her leg and had taken a pretty nasty beating."

"What did you do?"

"I dragged her inside and cleaned her up. I was so proud of myself for helping her but when she came around, she went nuts. Reamed me out for being a stupid little girl and opening the door to a stranger. Told me I was lucky I hadn't gotten raped or murdered."

"Yeah, that sounds like her," he said with a chuckle. "It obviously worked out though because you work for her now."

Pax thought back to that time with a smile. "It did. I stood up to her despite her terrifying me at the time. I may have lived in a gilded cage most of my life, but I have my grandmother's red hair and her spirit. I think Roz respected that. She stayed with me until she was healed and then kind of adopted me. I'd always been an organiser and she needed that."

"Do you enjoy it?"

Pax was a little shocked by his question. Nobody ever asked her if she was happy in her work. She had to think for a second before she nodded. "I do, yes. I get to do what I'm good at and play a part in making the world safer for innocents. I know I'm not as important as Bebe or Mustique—"

"Hey, no, don't do that." His hand went to the side of her neck. "You're just as important, if not more so. The lives of those girls that do the actual missions are in your hands and you're integral to their safety and success. A mission without planning and direction is a recipe for failure. Why do you do that?"

Pax thought about what he was saying. Maybe he was right, perhaps she was more important than she was willing to believe but she never felt that way. All the girls had done things as part of Zenobi, but they had always protected her from the genuinely gritty stuff or killing. She was definitely a behind-the-scenes woman and she was okay with that. Or was she? "I don't know," she said dropping her head.

Blake caught her chin in his hand and lifted her head to his. "Such beautiful eyes and so expressive."

She could feel his eyes wander over the rest of her face. Pax felt her heartbeat kick up a pace at the bright look of arousal in them. It was powerful and she imagined this was how deer felt when confronted by a lion. Half of her wanted to run but the other half, the side that craved the feel of his hands on her body, stilled her.

Blake's face moved infinitesimally closer until he was almost touching her mouth with his lips. The warm sweet breath on her skin making her ache for him.

"I want to watch you come." His dirty words whispered so close made wetness flood her panties. His lips touched her skin just to the side of her mouth and she swallowed as her hands dug into the sofa. "Do you want that, Gracie?" Pax knew he had used her name deliberately, that he had seen the effect it had on her. "If you don't, then say so now."

Pax stayed silent giving her answer and almost sighing in relief when his mouth touched hers. He kissed her slow and easy, teasing the response out of her until she sighed against him and opened her mouth. His tongue swept in and it was like a drug. She felt heavy and weak, and a desperate need began to build in her as they kissed. Blake didn't rush or grab at her, instead he mastered her, showing how much pleasure could be had from just kissing.

She felt like she was already on the edge of climax just from his mouth on hers and he hadn't laid a hand on her yet. Suddenly needing to feel his hands on her, she moved her body closer pressing her tits against his chest and letting out a moan at the friction that caused her nipples to harden and ache. She felt a chuckle move through Blake as he pulled back and moved his head to her neck.

"Easy, Pax, we have all night," he said but he took the hint and brushed his fingers over her aching nipple teasing and pinching until she was moaning. His mouth caught hers as he twisted and sat bringing her over him, so she was sitting astride him. "This will be easier on your ribs." His concern for her comfort above anything else showed her what a terrific guy he was.

Pax could feel the hard ridge of his cock as it pressed against her pussy, she moved slightly trying to ease the pressure in her body.

"So fucking beautiful."

His hands reached up to cup her face as she leaned into his touch before they travelled down her sides—his thumbs rubbing the stiff peaks of her nipples and moving gently over her sore ribs until they rested on her hip bones. He watched her for a second and Pax bent forward and touched her lips to his, kissing him until he took over, angling her head so he could kiss her harder. It was all consuming and she wanted more. She wanted to drown in sensation, to let go and just feel.

His hand cupped her pussy over her shorts and Pax gasped as he rubbed his palm against her mound until she began to move against him. He stopped and she let out a frustrated whimper before he slid his hand inside her panties. His finger glided through her wet slit finding the hard nub of her clit and began to move in slow, delicious circles that had her grinding into his cock.

Blake slid his fingers towards her pussy replacing his finger on her clit with his thumb. He plunged one finger, then two inside her and Pax threw her head back on a moan of pleasure breaking their kiss.

"So fucking wet for me."

She felt her pussy get wetter at his growled words. He kept working her clit as he fucked her slowly with his fingers building her higher but not giving her what she needed to push her over the edge.

"I need more," she pleaded as she ground against his cock and he hissed.

"I know what you need." Blake sat forward using his other hand to pull her top from her shoulders. The vest top fell to her waist and exposed her tits to his eyes.

Blake looked at her body with hooded, desire-heavy eyes. "You're exquisite." He palmed her breast bringing it to his lips slowing before taking it into her mouth. He sucked her nipple hard until it was almost painful then crooked his fingers inside her finding her G-spot.

Pax let out a keening cry, she was so close. The ache began to build as electric currents of pleasure moved through her. Her thighs began to shake. She felt Blake pull back when her head went back as he worked her clit harder.

"Look at me, Gracie."

It was his tone, the blatant masculine alpha demand that Pax cede her control to him that made her comply. Her eyes found his and at that moment, as he gazed at her as if she was the most beautiful woman in the world, she shattered. Her vision went hazy, her body shook, her mind a blank canvas of nothing but pleasure and sensation. A cry tore from her lips but it was mumbled and incoherent as she rode the wave of ecstasy.

She felt Blake's fingers go still inside her, sensing she was too sensitive to take any more and relaxed her body weight into him, every muscle drained from the intensity of the climax she'd just had. Blake removed his hand from her panties and wrapped his arms around her. He held her for a second before she sat up and looked at him,

"That was intense." Her words were mumbled, exhaustion hitting her.

"Yeah it was, and it was everything I thought it would be. Watching you come is my new favourite thing to do."

Pax laughed and felt his hardness against her core. "What about you?"

"This isn't about me. This is about you trusting me when I say I'm not going to fuck you and run. I want more, Gracie. I want us to build something together."

His look was filled with intensity and desire and she realised she wanted that too. It frightened her to death because a man like Blake—one who was sweet and kind, caring, dangerous, and sexy as hell, and could cook and give orgasms like that—was fucking lethal.

She had played down how losing Benny had affected her, and it wasn't until that second that she saw she had been picking safe men. Men who couldn't hurt her because she never let them get close. Choosing men she knew would fuck up sooner or later. Blake wasn't like those men. He had the potential to break her heart and she was terrified of that happening—terrified of him.

"I don't know if I can give you that." Her answer was as honest as she could be, and she tried to climb off him.

He stopped her pulling her closer and pinning her to his chest, played with her hair. "What are you afraid of?"

"You. What you could do to me. I like you, Blake. You're not what I thought and what I see I really like."

"I like you, too."

"Shut up. You know what I mean." She dug him in the belly with her elbow in punishment for his laughter.

"I do know. I can't promise we'll live happily ever after and have a house full of kids. I can't promise we won't have moments where we want to kill each other but I can promise to be honest with you and to put you first. Is that enough for now? Can we give this a go and see where it goes?"

Pax liked everything he said. It was honest and sincere, not flowery bullshit promises or declarations meant to manipulate. The fact was, she did want it. She had wanted it before, but Blake had been putting up barriers too. But now his were down and he was offering them a chance. Could she take it?

"What about Eidolon and Zenobi? They don't exactly play nice together. That's a pretty big stumbling block if Roz or Jack don't like it."

"It is but I don't believe Roz would stop us. She's a hard ass but she also knows what it's like to be in love and she and K make it work with Fortis and Zenobi. As for Jack, let's cross that bridge when we get to it. Maybe we make a rule that we don't discuss work at home. Lots of couples make that work. I'm sure we can find other things to do instead." His devilish smile made desire shoot through her.

"You have a one-track mind."

"Me? I was talking about watching boxsets."

Her smile was wicked. "Sure you were."

"There it is, the secret smile that first got my attention."

Pax felt herself blush. "I don't have a secret smile."

"Yes, you do. You smile like you have a delicious secret that no one but you knows about. It made me want to be in on that secret."

"Want to know what it is?" she teased and then lifted up and whispered in his ear, making him throw back his head and belly laugh. It was a sound she was growing to adore.

CHAPTER NINE

BLAKE LAY on the couch thinking about Pax. Watching her lose control and give herself over to the pleasure he'd given her earlier had been one of the most erotic things he had ever witnessed. His cock was still hard from the visual effect, his balls heavy and almost painful with the need to come but he wanted to give her time.

Pax was scared and it was obvious she didn't like the feeling. Nobody did, but with her, he sensed it was more than normal fear. She liked to come across as confident, but she didn't value herself as much as she should. He wanted to show her that she was important and had worth. He also wanted to wring the neck of the person that had taught her she wasn't either of those things.

He turned over on the couch which was comfy for a short time, but this was night three and he was over it. He knew he could have crawled into bed with Pax tonight, but he didn't want to rush her. So he lay on the couch and tried to sleep. When that didn't work, he got up and went to collect his laptop from the kitchen so he could see if he had any more emails from Will who had done as Blake suggested, and so far, had found nothing but he was going to go back further and see if anything broke.

As Blake passed the front door, he saw a shadow move. His senses went on alert as he listened for the slightest noise and heard nothing. Moving towards the living room he snagged his gun from the side table and moved towards the window. Staying hidden behind the curtain he peered out trying to see if he could catch any suspicious movement when a loud crash came from above his head followed by a scream.

Pax!

Taking the stairs two at a time he raced towards her bedroom and flung open the door. In a split second his eyes took in the broken glass all over her carpet and the brick that had landed there. His eyes went to Pax who was unharmed but shaking and disorientated in the middle of the bed. Blake was beside her in a heartbeat, holding her to him as he moved until she was between him and the wall.

Nothing would get to her without going through him first. He had no time to see if she was okay, he needed to find the threat and neutralise it.

"Get dressed and call Jack." He kept his voice low as he ushered her to the bathroom and threw some clothes inside. "Lock the door and don't come out until I say so." He handed her the gun he knew she kept in the drawer by her bed despite it being illegal here in the UK.

He watched her go without an argument. Her fear had gone, but she was following orders knowing she couldn't help him injured as she was and would only distract him.

Moving to the window he saw a man move across the lawn. Hitting the stairs, he raced to the back sliding doors and wasted precious seconds on the lock before he threw them open. He had his gun cocked as he stepped out and was hit by a wall of muscle that took him to the ground and knocked the gun from his hand.

Blake's body hit the decking with a thud as he and his attacker rolled jockeying for position. Blake managed to land a blow to the man's jaw and heard the grunt of pain. He couldn't see anything past the ski-mask, especially in the darkness. The man, larger than him with twenty pounds more muscle, caught Blake with an uppercut that sent him careening into the rattan garden furniture with a crash. Blake grabbed a pair of garden clippers to use as a weapon as he and the man eyed each other, waiting for the other to move.

Blake feinted right, his opponent read him, and Blake missed his mark and only caught the man across the bicep with the clippers instead of the chest like he had intended. The blow knocked the clippers from his hand. He had done a little damage though and he now had the advantage.

Blake blocked a kick to the head and threw a punch, but his attacker blocked and caught him with a ridged hand strike to the throat which caused him to lose balance, then the fucker took out his injured knee with a knee wheel strike that caused him to almost black out from the pain. Going to the ground, he turned to face his assailant, but the man had already taken off towards the hedge at the back of Pax's garden.

Blake knew he couldn't go after him as he struggled to stand, limping as he put weight on his injured leg. Motherfucker had known just where to strike which made Blake wonder who the attacker was after.

Blake heard the sound of cars pulling up outside with a screech and when he turned back, the only sign of the man who had attacked him ever being there was Pax's destroyed furniture.

Blake walked back through the sliding doors closing and locking them before casting his eye one last time around the surrounding area and finding nothing. He limped to the front door as he heard hammering on the door. He didn't need to ask who it was. Roz was more than making herself known.

"Open this fucking door or I swear I am going rip your balls off and feed them to you."

Her threat made Blake wince; he knew she was capable of doing just that. As soon as he opened the door Roz shoulder-barged past him, followed by Alex, Evelyn, and Jack.

"Will you calm the fuck down, woman." Jack's voice was a hiss as he followed behind Roz.

Roz had stopped in the middle of the room and seemed to be looking around for Pax. "Where is she?"

"I'm here." Pax's voice came from the top of the stairs.

Blake looked up at her with a glare. "I told you not to come down until I called you."

"Don't you fucking speak to her like that," Roz hissed rounding on him with fury and a barely controlled rage in her eyes.

"Is the area secure?" Jack turned to Blake with his question and ignored Roz and her outburst.

"Yeah. Just one attacker and they ran off over the back when they heard the cars."

Pax made it to the ground floor and moved towards him, her eyes on his leg that he couldn't hold weight on.

"Your leg." She'd come to stand beside him as Roz watched her every move.

"It's fine." There was no way he was going to complain in front of Roz.

"What the hell is going on around here and why does one of my girls look like she was fucking strangled?" Roz's quiet calm was more terrifying than the yelling and threats ever were. Roz was about to blow her top and someone was going to end up injured unless she was satisfied with the answers.

Evelyn took over then. "Let's take this into the living room. Why don't you go and make sure the house is secure and find out what happened?" Her last comment was directed at Alex indicating he, Blake, and Jack do the securing while her and Pax explained to Roz why she had been kept out of the loop.

It wasn't going to be an easy or a pleasant conversation and he had absolutely no doubt that the leader of Zenobi would take it badly. His instinct was to stay with Pax.

"You want me to stay, Gracie?"

Pax blushed deep crimson and the intimate name he used that

nobody else called her. He felt Roz's eyes shoot to him before going to Pax in question. "No. Go find the rock they threw, and I'll explain everything to Roz."

Blake winked back and moved away letting her have privacy for this. "I'm upstairs if you want me." His words were a reminder that he wouldn't be far.

Limping from the room he began the ascent up the stairs and moved to Pax's bedroom where Jack and Alex stood assessing the scene. "How come, Roz is here?"

Alex looked at him, "She was with Evelyn when Jack and I got the call from Pax. There was no way we could stop her from coming with us."

"I don't think it's going to go over too well with Roz."

"Can't say as I blame her," Jack replied.

It was no secret that the two leaders rubbed each other up the wrong way so Blake was surprised to hear him defend her.

"Why?" Blake was curious to hear Jack's reasons for defending a woman they all knew he didn't like.

"Well, I wouldn't fucking like it if one of my team got attacked and instead of telling me they sought help from an outside team after going to great lengths to hide what happened to them. That shit stings. Roz is a lot of things, but she's a good leader and deserves to know when her girls are under threat."

"I guess, but Pax had her reasons and I had to respect them." Blake wanted to make it clear whose side he was on.

"Got that but now she has to pay the piper and explain why she did what she did. If it was me, she would be gone. If your team doesn't trust you, they have no business taking orders from you."

"You'd fire her?" Alex asked.

"Abso-fucking-lutely." Jack tossed the brick he had picked up from the floor to Blake and nodded to the note taped to the brick with gaffer tape. "It's a warning."

Blake looked down at saw Jack was correct.

YOU ARE NOT SAFE!

"A clear message." Jack and Alex were both nodding their chins firm, jaws rigid.

"But for who?"

Jack asked the question Blake had been thinking and he had a distinct feeling it was for him. Something felt off about that attack. How did the guy know his moves before he did them? It was like they had sparred before, trained together and knew each other—and that knee wheel? It was a good move but not one used a lot. How did they know to go for his knee? It could have been a coincidence, but Blake didn't think so.

———

"WHAT THE FUCK is going on and don't even think about lying to me."

Roz stood in front of Pax's couch, her body perfectly still. Roz had a way about her when she was angry that seemed to suck the air from the room and Pax had the unexpected urge to open all the windows to let some oxygen back in. Instead she stayed still.

This moment was always going to come. She would have just preferred it in her own time.

"Roz," Evelyn began trying to calm their boss down.

"No, Evelyn, it's fine. This is my mess. Let me explain." Pax interrupted Evelyn, patting her on the knee. She looked up at the stunning face of her boss and swallowed. "Three nights ago I was attacked at the gallery. I was waiting for a client that had booked for seven pm. They were late and I started to lock up. I was just grabbing my backpack from the desk when two men attacked me. They beat me," she said waving at her face. "As you can see, I didn't exactly put up much of a fight. Then they warned me to keep my nose out of things that weren't my concern and my dad couldn't protect me this time. Then they left." She looked down at her hands, waiting for Roz to blow.

"Why was there no evidence on the security cameras?" Roz began to pace slowly.

"I erased it. But I did make a copy," she added quickly.

Roz swung back around to her and the look on her face was furious, her voice deadly quiet. "You fucking what?"

Pax met her look head-on. This was no time to wimp out, she had done enough of that. "I erased the footage."

"Why the fuck would you do that?"

Pax didn't answer for a second. How did she tell the person who had put so much faith in her that she was embarrassed because she wasn't as badass as they were? It was time to 'fess up and if Roz fired her then she would just have to find another job. Maybe something in Europe would be fun. A fresh start so to speak but then her mind went to Blake. She would miss him and what had nearly started.

"*Pax.*" Roz was obviously done waiting for an answer.

"I was embarrassed all right," she spewed standing herself, and pacing from the sofa to the window and back, rubbing her hands together in agitation.

"Embarrassed?"

Roz seemed confused and it was a tone Pax normally only heard when she was being told stuff about parenting. Roz was a feared assassin, a leader, and could probably take out a small army with her hands tied behind her back. But the girls she'd adopted after she'd rescued them from a sick piece of shit who planned to sell them, scared the crap out of her most of the time. She loved them with the fierceness of any mother but a natural Suzy homemaker she was not. It almost made Pax laugh—almost.

"Yes, I was embarrassed that I got jumped like that and couldn't defend myself. That would never have happened to the others. Shit, Bebe or you—any of you—would have wiped the floor with those jerks. I got my ass handed to me. So yes, I was embarrassed and didn't want you all to know. So I cleaned up and erased the file then drove home."

Roz sat down heavily on the couch beside Evelyn as Pax stopped pacing and watched her, waiting for the inevitable explosion, but it didn't come.

"I should fire you for gross misconduct. Wiping evidence and hiding shit that goes on in my organisation is a betrayal." Pax held her breath her heart breaking at the thought of losing her job, her friends, the women she had come to think of as family. "But I won't." She included Evelyn in her look. "Even though I should, I won't fire you either, not when it's my fault."

"Roz—"

"I'm talking now." Roz's glare stopped Pax from continuing. "This is on me. I'm to blame for you feeling this way. It *is* my fault. I should have made sure you had the same training as the others. Just because you're our support coordinator doesn't mean you shouldn't be able to step up and do other jobs. The problem is, and I'm not trying to make excuses, I can't afford to lose you from the office. Nobody can organise things like you do, Pax. If I asked you to arrange a military coup in a twenty-four-hour window you would do it."

"I don't know about that." Pax felt a blush creep over her pale skin and inwardly cursed her red hair and fair skin.

"I do. You are so integral to Zenobi that I don't know what I'd do if you wanted to go out on missions. But that's no excuse for leaving you vulnerable and for that I apologise. That said, you will start training as soon as your ribs are healed." Roz turned back to Evelyn. "I want you and Mustique to take over the office for a month while Bebe and I get Pax up to speed."

Pax was in a state of shock as she listened. *I'm not fired? I'm not the weak link?* "I thought I was untrainable—"

"What?"

"I thought you didn't think I had it in me to be like the others. That perhaps I was soft." She sat down suddenly exhausted.

"You are soft but that doesn't mean you can't be a deadly badass too. Look at me." Pax and Evelyn snorted with laughter at Roz's smirk. "You are every bit as important as the girls that go out on missions. Never forget that and if you decide that's the way you want to go, then I'll have to suck it up and find someone else to keep Zenobi running efficiently."

"I don't. I love my job."

"Oh, while I remember I'm going to need a copy of that CCTV footage."

"Of course, I have it here in my safe."

"Good." Roz's eyes turned wicked then, her grin huge. "Now, bring me up to speed on your sick as fuck father and how that sexy blond playboy is in your house in the middle of the night. And why is he going all alpha protective on you? That's hot as shit and makes me want to go home and wake K for some hot sex." Roz and Evelyn bumped fists as they both laughed.

"My father is trialling a new drug illegally and I'm going to stop him with Blake's help. As for what's happening with Blake, it's new but I like him a lot. He isn't the guy he shows the world. He's deep and sweet, and he cooks for me and washes my hair, and kisses like the devil."

"Good for you. Blake is a genuinely nice guy and it's good to see you opening up." Evelyn stood as they heard the men come down the stairs.

Blake walked straight over to her standing a few feet away and eyed her closely. "Everything okay?" he asked softly.

"Yes."

She moved forward a little and leaned her body into his as she settled herself with her arms around his waist, her head on his shoulder. Blake didn't hesitate in lifting his arm over her shoulder and holding her tight before dropping a kiss to her head.

She was making a statement and he got it. They were going to do this and see where they ended up.

CHAPTER TEN

"WE MAKE A RIGHT PAIR, don't we?" Pax laughed as she walked towards him with an ice pack and some ibuprofen. Blake was sitting on his couch with his leg on the coffee table trying to get the swelling in his knee down.

Last night they had decided it would be best to go to his place until her bedroom window was fixed properly. Jack had taken the note with the warning on it to get it tested for prints although nobody was hopeful of finding anything.

Pax and Evelyn had packed her a bag while the rest had secured her home. They had crashed here, falling asleep on the couch with Pax tucked into his side. It meant they both woke stiff and achy from the awkward position they had been in especially as they were now both injured. His knee ached like a bitch and had swollen up like a balloon.

Roz had granted Pax some leave to sort her father and the situation out as long as she promised to call if they needed back-up and she would commence her training as soon as she returned. Blake was fucking thrilled that she was going to get some training. Being able to protect herself from assholes would give her more confidence.

He laughed in agreement as he took the ice and applied to his knee. "We certainly do."

"Will we still make the flight tonight?"

"Yes and no. We're flying out tonight, but Jack has offered us the use of the company plane. We can sleep on the flight and it won't be so bad on your ribs." He took in the fading bruises on her face. "You also won't have to face as many people."

"That's kind of him. I need to make a list of things we'll need to do when we get there. I think pretending I'm not in the country is futile. My father has spies everywhere and judging by the attack on me, he knows I'm on to him." She said the words clinically even though her father having had men attack her must still smart—a lot.

"You don't have to be brave about that, Gracie. I know that hurts you." Blake laid a hand on her bare thigh just above her knee. Pax looked at him and then down at her leg, idly tracing the veins on his hand.

"I know but if I give in to it, it will only make things harder. He was my hero for so long and finding out he isn't the man I thought he was, hurts even now. As awful as it sounds, if it had been my mom, I don't think it would have been so bad. I love her but we aren't as close. But I was a daddy's girl growing up." She shrugged as if it wasn't important, but Blake knew it was.

"I get that. It's like the person you loved died and you need to mourn them, but don't believe it was all a lie. Even bad people can do good things sometimes and I'm sure he loves you in his own way." Blake surprised himself at the notion of shades of grey. He had always convinced himself that life was black and white but maybe that wasn't the case.

"Maybe. How's the knee?" She was changing the subject and he let her, knowing that she would talk about it when she was ready, and he would be there to listen.

"It feels a little better. You want to grab the first shower?" He had to fight the urge to suggest they share even though he wanted nothing more.

"Sure, then I can make some toast while you shower. Toast is my speciality."

"How can toast be a speciality?"

"You'll see," she said as she walked away to shower.

Blake smiled as he leaned his head back against the couch. He needed to check in with Waggs about this knee and he also wanted to know if anything had been found on the CCTV around the time of the attack on Pax's home. He couldn't shake the feeling that this was aimed at him not her.

Picking up the phone he dialled Waggs.

"What did you do now?"

"What makes you think I did anything?" Blake replied with a laugh.

"Because it's you, Blake."

"Yeah, well, it wasn't my fault this time. In fact, it wasn't my fault last time. I'm the victim here."

"So what did you do?"

"Some asshole attacked Pax's place. We fought, and the fucker did a knee wheel move on my injured leg."

"Fuck, that's going to potentially set you back weeks."

"Yeah, fuck. I've got ice on it, 'cos it's the size of a football again. Started the anti-inflammatories too."

"You had an X-ray or scan?"

"Nah, don't need one." Blake heard the shower go on and his mind instantly went to a naked Pax in his shower.

"Congratulations, man."

Waggs' words pulled his mind from thoughts of Pax. "What?"

"I didn't know you'd qualified as a medic and were now able to self-diagnose."

"Ha fucking ha."

"Seriously though, you need a scan to see if the ligament is damaged again. Can you come in for eleven and I'll get it done privately?"

"Yeah, fine. Meet you at Eidolon."

"No, meet me at the Nuffield, and I'll make the arrangements," Waggs said mentioning the local private hospital.

"Okay, see you there."

Blake hung up as he heard the shower go off. He sat there for a bit as water from the ice pack dripped down his calf. He was about to move when he saw Pax walk in with just his white towel covering her from chest to mid-thigh, her hair wrapped in a towel. Blake felt like he was going to swallow his tongue as he looked at her. The towel wasn't that revealing but knowing she was naked and wet beneath it made his dick harden. She stopped in the doorway like prey sensing danger.

Her hazel eyes locked on his face and she pointed at the bag on the floor by his feet. "I forgot my bag."

"Come and get it then," he said, and the invitation was more of a demand.

He sat motionless as she walked forward and stopped beside him. She looked down at him when he touched her leg, running his hand up her thigh until it disappeared under the towel. Her skin was like silk beneath his palm.

"So soft," he said as his eyes caught hers, both lost in the moment.

"Blake?"

He snagged her hand and tugged until she was on her knees on the couch beside him. "Do you have any idea how fucking beautiful you are?" he asked and saw her blush. His eyes followed the pink skin as it disappeared into her towel. "Come here." He pulled her gently until she was straddling his thighs.

Pax sat forward so her weight was nowhere near his injured knee. Blake looked up and then cupped her hips through the fabric as he ground his hard cock into the soft heat of her pussy.

A moan of pleasure slipped from her throat and Blake felt his control begin to fray. "That's how I've been around you since the minute I saw you. Hard as fucking stone."

"Do you have to swear so much?" she asked as she rocked against him.

Blake felt his mouth curl into a grin. "You love my dirty mouth."

"I do not."

"Care to test that?"

He tugged on the fold of her towel and let it fall open between them. Pax looked down at her naked body and then up at him without an inch of self-consciousness. And why would she? She was perfect.

Pale, almost alabaster skin, a flat stomach, perky rose-tipped tits that just begged for a man's mouth on them. Her pussy was almost bare except for a small landing strip of red hair. He lifted his hand and ran a finger down her cheek, over the pulse in her neck, and down through the middle of her breasts until he reached her navel.

He looked up at her eyes, their colour now greener than hazel. "Still want to test the theory?"

"Yes," she said, and it was a husky plea.

Blake used his other hand to lean her into him so he could take her mouth in a hot kiss. Pax responded instantly as he dragged his finger over her mound and through the soaking wet lips of her pussy. "Fucking drenched," he said and sealed his lips over hers before she could respond.

In all his years of whoring around, and it had been a few, he had never seen a woman with such an ethereal beauty as Pax. He'd had more than his fair share of beautiful women, some absolute stunners, but this right here in his arms was on another level.

Sliding his finger higher, he circled her clit with his finger as he broke the kiss and watched her face as he drove her towards climax. Her mouth fell open, lips wet and swollen from his kiss, face flushed with desire and he knew he would never get enough of this woman. His head went to her breast as he sucked the tight nipple into his mouth, and she moaned as she gripped his head tight to her body, stopping him from pulling away and she rocked against his hard cock trying to chase her release.

His cock was hard as a rock and he wanted nothing more than to be inside her, except maybe to watch her come from his hand first. In fact, he wanted to watch her come in every way he could make it happen. He pulled away and looked up at her. Her head was thrown back in abandon, wet hair cascading down her back.

"Look at me, Gracie." Her head moved as if it weighed too much and her sleepy sex-laden eyes found his. "Come for me, sweetheart." He plunged his finger inside her tight hot pussy and fucked her. Pax came hard, her thighs shaking, hands gripping his shirt, her pussy clenching around him and she let out a longer keening sound that made his balls ache.

That was the moment he knew he was in trouble. Now he'd had his second hit of her, and it was just as good as the first, he knew he would crave more and more.

"Want to fuck you." he growled not able to hide the husky desire from his voice, his fingers still inside her.

"Yes."

Pulling away he watched her face as he sucked the taste of her from them. She was sweet and musky, and he wanted to eat her until his hunger was satiated but not now. Pax began to undo his zipper, sliding her hand in and taking hold of his cock, her thumb swiping off the bead of pre-cum and making him arch into her hand.

Now he needed to be inside more than he needed to breathe. Snagging his wallet from the side of the couch where he had thrown it earlier, he unwrapped a condom and slid it on as Pax fondled his balls, almost making him embarrass himself like a teenage boy.

"Lift up." He positioned his cock at her entrance and watched as she sank down on him, taking his entire length until she was buried to the hilt. He held her hips still against him so she could get used to the feel of him inside her. Pax started to squirm, and he knew she needed to move.

"Ride me, Gracie."

She did. Slowly at first, then finding her rhythm as she drove them both crazy.

He felt her movements get un-coordinated and watched her falter and swore. "*Fuck.* Your ribs."

He slid out of her and she moaned. He lifted her off his knees and stood, turning her around and pushing her so she was bent over the couch, her ribs against the cushion, her feet on the floor. "If it hurts you fucking tell me," he growled as he slid inside her from behind.

The position allowed him to go deeper, to control the movements. He would take her slow next time but now he needed to come. Blake fucked her as his fingers toyed with her nipples, pinching and rolling them until she whimpered. Pax liked it a little rough and he loved that. They would definitely be exploring it more when they were both healed.

Moving his hand down her belly he rolled her clit, but with not being able to put weight on his leg, he couldn't hold the position. "Tease your clit, baby. Pretend it's my fingers on you."

He moaned as she did, allowing him to grip her hips harder as he fucked them both to climax. His balls tightened and his legs shook as he came so hard, he saw stars. He heard the sound of her orgasm, felt the clench of her walls against him, milking every last drop of his come from him.

They stayed still for a second, breathing hard as they let the last vestiges of pleasure leave their bodies.

"You've killed me for all other women." He kissed her shoulder and pulled out of her.

He heard the chuckle from her as she stood and turned to face him. "I'm sorry, I couldn't—"

"No. Don't say that. If you're hurt or we do something that's painful or uncomfortable or you just plain don't like, you tell me, and we deal with it together. Sex isn't about one person getting off at the expense or the enjoyment of the other. In fact, if you pull a stunt like that again and don't tell me, I'll be pissed," he said firmly leaving no room for argument.

"Okay," she said with a small grin as she bent to pick up her discarded wet towel. He admired her ass unable to resist running a hand over the curve.

"Perfect." He kissed her softly exploring her mouth and wishing he had time to fuck her again, but knowing he didn't, he pulled away. "You all right?" He wanted to make sure she was okay with the sudden change in their relationship. He had planned to wait but then she'd walked in looking like a fucking dream and he was done.

Pax rested her nose against his and smiled "Perfect," she repeated his word.

"Right. I need to get showered and you need to get dressed and stop distracting me." He laughed as he patted her ass gently and moved to get ready for his MRI scan.

"Bossy."

He loved the fact she felt secure enough to sass him, and he smiled as he watched her walk away swinging her hips even more. Blake's grin got wider. She was going to kill him, and he would love every second of it.

CHAPTER ELEVEN

THERE WAS no disguising her sex-tousled hair or the just fucked glow to her skin, so instead of trying to hide it she went with it. Leaving her hair to curl naturally and piling it into a sloppy bun on her head, she added lip gloss and mascara to her rosy-cheeked face. A green and white palm print skirt to mid-thigh and white camisole made her look relaxed and carefree, which was how she felt for the first time in years. Flat metallic ankle strap sandals completed the look.

Pax stepped from the bedroom and saw Blake already dressed in navy cargo shorts and a white tee with white Converse shoes on his feet. He looked good enough to eat. His hair was still wet, his chin slightly stubbly making her wonder what it would feel like between her thighs.

Sex with Blake was all consuming. It stole her breath, her thoughts, and made her feel as if nothing else mattered but him and how he made her feel. It was heady and terrifying, but she couldn't make herself care. Blake made her feel more in one electric episode of lovemaking than she'd ever felt with anyone else. She was going to go all in with this and see what happened. They may not work out, it all might go horribly wrong and she could get her heart broken, but she was done hiding from life.

She had used Zenobi to hide behind and stopped taking chances. She had lost the brave girl who'd walked out on her family years ago. Buried her under fear, sadness, and loneliness. She hadn't realised how lonely she was until Blake had barged into her life and demanded to stay. Now she found she liked the sound of him in the living room while she dressed. Listening to him as he hummed a song off-key while he cooked.

It had only been a few days but already she felt comfortable with him around, like this was normal and how it should be. Her body was still tingling from the orgasms he had given her earlier. He had seemed to know what she'd needed before she did and given it to her. His lecture afterwards had been bossy, but oh, so sweet. He was looking out for her and proving they were a team and she liked that.

"You gonna keep staring or get your ass in the car before I decide to forgo the MRI and fuck you instead?" Blake moved into her body and put his arm around her waist.

Pax tilted her head as she studied him. "I'm trying to decide if you're threatening me or promising?"

"There it is." He fingered her lip.

"What?" she asked.

"Your secret smile again, and best of all I got to put it there." He kissed her cheek tenderly and her throat clogged with emotion.

"Softie." She pulled away breaking his hold on her emotions. Blake quirked an eyebrow as he grabbed her bag and handed it to her and pocketed his keys.

He smiled at her as they got in the car. "Let's keep that our secret, I don't want everyone to know."

He had insisted on driving despite his injured knee. They drove to the Nuffield in comfortable silence. The weather was still warm, and Pax turned her face to the sun, enjoying being out for the first time in days.

They pulled into the carpark and were met by Aiden Wagner

and realised he was the 'Waggs' Blake had mentioned. She'd met him once at a party held by Fortis Security, but hadn't connected him with the nickname. The owner, Zack Cunningham, had married a fellow American and she and Ava had gotten on well.

Aiden was slightly older than the rest of the team except perhaps Mitch. She guessed he was in his early forties. He had blond hair that was already showing signs of grey at the temples, a short-trimmed beard, and square jaw. He was around six feet with a muscular swimmer's build and was incredibly soft spoken. Pax didn't know a lot about him other than he was American, an ex-Green Beret Medic, and didn't go out socially a lot.

She and Blake exited the car which she was in love with. Audi was her favourite car and she had been considering a TT but decided she was getting one of these babies. Blake's hand found her back as they approached Waggs.

"Blake, Pax," he said with a nod at them both.

He studied them for a second before he nodded again and moved to the door leaving them to follow. Pax could have stayed at home, but she needed a few things to take with her to the States and was sick of being housebound. She sat with a mostly silent Waggs while Blake followed an older guy in a white lab coat to get the MRI done.

He was noticeably limping now, and she worried that perhaps she had caused him more damage when they had fucked earlier.

"Do you think he tore the ligament again?"

Waggs' head turned to her and his pale almost ice blue eyes watched her for a second before he answered. "Yes, most probably."

"Shit," Pax said worrying her lip with her teeth.

"It wasn't anything you did."

Her head snapped up. Waggs was looking towards the door watching every time it opened. He had read her mind, and if she wasn't mistaken, was totally aware they were having crazy sex over couches before MRI scans.

"How did you know? Did Blake—?"

Waggs shook his head. "No. Blake might be a slut, but he doesn't kiss and tell so you're safe there."

"Then how?" She was genuinely curious now.

"Blake steers clear of commitment. He doesn't even have house plants for fuck's sake. So the fact that you're here and the way he all but pissed on your leg when he walked towards me was a bit of a giveaway."

Her instinct was to deny it, to say he was wrong, that nothing had happened but that would be wrong. Mainly because it was a lie but also because it would diminish what they had agreed to start. "I like him." She found herself wanting to snatch the words back as soon as she made the admission.

Waggs merely nodded. "Not blind, woman. Blake is one of the good ones despite what he might have you think. Don't let him hide from something that could be beautiful because of what happened in the past."

Pax wanted to ask what he meant. What had happened in his past? But Blake appeared with the results of the MRI in a folder which he handed to Waggs.

He smiled at her as he moved closer, until their shoulders were touching. "Miss me?"

"Sure. I can't go twenty minutes without you now that I've had you."

"Pax, not in front Waggs. I'm shy." His look was one of mock offence.

Pax laughed and rolled her eyes at him. "Of course you are!"

"Well, the ligament is fucked good and proper this time."

Waggs' assessment wasn't something he hadn't already figured out. "Yeah, I kind of guessed that."

"There's no way Jack is going to let you go off on this mission with Pax without back-up."

Pax felt Blake tense. "Jack can't fucking stop me," he replied bristling with aggression.

"No, he can't, but you would be a fool to disobey him."

"I'm not leaving Pax to handle this situation on her own."

Pax felt increasingly guilty for the hassle she was causing. "I can—"

Blake pinned her with a look. "No, you can't."

Ignoring the instant knot of desire at his sexy growl she went on the defensive. "Don't you tell me what I can and can't do."

"Like you when you're all sass and sexy but I won't give on this, Gracie."

His use of her real name caused a pang, and Pax softened her tone really liking that he called her sexy and sassy but not willing to back down either. "I know you want to help but with your leg like it is you could get hurt."

"I love that you care about me, Gracie, but I've got a dick and that dick means I don't let my woman go across the other side of the world to confront her asshole of a father who had her attacked. You are mine, and I protect what's mine." He curled her closer to his body as he said the words and looked at her lips before lifting his eyes to hers.

Pax felt her body relax into him. He made her feel cared for, protected, and so fucking turned on she wanted to jump his bones right then and there.

Waggs rolled his eyes at them both. "Oh, for fuck's sake. Will you two stop with the foreplay? I'll come with you and I can see if Reid will too, or maybe Decker. I have a few days leave owed me anyway." Pax felt Blake tense slightly at that and wondered why.

"I can't ask you to do that," Pax said.

"You ain't asking. I'm offering so I don't have to watch you two flirting with each other anymore" He pulled out his phone as he walked away.

"Fine, call Jack." She felt Blake tense again wondered what had caused the sudden change in him. He seemed on edge all of a sudden.

"You okay?"

"Got you in my arms, haven't I?"

Pax felt a smirk cross her face. "You like me."

"Yeah, babe. I like you," he replied as he watched Waggs pace and talk a frown still on his face.

Pax let him get away with his evasive answer, but she knew he was hiding something and all of a sudden Waggs words came back to her. Was he hiding something big from her or was she doing her usual trick of self-destructing before she could get hurt? Determined not to let that happen she pushed the gloomy thoughts away and kissed him lightly.

Waggs moved back towards them as he slid the phone into his pocket. "Decker, Reid, and I will be going with you. Also, Jack wants you to call him as soon as you can. He said you know what about."

"Cool. Thanks, Waggs."

"Sure. Just ice that fucking knee and we'll see you at the airport," Waggs said as they parted at the entrance of the hospital and he walked towards a beefed up Ford Ranger pickup.

"Let's get what you need and go home. I need to ice my knee and call Jack."

CHAPTER TWELVE

BLAKE WAS EXHAUSTED. He had spent the eleven-hour flight to Los Angeles going over details of Sana Pharmaceuticals with Pax. She had told him everything she knew, including who the shareholders were. That list had included both her parents and her maternal grandfather, which he had found odd until Pax explained that it had been his financing that had allowed her father to start the company.

The company was solidly in the black, making an obscene profit each year. It had quite a few lawsuits but nothing above the norm for a company of its size. They had decided between the five of them to divide and conquer. He and Pax would start with her parents and the board members, while Waggs, Reid, and Decker would look into the lawsuits, the current trials, and see if they could find any discrepancies.

Pax had slept most of the flight, her body curled into his, legs tucked under her bum, head on his shoulder. Blake hadn't slept. He had been watching the three men with him, one in particular. No matter how many times he'd thought back to his recent and older interactions with him, he couldn't find any memory that sparked anything or indicated he could be the traitor.

His posture was relaxed as it always was, face open. But Blake knew liars were masters at hiding things. Add to that some specialist training like could be found in the military or FBI, and you had someone who could have a pint with you while they stabbed you in the back.

It was a sickening and terrifying thought and one that made him angry, so angry because this team had become extended family to him. There wasn't one of them he wouldn't die for and now one of them was causing him to question the entire team.

Blake had closed his eyes and faked sleep the rest of the flight until landing, not wanting to talk to anyone. They had collected their bags with Reid, Decker, and Waggs doing most of the carrying due to his bum leg and taken two cabs to the hotel. Pax had been almost silent the entire time and he could still feel the tense worry coming from her even now as they settled into their room.

She had been on edge since the moment she'd woken for landing and it hadn't dissipated. He watched her walk out of the bathroom, having washed her face, brushed her hair, and wringing her hands together. It was a gesture he hadn't seen from Pax before and he didn't like it one bit.

The woman he was falling for was not nervous and edgy—she was confident and relaxed. Perhaps a little unaware of her own worth —something he was going to rectify with a bit of time—but she wasn't this nervous wreck who kept watching the window and rubbing her palms together.

"Come here, Pax," he said softly.

She looked up as if surprised to see him standing not five feet from her. Then she walked towards him without question. He opened his arms and she walked right into them planting her head on his chest and letting him hold her. "Talk to me."

She stayed silent so long he thought she wasn't going to share what was on her mind. "It just feels wrong being back here in this city where I grew up. I feel like I don't fit here anymore. I was always the girl with lots of friends in the in-crowd. I thought I was the shit. I was superior and snooty, went to all the best parties, had the best clothes, best car, everything. But deep down I hated it all. The only person who ever saw that was Benny. He was my best friend and called me out on it all. He made me see that it wasn't the real me. Then he was gone, and I was alone." She went quiet for a minute and Blake sensed she wasn't done. "I just hate this place and these people. They make me feel dirty, remind me of who I was, and I don't like who I was."

"You're too hard on yourself, Pax." He pulled back a little but didn't let go of her. "Teenagers the world over think they're superior. You got caught up in it, but you didn't become the same adult. You saw yourself and what you were becoming and were mature enough to recognise that. I'm glad you had a friend to help you with that, but I have no doubt that you would've seen it on your own eventually. Look at what you've achieved. You help people in difficult situations. You're the backbone of Zenobi—Roz said so herself. You need to stop being so down on yourself and start seeing what the rest of us do."

"What do you see Blake?"

He saw the vulnerability in her eyes at the question. "I see a woman who is brave and strong, beautiful and kind. A woman who makes me want to be a better person so I'm worthy of her."

"Blake," she said in a whisper as she lifted her head and kissed him.

It was passionate and yet so sweet. It made his blood pump harder as he moved in closer to deepen the kiss.

A knock on the door had him pulling back with a sigh. "Time to suit up, baby," he said with a grin. "We have to go visit the parents."

She made a sound somewhere between a moan and grimace and he laughed as he checked the peephole and saw a grinning Reid.

"Y'all ready?" Reid leaned against the door jamb looking like he was about to go join a biker gang. Tattoos covered him from head to foot including his hands and neck, his hair was long on top and slicked back with an uppercut underneath. His accent seemed to have deepened into his southern drawl since they'd landed on US soil.

"Your South is showing," Blake said with a smirk.

Reid's slow grin was infectious as he replied. "Ladies love some Southern charm."

"Yeah, I bet they do." Blake laughed. "Give us ten minutes. We'll meet you downstairs in the bar for a quick chat before we leave."

"Sure thing." With a nod he sauntered away.

Blake shook his head and smiled. Reid was a cool guy, a fantastic team member, and had earned a fearsome reputation with the FBI's HRT team. It made it that much harder to consider him as a possible traitor. Closing the door he turned to see Pax pulling a pair of wide-leg cream trousers and a pale blush blouse from her case.

"What are you doing?" he asked slightly confused.

She looked up and tilted her head. "Getting changed to go see my parents," she answered as if he was being ridiculous.

"You don't seriously dress up to see your parents, do you?"

Pax smirked. "You most certainly do." She indicated her skinny jeans, ballet flats, and green peasant top which he thought looked fucking fantastic on her. "My mother would skin me alive if I turned up like this."

He couldn't imagine having to dress up to see his family. They had seen him hungover, sick, drunk, and lounging in his pants on the couch. He had never felt judgement from them. They were his family and they loved him regardless of what he wore. For Pax though, he would do what it took to make her feel comfortable. He grabbed his case. "I guess I better change too then."

"Oh no, you don't have to. I'm the only one that will be found wanting. My mother will eat you with a spoon—literally—if you let her," she said without humour.

Blake continued to pull his case towards him. "Regardless, if you're changing so am I. Strength in numbers, right?" he said with a wink.

Pax smiled and cupped his face with her soft hands, a strange look passing over her face. "Thank you," she said simply and with that disappeared into the bathroom.

Twenty minutes later she emerged while he was texting Reid to say they would be down soon. He looked up and saw she had done a bang up job of hiding most of the bruising on her face. He could still make out some near her cheek but all in all, it was a good job. Not that anything, even black eyes, could take away from her beauty. The look she had gone for was pure Pax—elegant, sexy, sleek, and sophisticated. It suited her. She was stunning, but he still preferred her in jeans or a simple summer skirt and vest top. Not that he got or deserved any say on how she dressed. She was her own person and he had no intention of telling her how to be her awesome self.

This though, this was armour and he was going to find out what she needed it for if it killed him.

"You changed," she said as she picked up her bag from the bed.

"Yeah, it's no big deal," he said indicating the navy suit and white shirt sans tie he wore.

"It is," she said with a wrinkle of her nose. "I feel like I need to pee on you to stop my mother from flirting with you."

"Yeah, not really my kink." He laughed as he put his hand to her back and ushered her to the door.

"No, me neither."

She had relaxed a little, but he couldn't help feeling the nerves that were emanating from her as they rode the lift to the ground floor. They stepped off and walked through the foyer towards the bar where he could see Reid, Waggs, and Decker standing at the bar with women admiring them like they were pastries in a bakery.

Blake stopped short when Pax froze in front him, almost making him walk into her. She was staring towards the front door, her eyes wide. He followed her line of sight and saw two men with heavy builds in black suits. Typical bodyguard attire—he would know, he'd worn it for long enough as a PPO. Both men were more than likely armed, one bald, the other had long hair pulled into a low ponytail.

"Who are those men?" He already had an idea but wanted Pax to confirm it.

"My father's personal protection, Eddie and Pete." She sighed. "They're okay. I just wasn't expecting them so soon."

"How did they know you were here?" He didn't like that they were being ambushed.

Pax turned to him and shrugged. "We didn't exactly hide the fact, and like I said, my dad knows everything."

The two men waited a respectful distance away not attempting to approach her.

"Let's have a quick word with the guys then we can leave but we take a cab. I'm not being dictated to by them."

Pax nodded her agreement as he took her hand and they walked towards the bar area.

Waggs saw them and quickly shooed the clearly irritated young women who were hanging on their every word away. One had the audacity to glare openly at Pax. He felt her prickle beside him.

Instead of cutting the girl to ribbons with her tongue, Pax smiled sweetly at her.

The young woman confused by Pax's smile huffed and stormed off as Decker chuckled. "You probably just cost her three weeks in therapy."

Pax shrugged her shoulders and smiled, although it didn't reach her eyes. Blake quietly and swiftly brought the guys up to speed.

"Keep in touch and if we haven't checked in by eighteen hundred hours, call Jack, and let him know we're not back."

He didn't believe that would happen. Pax's father wasn't stupid and even if he was, Blake had a little plan up his sleeve to keep them safe in the short term. Pax had been unsure but eventually agreed. It was smart even if she didn't like the idea.

With his hand in hers he kissed their joined hands and grinned. "Let's go meet the parents."

Pax laughed lightly as he wanted her to, erasing the look of tension that she had worn for the last few hours.

They walked towards the doors and Eddie and Pete nodded.

"Miss Paxton."

"Hi, Eddie, Pete."

The two men fell in behind them. To Blake it all felt surreal. He had always been the PPO and now he had two men watching his back similarly. He didn't like it and he didn't need it. He had to grudgingly admit though, as Eddie slipped in front of them to get the doors and proceeded them, they weren't bad at it.

Light flooded the entrance and a cache of photographers and journalists jostled to put microphones in front of their faces as Eddie and Pete hustled them to a car.

"Miss Paxton, what happened to your eye?"

"Miss Paxton, is true you are to marry an Englishman?"

"Miss Paxton, are you back for good?"

Questions came from all angles and Pax handled it with the same calm composure she handled everything else. She held her head high and smiled her unique smile. "If and when there is anything to tell, I'll tell it."

Eddie ushered them into a waiting car and Blake let him. It would have raised questions if they hadn't. The door slammed on the limo and Pete pulled away from the curb seconds later.

Pax sighed and leaned into him, letting her mask slip.

He rubbed her hand with his thumb. "You okay?"

"Yes. I just forgot how bloodthirsty they were." She sighed again. "Sorry you got caught up in this, Cal."

She'd used his given name for the first time, and it made him want to kiss her until she could hardly catch her breath. There was something very intimate in her using the name that only his family used. He liked it—perhaps too much.

"Don't be sorry, this isn't your doing. I'm glad I'm the one you came to for help."

Pax quirked her head at him, obviously waiting for him to expand on his remark.

"If you had gone to someone else, I wouldn't have gotten to know the sweet beautiful girl underneath the stunning sexy woman." He saw her face soften even as she dipped her head to blush beautifully.

Blake let her have her moment and tapped on the window.

"Hey, Pete, stop the car and find us a cab," he said when the window came down.

"But..."

Blake cut him off. "Just do it." His tone brooked no argument.

"As you wish." Blake could tell Pete wasn't happy from the way his jaw was clenched tightly as he cast a look at Eddie who shrugged.

The car slid to a stop and Eddie stepped out to hail them a cab. Blake followed suit and as soon as the cab skidded to a halt beside them, helped Pax out. Once they were safely inside the cab, he gave the driver the address.

Then they sat back silently, Pax shoring up her emotional defences against the upcoming meeting with her parents and Blake trying to decide how he would play this. Either way, he was going to let Mr and Mrs Paxton know that Gracie was off limits to them from now on and if they didn't like that, then it was tough shit. The woman who was almost statue still at his side meant something to him. She meant a lot and he wouldn't let her be hurt ever again.

He didn't delve deeper into his thoughts knowing now wasn't the time. But later he would, and he would see what Robert Paxton saw the minute he opened the door.

CHAPTER THIRTEEN

As THE CAB pulled up behind the limo at the first of the two security gates, Pax felt her stomach knot painfully. This had been her home her entire childhood and most of it had been happy, if a little lonely. She felt Blake grip her hand anchoring her to the present. She gave him a shaky smile that felt false even to her.

As they drove, the lights over the beautiful Tuscan style home came into view. It was a stunning house and the view over the mountains and canyon were breath-taking. The cab stopped and she took a deep breath as Eddie opened the door and Blake got out holding out a hand for her. She waited as Blake leaned in and offered the driver some money and took a card with the number to call him back on.

Blake held on to her hand tightly as they walked to the front door and he rang the bell as she had done since the night she'd left, and it had stopped being her home. Blake stood close, his arm touching her shoulder, the warmth from it comforting her and giving her strength. The door swung open and there he was—the man who had raised her, who had been her idol and the first man to break her heart.

She watched him pale underneath his permanent Malibu tan.

"Grace!" His eyes traversed her face and if she didn't know better, she would say he looked shaken.

"Hey, Dad," she answered her voice sounding stronger than she felt.

He pulled the door open as if remembering his manners and ushered them inside. "Come in, come in," he said regaining his usual aplomb.

She stepped through and felt the familiar ache in her chest at the house that used to be her home. It was spectacular with large open spaces, marble floors, and a large double staircase leading to the second floor. An entranceway ran through the middle with the kitchen and dining room to the left and the living room and library to the right.

"Dad, this is my boyfriend Calvin Blake," she said introducing the two men. "Blake, my father Robert Paxton."

The two shook hands and she could feel them sizing each other up. In a normal situation this would have been the two most important men in her life meeting and would have been significant. Maybe in another life but not now. It was funny to think that without the rift between her and her father she never would have had the life she did now. She never would have met the man who was fast coming to mean everything to her.

"Your mother is by the pool; we've just finished a late lunch." Her father seemed to be trying to fill the silence as he led them through to the back patio and pool area.

"You have a beautiful house."

Pax felt it significant that Blake didn't say home and tried to see it from his view.

This house had been her home but as she looked around at the stylish residence with priceless art and not a single thing out of place, she realised she wouldn't swap her tiny home for it. Her home was filled with warmth and candid snaps of her and her friends in frames.

The only pictures in frames in this house were the stuffy portraits that she'd hated having done.

The sun was starting to wain as they stepped out onto the patio, it was spectacular, and she could see all the way over the manicured lawns to the canyon and beyond. Her mother Henrietta Paxton was a beautiful woman. She stood from the sun lounger as they approached, her long shapely legs on full display as she sashayed towards them.

"Grace, my darling, what happened to your face? You look awful."

Pax felt Blake squeeze her hand and looked up to see his face had hardened. Pax definitely got her looks from her mother who was tall, slim to the point of being almost too thin, and constantly reminded Pax how she should watch her weight. Both had red hair although her mother's hair was more blonde than red now. Her mother had blue eyes though, while Pax followed her father for that. She also had her mother's creamy complexion which her mother was very proud of, hence the reason she wore a sheer cover-up to protect her skin. At fifty-two she was a beautiful woman and Pax had always felt like the ugly duckling to her mother's swan.

"I was mugged." Her eyes landed on her father to see if he reacted at all to what he'd had done to his only child.

"Well, you should really be more careful," her mother admonished.

She could have sworn she heard Blake growl but dismissed it as she watched her father.

"Henri," her father said sharply and angrily, if she wasn't mistaken. He seemed furious and concerned filled his face when he turned back to her. "Sit, please, both of you." He rang a bell and a pretty maid in a white dress came through. "What would you like to drink?" he asked as she and Blake took seats on the cream sofa.

"I'll have sparkling water."

"I'll have the same." Blake held on to her hand as if he knew she needed his touch.

The maid ran off to get the drinks as her parents sat opposite.

"Tell me about what happened. Did you call the police?"

She felt an odd moment of doubt. Her father seemed so genuinely concerned for her it made her want to weep.

"No, it was dark. I didn't get a good look at them." She watched his reaction.

He went still at her words. "Them? There was more than one? Oh, Grace, I do wish you would come home where I can look after you."

"She'll be looked after in her home from now on. I'll see to it personally."

Her father must have realised he had ruffled Blake's feathers. "I meant no disrespect, Calvin. I'm merely worried about her safety. I'm heartened to see my Grace with a man such as yourself. You have an excellent reputation in your field as a PPO. To the Queen no less. Knowing she has you makes me feel happier. Although our relationship has been somewhat strained over the last few years, she is my daughter and I love her with all my heart."

Pax had to swallow the tears down. He sounded so heartfelt. She wanted desperately to believe him but then she thought back to the terrible night she'd found out the truth and hardened herself to his words.

The maid came back with their water and talk turned to other things—her job at the gallery, Blake's work in private security. Her mother flirted with Blake every chance she got, touching his arm or knee in a mock-friendly way which Pax ignored. She'd seen it done to every boyfriend she ever brought home until she stopped bothering after she found her mother and the last one in a very compromising position.

Her father stood, bringing her out of her reverie and glanced at his wife for a second, a warning look in his eyes before he turned to Blake then his eyes came to rest on hers. "Pax, may I have a second of your time? I need to discuss a personal matter with you."

Pax looked at her father with a surprise for a second, her instincts telling her she should listen to what he had to say. Her father could be ruthless, but he wasn't an idiot and with the press knowing she and Blake were here, they had secured their safety for now.

Pax felt Blake squeeze her hand gently to get her attention. She looked at him and he gave her a barely perceptible shake of his head. He didn't want her out of his sight, the thought made her happy, happier than something so simple should. She gave him a reassuring smile and moved to kiss his cheek then slid her eyes to his before lifting them towards her mother. "It will be okay. Just keep on eye out for my mother."

She knew he didn't like it by the way his jaw tightened but he didn't fight her on it, just nodded. Pax stood and followed her father from the deck into the house. An older maid walked across the hallway with her head dipped low. She wasn't one Pax recognised, her mother had very exacting standards and didn't particularly like the prettier maids; hence they didn't last long.

Her father led her into his study and a flood of memories hit her as the familiar scent of leather and musk filled her nose. The melancholy pain in her chest was almost overwhelming. She rubbed the ache there and looked around the room she'd spent so much time in as a child and saw not much had changed. Large, high windows looked out towards the vast mountain, and a magnificent oak desk sat in the middle of the room with a brown leather desk chair behind it. The wall to the left was covered in a bookshelf, opposite that sat a drinks bar and stools. It was the original man cave and yet she had been happy in here. Painting and colouring as her father worked.

Pax pushed the feelings of sorrow away, straightened her shoulders and faced her father "What did you want to discuss?"

She watched her father flinch at the cold tone of her voice before his shoulders drooped a little. Pax didn't want to acknowledge it, but she felt guilty. Considering what he had done, it was silly, but she wasn't someone who enjoyed hurting others.

He walked to the bar and poured himself a brandy before turning to offer her one. She shook her head no and waited, her back ramrod tight wanting him to get on with it.

"Talk to me, Grace."

"Talk to you?"

"Tell me what happened to you." He stepped closer and she held her ground and fought the tears and the tender look in his eyes. "We were always so close." He looked away as he turned to the window. "I don't know what went wrong."

Pax felt her heart rate increase as anger took over. His innocent act more than she could bear. Crossing her arms she leaned back on one hip as she tapped her foot in agitation. "How can you say that? You viciously betrayed me and then acted like it was *nothing*."

Her father spun and stepped back as if she had struck him. "I made a mistake, Grace. Am I not allowed to be human?"

"A mistake? Is that what you call it? You let my friend die! That is not a mistake." She threw up her hands in frustration. "A mistake is choosing the wrong school or forgetting a school play."

"Which I never did. Not once did I miss anything you did at school or out of it. I love you. You are my only child and I would die for you."

"And yet here I am with the bruises to prove that wrong."

Her father blanched at her words. For a second, she thought he would pass out as he staggered to the chair behind his desk and fumbled in the drawer for something. He pulled out a bottle of pills and unscrewed the lid before washing two down with the brandy. She stepped forward as if to help and had to steel herself from going to him.

Her father looked old all of a sudden weak and despite everything she hated that she cared. "What are those tablets for?"

He looked up and she saw sweat bead his brow. "I have angina, it's nothing serious." She could see the colour was beginning to return to his cheeks. "What did you mean about the bruises proving me wrong?"

Pax felt incredibly tired all of a sudden. A headache was forming behind her eyes as she tried to keep up with the barrage of emotions she was dealing with. She was angry that her father insisted on keeping up this charade when they both knew he was behind it.

Rubbing the temples she sighed. He seemed determined to make this play out and she just wanted to go back to the hotel take a long shower and sleep. "Stop, Dad. Just stop. I know you were behind it. I know you sent the two men to warn me off pursuing this latest illegal drug test by your company." She walked to the door and stopped, hand on the doorknob and turned back to him taking in his pallor and the despondency on his face. She hardened her heart. "It won't work. I *will* get justice."

"I don't know what you think you know but I would never harm a hair on your head or order such a thing. I don't know where this is coming from. I know you blamed me for Benny dying but I can assure it wasn't my fault. All I did was try and help. Maybe I could have handled your accusations better than I did but I'm only human, and I lashed out at you. In doing so I lost you. I'll take that regret to my grave." He dipped the crystal glass and finished the brandy before he continued. "As for the rest, I have no idea what's happening at Sana these days. The board voted to replace me when your grandfather found out about my health issues."

Pax rocked back on her heels at the words. Sana was her father's life. For him not to be in charge was unthinkable. She knew he and her grandfather—her mother's father—had their issues but to vote him off was a shock. It also made her pause and consider that maybe things were not quite as they seemed.

Either way, it didn't eradicate her father's wrongdoing with Benny. He had all but admitted he had given the drugs to Benny. Pax thought back to the night she'd found out and the familiar feelings of betrayal rose. She and Henrietta had never had a touchy-feely mother-daughter relationship. Half the time her mother resented her, the other half she was distant, but Pax knew she loved her.

If it hadn't been for her mother getting drunk and revealing the truth about Benny and her father, Pax would most likely never have found out what kind of man her father was. As much as it had hurt, and it had been the single most painful thing of her life, she was grateful for her mother's honesty that night.

Pax took one last look at her father and left the room almost crashing into Blake who looked ready to commit murder.

CHAPTER FOURTEEN

HE FELT like smoke would start spewing out of his ears if he didn't get out of this pretentious place in the next few seconds. How Pax could have grown up in such a cold environment with a praying mantis for a mother he had no clue. In fact, the only warmth and genuine behaviour stemmed from the man Pax thought betrayed her.

That was another thing that had his instincts humming—her father's reaction to her injuries. While Henrietta seemed to criticise and almost blame Pax, her father had seemed genuinely concerned and that didn't fit with the man Pax described. Either the man deserved a fucking Oscar, or he had no idea about the attack on her which threw up a whole host of questions. He needed to find Pax and get the hell out of here.

He had never hurt a woman but when Pax and her father left the patio and Henrietta had slid closer and started rubbing his leg, he had been tempted to break her hand. He had resisted and as she went to grab his cock, he had merely pushed her away and stood up.

The woman was not deterred though. As he had moved towards the pool to look out at the magnificent vista, she had sidled up to him and draped her body over his side, leaning her breasts against his arm. Not wanting to cause a scene and embarrass Pax he had stayed still.

"Did you really protect the Queen of England?" she asked as she rubbed the muscle of his bicep.

Blake had never felt more uncomfortable in his life. Not even when he was younger and his best friend's older sister had tried to seduce him. Although try was the wrong word—she had definitely succeeded. "Yep."

"You must be so brave and you're so strong. I wonder what it would be like to have a man protect you with his body?" She carried on caressing his arm, her intent and the way she said body made it clear what she meant. He fought the anger that this woman would behave this way towards her daughter's boyfriend.

"It is just a job." He disentangled himself from Henrietta and faced her with space between them. "Protecting your daughter however is my honour and a gift. She is a very special woman." Blake saw the calculation in Henrietta's eyes before she hid it behind fake laugh as she sashayed to the table and picked up a slim cigarette holder and lit one.

"Grace is a stubborn girl, but she's pretty in a plain way." Her hand waved in the air flippantly. "She's lucky to have bagged herself a man like you."

Blake sawed his jaw back and forth as he ground his teeth to keep from saying anything he might regret. Instead, he tried to use the time with Henrietta to get information useful to the investigation. "I don't think I would agree with that. Are Grace and her father close?" he asked as he moved to sit back down.

"They were. He would have done anything for her, she was his little princess."

Blake detected jealousy in her tone. "What happened? Gracie said they had fallen out but not why." The lie was boldfaced, and he didn't care.

Henrietta sat opposite him crossing her long legs to reveal an ample amount of thigh. She was an attractive woman, but she didn't hold a candle to Pax. Pax was beautiful inside and out, her sparkle and humour one of the first things he had noticed about her. All of it wrapped up in a stunning package of grace and beauty that left anyone else in the shade.

He waited for Henrietta to continue knowing most people would scramble to fill a silence.

"Grace found out her father was not the man she thought he was. She had looked up to him, worshipped him even. They were like two peas in a pod. He never missed a single recital or parent's evening at school. Whereas an anniversary meant nothing to him. Then one night she found out the truth." She rolled her hand in the air and ash dropped from the cigarette on to her leg. She brushed it away and sat up taking a sip of her drink.

"That must have been difficult for you being the outsider?" He offered the false sympathy hoping it would encourage her to be more forthcoming.

Her eyes met his and he saw a flash of hatred spear through them before she masked it, her face falling into that of the perfect wife, mother, and hostess. "Not at all. I love my husband and my daughter. I would rather he be a perfect parent than a perfect husband. I know what it takes to be an adult woman in this world. My Grace did not. Maybe now she has a man to take care of her she will realise." Henrietta stood gracefully. "If you will excuse me, I have a migraine attack coming on."

Blake nodded and watched as she walked away. This place was poisonous. He needed to find Pax and get out of there. He moved back inside the house and followed the sound of voices and was about to knock when Pax burst out of the room like the house was on fire almost knocking into him. Blake reached for her shoulders to steady her as his eyes scanned her face. She looked shaken and upset and the desire to walk inside and tear her a strip off her father for upsetting her warred with the need to get away from here.

"Hey, you okay?"

Her eyes were wild and confused as her hands grabbed on to his forearms. "I...yes. I want to go home. Back to the hotel," she clarified.

Blake tucked her under his arm as he steered them towards the door and dialled the number the cab driver had given him and asked him to come and collect them. "Come on, let's go wait outside."

The early evening sun touched their skin as they left the property and walked down the drive towards the gate. Blake turned and saw Eddie watching them from the front door, clearly making sure they left the property like any good guard would.

As they reached the gate, the cab swung in and Blake moved to open the door for Pax to proceed him inside. He slid in beside her and took her hand in his letting her have a moment to compose herself as they were driven back to the hotel.

The cab stopped and Blake chucked some money including a hefty tip at the driver who nodded and tipped his baseball cap. "Cheers."

A few photographers were still hanging around and he leaned in to help Pax out, not for show but because he needed to touch her, to protect her from anything that would hurt her. She took his hand and gave him a small genuine smile as she slid from the car with all the finesse of a seasoned celebrity. Her large glasses covered her eyes and Blake made sure his aviators were in place as the evening sun shone on them.

He ushered them inside ignoring the flash of the camera knowing that this hotel took its guest's security seriously. It was his job to know such things and whatever else anyone said about him, he was good at his job.

Blake glanced at Pax as they travelled up in the elevator, her silence in the car was causing him to worry now. He bit back the need for answers knowing she would talk when she was ready.

Leaving the elevator they moved to the door of their room and went inside. Blake did a sweep of the room for bugs and found none, not that he was surprised but he would rather be overly cautious than under.

He sat on the bed beside Pax who had flopped on her back, arms out, hair all around her.

"Talk to me, sweetheart," he coaxed gently.

Her closed eyes opened, and she watched him with a strange look on her face. She didn't answer his question but posed her own. "Did she make a pass at you?"

Blake had no intention of lying to her, but he didn't want to hurt her. "Yes, she did. I take it that's not the first time?"

Pax shrugged a delicate shoulder as if it meant nothing, but Blake was no fool. "She did it with every boy I brought home. I stopped bringing them home after a while." She moved to sit up tossing her hair over her shoulder as she faced him. No sadness or surprise marred her pretty face. "It's not her fault. She can't seem to help herself and she doesn't mean anything by it."

Blake was shocked. Hearing her defend her mother's behaviour was confusing and a little unsettling. "Gracie, it most certainly is her fault and she can definitely help herself. She's a grown woman for God's sake." He stood and brushed his hair back from his forehead in agitation. Pax looked up at him a look of surprise and confusion there. "Pax, can't you see this isn't normal behaviour from a parent?"

"I know that but what the hell am I supposed to do? She's my mother and she doesn't mean to hurt me!"

Blake sat down beside her and took her hand. "Gracie, how do you not see her for what she is? She belittles you, criticises you, and treats you with contempt." He saw her wince and tempered his tone. "You are worth ten of her." Blake stroked her hair back from her cheek looking deeply into her eyes.

Her mouth opened and he knew she was going to argue so he did the only thing he could he showed her how special she was. His mouth came down on hers in a drugging kiss that was at once gentle and powerful. He wondered how he had managed to think he had lived without the taste of her. She opened for him immediately, her body leaning into his as she lit up in his arms.

His hand moved to cup her neck as he kissed his way down her neck, nibbling on her pulse points as he pushed the material of her top from her shoulders exposing the pearly perfection of her skin to his eyes and lips. Reaching the curve of her breast he pulled the lacey fabric down and sucked her pink nipple into his mouth. His voice was husky as he broke away and looked at her heavy-lidded eyes. "Perfection."

Her mouth tilted into the smile that made him crazy and he knew he was falling for this woman—hard. She had the power to destroy him and he didn't care. He saw something in her, something special, something beautiful, and he wanted it all for himself.

Grace Paxton was strong and gentle, kind and sweet with an air of vulnerability that spoke to him. For the second time in his life he was in love, except this time he had a chance at something—a chance to make something profoundly beautiful and he wouldn't give it up.

Pushing her back on the bed he took his time stripping her of her armour, kissing every place he touched until she was whimpering beneath him with need. He wanted her to see what he saw, what the world saw when they looked at her.

When she was completely naked before him on the bed, he stood to gaze at her. His cock was hard as rock begging for relief. Every part of him wanted to bury himself in her perfect pussy that was made just for him. But he wanted to take his time, to show her what a prize she was. Show her she wasn't second best to a mother that didn't value her, or a boyfriend that didn't realise how fucking lucky he was that she would even look at him.

Stripping his clothes he went to his knees in front of her, his eyes travelling over her flushed skin. Bending, he ignored the pain in his knee and tunnelled his hands underneath her, grasping both her ass cheeks in his palms and squeezing gently. Lowering his head he nipped at the soft skin of her thighs before licking his way upwards from the bottom of her slit until he found her clit.

Her head went back, her chest leaving the bed, her magnificent hair making her look ethereal and otherworldly. "Blake, oh God, don't stop."

Her hand on his head stopped him from moving as she chased her climax while he worshipped her. He didn't answer but kept up his assault on her senses until he felt the first flutter of her climax. Using his tongue he fucked her until she was writhing and screaming his name as she came apart.

Her hand left his head and he looked up at her with a devilish smile. "Fucking beautiful. You have no idea how amazing you are, but you will. We won't be leaving this bed until you understand what you mean to me and what a gift you are to those around you."

She smiled as she reached for him and he covered her body with his being careful not to put any weight on her ribs. He looked down at her lips swollen from his kiss, her body flushed from her orgasm and he wanted to spend every day like this with her. "You are special."

"So are you," she replied her eyes soft as she caressed the stubble on his jaw.

He kissed her then and proceeded to spend the next few hours making her see how unique and amazing she was.

Hours later as he lay in bed with Pax asleep on his chest, he looked at the ceiling trying to resist the temptation to go back and wring her mother's scrawny neck. He knew she was the reason for Grace's lack of self-worth. The reason she saw herself as somehow less than those around her. Her father wasn't the one who had done the damage, it was Henrietta. Which begged the question, what else had she done?

He had been doing this job a while and his instincts had kept him alive more than once. Now his were telling him that her father had been genuine when he had reacted to her appearance. The way he was with Pax wasn't an act, he really loved his child. Henrietta, on the other hand, only seemed to love herself.

Was Pax wrong about her dad or was he not seeing something? He needed to ask Pax what her father had said to her in his study. She had clearly been upset when she'd come out, but he hadn't wanted to push her. But time was of the essence and he needed to be back in the UK before Jack went away.

It would be easier if he could tell her what was happening with Eidolon, but he would never betray Jack in that way and as far as he knew, it wasn't related to Pax's situation in any way. At least, he didn't think it was. His mind went back to the attack at her house and how the person had known to target his injured leg. That hadn't been a coincidence and he didn't like it touching Pax. He now had multiple threats and he wasn't sure exactly where any of them were coming from.

They needed a better plan. Part of that would involve looking into Henrietta Paxton further, as well as her father. Both were guilty of something—they just needed to figure what and how it affected Pax if at all.

His phone buzzed beside him with a text and lifting up he snagged it with his free hand and saw it was from Waggs.

MEET US IN THE BAR AT 9. WE HAVE A LEAD.

Blake shot back a reply and dropped his phone.

It was time to get serious and eliminate the threat once and for all. Then he would see if he and Pax were leading where he hoped they were. His mother would be giddy if he took Pax home to meet her. The thought made him smile as he turned and kissed her shoulder intent on waking her up in the nicest possible way.

CHAPTER FIFTEEN

BLAKE CHEWED on a piece of the medium rare fillet steak before glancing at Pax who was picking at her salmon. "Tell us about Benny's family."

The team were seated around the table eating a late dinner and discussing the case. Initially he had wanted to do this in private, but she hadn't wanted to explain it twice which he understood so they had met Reid, Waggs, and Decker in their suite for dinner. Luckily for them the suite they were in also had its own dining area where they could eat so they had the privacy and security he preferred.

Waggs and Reid were happily tucking into rare cuts of fillet steak, while Decker ate quinoa and spinach meatballs with gluten-free pasta. Decker very much followed that his body was a temple and would only eat organic, healthy food. Blake had tried the whole 'healthy eating' thing and while some of what Decker ate was good, most of it tasted like cardboard to him. What was life without a greasy burger or doughnut now and then?

Pax lifted her eyes to his, and he saw sadness flicker through them before she banked it. She had woken up to his mouth on her and after making love to her in the shower she had seemed almost back to her usual self. She was still processing her visit to her parents and he knew she would talk about it when she was ready, but they needed the information from her to help solve the case.

He hadn't wanted to push her and in normal circumstances, he wouldn't, but time was of the essence and he'd been left with the feeling after leaving her parents that more was at play here than they knew and he didn't like it.

"Benny Castillo's family were originally from Sacramento." She paused to take a sip of water. "They moved to Loma Linda which is about an hour's drive from Palm Springs. His mom Sally was transferred with her job to the area when he was thirteen."

Reid sat back in his chair. "What did she do for a living?"

Pax glanced at him and Blake followed the interaction. "She was an account manager for an advertising company. I forget the name, but I can find out." Pax sat forward and pushed her plate away to lean on the table. "Anyway, from what Benny told me his father was a deadbeat lowlife. He was serving fifteen years in prison for armed robbery and assault. Benny had nothing to do with him."

Blake took a sip of the beer in front of him. "What about siblings?"

"Two younger brothers. His mom remarried Frank Nixon just after they moved here. That was another reason for the move. Her husband worked for the company too. The youngest was only two when Benny died." The sorrow in her voice made it catch on the last word and she cleared her throat. Everything in him wanted to reach for her but he knew she wouldn't want to appear weak in front of the others.

Waggs, ever the medic, chimed in then. "Tell us about his illness."

"He started getting bad headaches when we were in eleventh grade. He kept blowing it off as too much studying. Benny was an A grade student, but he worked his ass off to keep his grades up. He wanted to be a marine biologist," she said wistfully.

"When did he go to the doctor?"

"When he collapsed at school. They diagnosed him with a brain tumour, and he began chemo right away. The tumour was inoperable."

Waggs nodded in understanding. "It didn't help?"

"No. That's when Sana got involved."

Blake stood and walked to the writing desk in the lounge area of the suite and grabbed a piece of paper and a pen. He handed it to Pax. "Can you write as much of the details down as you can including the major players? Also his biological father's details. We can't discount anything at this point."

Pax nodded and took the paper. "Yes, of course."

He began to pace his leg aching from being seated for so long. "We need a plan. I think Pax and I should visit Sally Nixon and find out exactly how Sana became involved." He turned to Pax and gave her an assessing look. "I have to say, Pax, after today I'm not convinced your father is as involved as we thought. He looked ready to stroke out when he saw you."

Pax was nodding slowly. "I agree. When we were in his study, he kept saying he had no clue why I was angry at him or what he had done. He also said he'd been voted out as managing director by the board."

Decker who had been relatively quiet up to this point spoke up. "What for?"

"He has angina, and get this, the person to instigate his removal was my grandfather."

"His father?"

"No, my mom's father. He put up the money for the business initially, so he was a managing partner. My mother is too, but her role has always been silent."

Blake let this information sink in. Was her mother a silent partner though, or was his dislike of the woman clouding his judgement? "So if he didn't order the hit, who did, and is he behind the original drug trial or was someone else?"

"I honestly don't know."

"Okay, we need to investigate all the known players including your mom, grandfather, and the members of the board. Also any trial nurses or doctors that were working back then."

"Yes, but how?" Pax angled her head and rubbed her the back of her neck. He could see the toll this was taking on her.

Blake smiled at her and moved closer, sliding his hands under the sleeveless top and massaging her shoulders. Her head fell forward giving him greater her access. "I suggest Decker poses as a journalist writing a book on the fast-rising business of this century." Blake looked at Decker. "You already have a cover in place for that, don't you?"

Decker nodded. "Yes, I do. Hopefully that will get me access to the board members."

Blake looked at Waggs. "Feel out the staff, find out where they hang out and use some of that hidden charm. Pax and I will start with Sally first thing tomorrow. Reid, can you trace the father, find out where he is and what he's up to now? I don't think he's involved but let's rule him out."

Reid nodded slowly as if he was thinking but remained silent. The others nodded and began to walk to the door. Decker and Reid walked out with a wave, but Waggs stopped and looked at him. "Ice that knee."

Blake saluted him and nodded as he closed the door. His hands left Pax and he moved to her front and pulled her from the chair and motioned to the veranda. "Come on, let's go out and enjoy this spectacular view with a drink."

Pax followed as he picked up their drinks, keeping her hand in his.

Their room looked out over the pool bar with the twinkling lights of a few surrounding buildings off in the distance. He sat on the rattan sofa and looked up at Pax as he set their drinks on the low glass table in front of him. He heard a sigh from her as she settled beside him, lifting her long sexy legs to the glass edge of the table. Pink painted toenails made her look delicate and hot as fuck.

Tilting his head to the side he looked at her. "You okay?"

She angled her head to him and let out another small sigh. "I guess."

"Want to talk about it?"

Pax reached out and twined her fingers through his as she dropped her gaze. "My father was my hero. I adored him, and it was mutual. He never missed a single thing I did. The happiest times of my life was drawing and colouring in his study as he worked." She looked up and he saw the echoes of grief in her eyes. "Even on the day I found out what he had done, I didn't want to admit it. My heart was broken about Benny. I had been barred from his funeral because his family blamed Sana."

Blake felt a tendril of unease curl through him at the thought of Pax being blamed for something which she had no control over. He shouldn't but he felt angry towards Sally Nixon for taking her grief out on a child. His rationale told him it was not her fault. For a mother to lose a child was incomprehensible but when it came to Pax, he had no impulse control. "It wasn't your fault, Gracie."

"I know that now, but it hurt. I had spent a lot of time at Benny's place and they had treated me like one of the family, then all of a sudden I was like a leper."

He pulled her closer and kissed her head in a comforting gesture. "It must have been hard."

Pax was silent for a little while before she spoke again. "It was like he had no clue the damage he had done, no concept of the pain he had caused. He just saw the bottom line for the business and this drug would have done good things for Sana if it had worked." She was tracing the veins on his arm as she spoke, completely absorbed in a time gone past. "That night I packed my stuff after fighting with my father and left. I never went home."

Blake stayed silent feeling she wasn't finished as she cuddled closer to him lifting his arm so she could rest her head against his shoulder.

"The sad thing is, when he was pleading his innocence today and telling me about his angina, I had to fight everything in me to turn and walk away from him." She lifted up and looked at him tears in her eyes. "How is it that I still love him? Am I just a glutton for punishment?"

Blake took her face in his hands and made her look at him. "No, Gracie, it makes you human. Relationships with parents are complex. You can dislike them but still love them, hate them but still seek their approval."

A single tear tipped over the edge and slid slowly down her cheek breaking his heart.

"I don't know exactly what happened with Sana and Benny and if your father was involved or not, but we'll find out—together. I promise you." He swiped the tear away with his thumb as she nodded. They sat in silence for a while, content to just be with no need for useless words to fill the void.

Pax shifted and her eyes came to his. "What's the most embarrassing thing that has ever happened to you?"

Blake could see the playful look in her eyes replacing the sadness of earlier. "Hmm, let me think." He brushed his fingertips over her arm as he thought. "When I was fifteen my mum had to go into hospital for a minor operation." He leaned forward and set his glass on the table. "My dad had gone with her and I was watching my sisters for a few hours. I was in my room playing Xbox when my youngest sister Erin came in and said Natalie was crying.

"Nat is three years younger than me. I was pissed because I had just managed to get past a new level on Call of Duty and wanted to play it, but Erin insisted. My baby sister can be very demanding when she wants something." He laughed at the memory of her badgering him.

"When I went to Natalie's room I knocked, and she told me to go away. I was tempted to just walk away but she was crying so I knocked again and asked what was wrong." Pax was hooked to his every word, her lips parted. "She came to the door and opened it a pinch. She was distraught and didn't want to tell me what it was, but I kept on. I can be a persistent bastard." He laughed at that.

"What was wrong?"

"I eventually managed to get it out of her that she had started her period for the first time and had no supplies. I didn't know whether to run and hide or puke. This was my sister. I did not need to know that —ever, but I couldn't just leave her. I told her to wait there and I took Erin and we walked to the local shop. I nearly died when I saw all the choices. I had no clue, there were so many different kinds."

Pax laughed, throwing her head back and he grinned at her, taking in her beauty and knowing she had no clue how gorgeous she was.

"It gets worse! Not knowing what to do I chucked one of each in a basket, added a tone of chocolate and a heat pad thingy, and went to the till only to find Janie Lawson and Dylan Jenkins at the checkout. Janie was the girl I was crushing on and Dylan, her boyfriend at the time, was my arch enemy. I wanted the ground to open up and swallow me. I went so red I swear my cheeks were burning. Erin was no help, she told them all the details leaving nothing out—little brat." He said the last with affection. Pax was wiping her eyes from tears as she laughed making Blake chuckle. "Hey, be nice, he teased me mercilessly for months."

Pax reached over and kissed him softly before pulling back. "Poor baby, and you did such a sweet thing for your sister."

Blake shrugged. "What else could I do? I couldn't let her suffer and it turned out okay. I got to steal Janie from Dylan because she thought I was sweet for doing what I did."

Pax climbed across him, settling herself across his thighs as she ran her hands up his chest. "You are a good man, Calvin Blake."

He ran his hands over her hips and ass loving the feel of her against him. "If you could read my mind right now you wouldn't think so."

Pax pressed her firm tits to his chest as she twined her arms around his neck. "Oh?"

"The things I want to do to this body are illegal in some states."

"Why does that make you a bad man?" She nibbled on his ear biting down. "I think it makes you a very," she said it slowly, "very good man."

Blake felt his dick harden at her sexy languid voice in his ear.

Standing he swept her up into his arms and she shrieked as her hands grabbed his shoulders. He was about to carry her to bed and show her exactly how good he was when the ping of a bullet hit the toughened glass of their balcony.

CHAPTER SIXTEEN

ONE SECOND, she had been teasing Blake, the next she was on her back on the floor of the balcony with Blake's body pressing her into the hard surface. She heard the unmistakable sound of a bullet hitting glass and tried to peek out from the man on top of her.

He lifted his head and looked at her "We need to get inside."

Pax nodded her assent, her heart beating hard in her chest. Taking her hand in his, Blake rolled and shoved her in front of him, his hand on her head keeping her low as they dove for the sliding glass door. She felt another bullet hit the wall next to her ear as they reached the door and she fell inside with Blake behind her.

He closed the door and locked it before quickly hitting the button on the electric-close curtains to stop the shooter seeing in and having an open target. Not satisfied with that, Blake grabbed her hand and moved them towards the bedroom. The window in there faced a different outlook and the curtains were already drawn.

Not letting go of her, he pulled her closer and took out his phone. "Waggs, it's me. We have a sniper on the roof of the building opposite our balcony. Fucker just shot at us." Pax watched him nod. "Come here first, I'm coming with you."

The look on his face was determined as he hung up. Without a word he hooked her around the back of her neck with his hand and brought her head to his chest, kissing the top in a tender gesture which bellied the situation.

He held her for a second in silence. "Thought I was gonna lose you then, Gracie."

Pax pulled up and saw the anger and fear in his eyes. Her heart beat harder but for a different reason now. "You would never let that happen, Blake. You're too good at what you do."

Blake shook his head. "Not good enough. I never should have taken you out there. It was fucking stupid."

Pax hated that he was beating himself up over this but had no time to reassure the stubborn man as a knock sounded on the door. Letting her go, he strode from the bedroom to the door like a man on a mission. Pax stayed by the bedroom, her shoulder leaning on the jamb.

Checking the peephole, he unlocked the door and Decker, Reid, and Waggs walked inside. Decker moved closer to her and Reid and Waggs stayed close to the door.

Blake headed back to the bedroom and grabbed his gun from the side of the bed, tucking it into a holster at his shoulder. Shrugging a jacket on, he moved to stand in front of her and grasped her hips pulling her close. "Decker is going to stay with you while we check things out. Do what he says and stay away from the windows. I don't trust that they won't start shooting randomly. I'll be back soon."

Pax nodded. He kissed her hard and quick and then he was gone the door closing behind him. Decker locked it and slid the chain across as an added measure.

Pax shivered feeling the cold as her adrenalin crashed. Her ribs ached from hitting the ground but that was nothing compared to the fear she felt knowing Blake was out there facing a crazy person with a gun.

Moving to the coffee machine near the bar she made herself a cup and held it up. "You want coffee, Decker?"

Decker shook his head. "No, thanks. I don't drink it."

Pax pulled back with a frown. "Really?"

Decker chuckled, his eyes crinkling making him look even more devastating. Decker was slim, tall, fit, and wore a suit like Captain America wore spandex—like it was made for him. Which if the label was any indication, it probably was.

"I limit my coffee intake to one a day. That shit's not good for you if you drink it like pop."

Pax took a sip of the fragrant brew and shrugged. "I'll take my chances."

Pax moved to the sofa that was out of the line of the window and sat, curling her leg underneath her and cupping the mug for comfort. Decker was on his phone doing something and she took the time to go over the shooting in her mind. It had played out so fast she hadn't had time to think—just react.

It was difficult to tell who the shooter had been aiming for, her or Blake. She assumed her as this was her nightmare they were trying to figure out. But equally, Blake was sure to have made enemies over the years doing what he did. Another thing she realised was that either the person shooting at them was incompetent or he hadn't wanted to kill them. They had been like sitting ducks out there. A true professional like Lucy or Mitch would have hit their target with no problems. The night was clear and dry with nothing to impede the shot.

"They shouldn't be long," Decker said as he came to sit beside her leaving a foot of space between them.

"Good."

She was anxiously watching the door when her cell phone rang. Lifting it from the table, Pax saw it was her mother, which was odd. She never called unless it was to berate her for not visiting. She hit decline not wanting to deal with her mother again today. Pax could feel Decker watching her. Her phone rang again, and her senses sharpened as if knowing something was up.

Knowing she couldn't ignore it a second time she sighed and answered. "Hello, Mom."

"Grace, where have you been?" The urgency in her mother's voice made her sit forward and put down her mug.

"What's the matter?" Her mother was always calm, almost to the point of boredom.

"Your father had a heart attack." Her mom's voice cracked on the last words, and Pax heard the sound of tears in her ear over the sound of her heart thundering in her chest.

"Oh my God! Is he okay?" Pax was on her feet now, shoving her arms into a jacket as Decker watched with a question in his assessing brown eyes.

"They're taking him to St Vincent's Memorial by life flight."

Pax didn't need any more. If they were life-flighting him instead of taking him by road it was bad. St Vincent's was a cardiothoracic specialist teaching hospital too.

"Okay, where are you now, Mom?"

"I'm in the car. Pete is driving me. I was too shaken to drive."

She actually did sound upset. Her parents had a complicated relationship and not one she wanted to try and figure out. "All right. I'm leaving now and will meet you there."

"Okay."

Pax hung up and turned to Decker. "My father has suffered a massive heart attack. They're life-flighting him to St Vincent's now."

Decker picked up his phone and called Blake and relayed the situation. He hung up and looked at her his face completely unreadable. "Blake is on his way back now." Decker didn't elaborate or give her any clue as to what had happened, but his jaw was tight, and she wondered what that meant.

———

HEAD LOW, body crouched close to the ground, Blake went in behind Reid and cleared the entrance to the apartment building that was the most obvious choice for the shooter. Waggs moved ahead and cleared the corners as they hit the stairwell. Moving in formation they secured each level until they found the door to the roof.

His leg hurt like a motherfucker, but Blake ignored it as he covered the door for Waggs to go first. The lock was broken and hanging loose, probably from being hit with the fire extinguisher that was leaning up against the wall. Waggs went through with Reid close behind him both highly trained operatives in this situation. More so than he was. He was more about seeing the threat and evaluating it before it got to this although he'd had his fair share of situations involving breaching doors and risk.

His gun arm up he swept the rooftop, his eyes out for any threat that might be hiding in the shadows. His gut told him it was clear, but he would never assume that without knowing for sure. He liked his life and he sure as hell wasn't going to get himself killed because he was a sloppy idiot.

Once they were certain the roof was clear, Blake moved to the side that faced his and Pax's room. He looked over the three-foot-high wall that stopped anyone from tipping over the side and saw the closed curtains of their suite. It was almost on the same level as the roof and although it was a fair distance away, it was a relatively easy shot for someone with any skill.

Reid moved up beside him and cast his eyes over the wall then looked down and around the floor. "No casings."

That meant whoever had shot at them had picked them up and taken them away so as not to leave evidence. That could mean the shooter was a pro or it could mean they watched CSI. Blake walked the length of the wall looking for any clue as to who had been there and shot at them. If it had been a professional, they wouldn't have missed that shot—unless they wanted to. Could it have been a warning for Pax or was it someone closer to home?

The other alternative was that they were dealing with an amateur. One that wasn't good enough to make the shot but watched enough 'police procedural' shows on TV to know to pick up the casings. Either way, he wasn't going to get any more answers up here.

With a final sweep of the roof they decided to go back to the hotel and get some sleep. He would have their stuff moved into Waggs' room and Waggs would take the suite tonight.

They were moving down the stairs when his phone buzzed in his pocket. The silent vibration sending a tingle of apprehension through him when he saw Decker's name appear. He stopped and the other two looked at him as if sensing his worry.

"Yes?"

His back went stiff when Decker told him that Henrietta had called, and Robert Paxton had had a heart attack. His first thought was it was a trap and they should not go to the hospital, but he knew Pax would want to go. "Keep her there. We're on our way back now."

He hung up and looked at Reid and Waggs. "Robert Paxton had a heart attack. They're life-flighting him to St Vincent's." Blake saw the look of suspicion cross Reid's features. He seemed to be thinking the same as Blake.

"Not to be a dick but that is some coincidence."

"I agree."

Waggs walked beside them as they crossed the road and having tucked their weapons from sight, moved into the lobby of the hotel. "Agreed, but a life flight is some serious shit and St Vincent's is the cardiothoracic teaching centre, so if he has had a heart attack, he's in a bad way."

Blake understood what Waggs wasn't saying. There was a very real chance Robert Paxton would not pull through, which meant for Pax's sake he needed to take her to see her father because if he didn't pull through and then was cleared, Pax would never forgive herself.

CHAPTER SEVENTEEN

PAX CHEWED the skin around her fingernail until it bled as she waited for Blake to arrive. She jumped visibly when the knock on the door came. Her instinct was to run to the door but as she moved forward, she felt Decker's hand on her arm.

"Let me."

Pax nodded and stepped back, her heart racing, nerves frayed for so many reasons. She just wanted Blake to hold her, to centre her as he seemed to do every time. Decker moved to the door and looked through the peephole his hand on the weapon at his hip. Pax saw him relax and proceed to open the door.

Pax planted her feet not wanting to run to Blake and throw herself in his arms in front of everyone. The look of concern for her on his face when he walked in, and the open arms he met her with, had all of that flying out of the window. Her legs were moving, and she was wrapped in his arms, head buried in his neck inhaling the masculine scent of the man who was coming to mean everything to her.

Taking her first deep breath since her mother had called, Pax felt the shudder run through her as he held her tightly not letting her go or pulling back. He gave her what she needed kissing her hair. When she had gotten her emotions under control, she took a last calming breath and pulled back. "Did you find anything?"

Blake shook his head "No, whoever it was is long gone." He stroked her cheek softly the pad of his fingers slightly rough. "You want to go to the hospital?" he asked as if he sensed the inner struggle she was having. Pax nodded not able to voice the words to explain her messed up feelings towards her father.

Blake nodded and kissed her head. "Get yourself ready then and let me talk to the guys."

Pax frowned. "What about the investigation?"

"The guys can carry on as before and when we've visited your father, we can reassess and decide if we're still going to visit Sally Nixon or Waggs goes to see her instead."

That made sense to her. Once she knew her dad was okay—or not—then she could figure out this mess with Blake's help. She didn't allow herself to go down that path of her father dying, she didn't even know how to feel about that. Yet she did. The pain in her chest told her how she would feel about him dying. Her hand flexed against Blake's bicep and he looked at her as if he somehow knew how she was feeling. His smile was one of reassurance that left her incredibly grateful that he was here, but his eyes filled her with warmth and a sense of protection came over her she'd never felt.

She looked up at the serious men who were talking across the other side of the room near the sliding glass doors trying to compose herself. These men, all of them, were here for her and suddenly it hit her like a truck that she was not alone. For the first time in forever she was allowing people to help her and not pushing them away believing that she wasn't good enough.

Blake ran his hand to the back of her neck and pulled her closer, so she stood hip to toe with his hard body. He gave the back of her neck a gentle squeeze as he dropped his voice low. "You good, baby?"

Pax took in the softness of his voice, the heat from his body and nodded. "Yeah. I am." And she was because he was there, and he was reading her mood and giving her what she needed.

He didn't pull away but dropped his forehead to hers. "That's good, Gracie." He let her hold him for a few moments before he gently pulled back and eyes locked to hers kissed her softly just a touch really but enough to ground her in a way she needed. "Go get yourself ready and then we can go."

"Okay, Cal," she returned.

She headed to the bedroom and closed the door behind her before quickly pulling on a pair of ripped skinny jeans, a sleeveless cream blouse, and shrugging on a khaki military style jacket. She put her hair in a messy top knot and kept her make-up light to save time. While getting ready she didn't once think about what her mother might think. No, her only thoughts were about the man who was trying to fix this situation with her. Her feet slid into khaki stilettos that made her legs look ridiculously long, and she grabbed her over-sized navy bag and shoved a few essentials into it before she stepped out.

Blake's head snapped up as she closed the door and Pax saw him do a head to toe before a seriously sexy smile crossed his handsome face.

Not letting it show how much that pleased her she walked directly to him where he was now standing with the others. Wanting to show him how much his support meant she didn't hesitate to slip under his arm that automatically came around her as if they had been doing it for a long time and not just a week.

That was the thing with them, it felt right in a way nothing else had. Not even her relationship with her family had been this way. She loved her parents, but she was coming to realise she didn't like them. Her father had hurt her, breaking her heart in a way that it would never be the same yet that was okay. She knew that what she had now would never have come to be without that heartbreak, and for the first time, she saw that.

Her mother was different; they had never fallen out as such, but they had also never been close, not how a mother and daughter should be. Ever since she had become a teenager her mother had been jealous of her, making remarks that put her down or made her feel smaller than her and not worthy.

It hurt but she'd been able to handle that so much better than what her father had done. It hadn't always been that way. When she was a child her mother had been wonderful. Never the cookie making kind but fun and sweet. Everything had changed when she had been around thirteen.

Pax shook off her thoughts as Blake and the others resumed their discussion. "I don't want you guys anywhere near the hospital. It will slow shit up if we have to find a different way to interview everyone."

Reid pushed back a hank of hair that had fallen over his eyes. "We should get Lopez doing background checks on everyone, including Benny's biological father. See if anything pops."

Blake nodded. "Good call. Can you do that, Decker?"

Pax found it odd that he'd asked Decker when Reid had been the one to suggest it. She was about to shove it off as how they did things when she saw Reid's jaw tighten angrily. He kept quiet and so did everyone else.

"Yes, of course," Decker replied hitting a speed dial button on his phone and walking a short distance away. It was close to midnight now, but in the UK, it was around eight in the morning.

Blake gave her a light squeeze to get her attention. "You ready?"

"As I'll ever be," she answered knowing that she had been stalling a little. She wanted to go see her father, but she was also terrified of what she would find.

Blake nodded and led her to the door with Waggs and Reid covering them. They made it to the car park, and she saw a shiny black Chrysler sedan waiting for them. Waggs clicked the locks and handed the keys to Blake. "Be in touch in a few hours or before if we have anything to tell."

"Cheers, Waggs."

Blake helped her in and crossed to the driver's side and got in, clipping his belt before resting his arm on her headrest. He turned to look over his shoulder as he reversed out. Something about him doing that was incredibly sexy.

Pax had no idea what it was, but she found it turned her on more than it should. A smile curved her lips and she looked out the window to hide it, she needn't have bothered though because Blake missed nothing.

"What was that smirk for?" His eyes slipped to hers before concentrating back on the road. It was just over an hour to St Vincent's from where they were. Luckily, they would miss any traffic at this time so she figured they could make it in about forty-five minutes.

Pax continued to look out the window and decided to toy with him to distract them from the shitty situation she had gotten them in. "What smirk?"

"The one you were wearing a few seconds ago."

"Can't tell you. If I tell you I'll have to kill you," she said in a playful tone.

Blake caught on to her mood quickly. His eyes moved the length of her thigh before the hand that was closest to her rested on her leg. Warmth and heat radiated into her from his touch. "If you tell me, I'll tell you what I wanted to do to you when I saw you in those sexy as fuck jeans."

Pax's eyes flashed to him and she felt the warmth spread through her at his words. "Oh, yeah?"

"Yeah."

"Well then, in that case I guess I could tell you." She didn't elaborate wanting to draw the flirtatious banter out a little as the car ate up the miles on the freeway.

She waited for a beat and he glanced at her. She could feel the blush that crept over her cheeks, making her damn her fair skin once again.

"Well?" he asked.

"I was smiling because..." She paused then. "You know when you put your arm over the back of the headrest to reverse?"

Blake looked at her and frowned obviously confused. "Yeah?"

"Well, it's hot."

Blake looked across at her again; his lips teased into a grin. "Hot? You think it's hot when I do that?"

"I think you're hot breathing," she muttered under her breath.

"Pardon? What did you say?" he said hand to his ear.

"I said, yes, you're hot when you do that."

Blake suddenly pulled the car to the side of the road causing Pax to brace as he hit the vehicle into park. She glanced at him, surprised but had no time to react before he leaned in and kissed her hard and wet. The tip of his tongue touched hers and her mind went blank of all thought except how it felt to have Blake kiss her like she was the only thing in the world that mattered at that moment.

He slanted his head as he drove his fingers into her hair and cupped her head using her hair to gently pull and angle her so he could go deeper until she was squirming in her seat. Eventually, after what seemed like minutes but were probably only seconds, he pulled back. He didn't release her though, he held on to her hair, cupping her head as his blue eyes smouldered in the darkness that was lit only by passing cars.

"So fucking beautiful and you gave me that when I know you're worried about your dad. You still had time to give yourself to me."

Pax remained silent not knowing what to say because it hadn't felt like she was giving to him. It had felt natural.

"Want to fuck you," he growled, and Pax felt her body go liquid. "Haven't got time and what I want to give you needs time. But I will say this—what we have, Gracie, is special. Seeing the crack in that glass tonight where the bullet hit drove it home to me. You are it for me. I'm all in with us. No holding back, none of that shit. We do this. We do it and we do it to build a life together." Her heart cracked at his words and she felt the second it healed back into a healthier place. "You want that, baby?" he asked his voice growling and rough.

Never in her life had she wanted anything more than to build a life with this man. He was everything to her. Although she recognised it had been since Monaco that she had been falling for him. Now she felt like the fall was complete. She didn't give him that yet. She didn't want to tell him she loved him and frighten him. Despite his words, Blake had been a ladies' man. He was a good man, a kind honourable one but starting something and being all in was different from declaring love for someone wasn't it?

"Yeah, I want that."

Blake nodded and she saw an understanding in his eyes as well as relief. "Let's go see your dad so I can show you what those sexy jeans do to me. Sexiest ass I ever did see," he said almost to himself as he pulled back onto the road and into traffic.

"Cal?" she asked as she left her hand in his as he drove.

"Yeah, gorgeous?"

"Thank you."

"What for?" He seemed perplexed.

"Everything," she said throwing up her hands to encompass the car.

Blake gave her a smile that made her heart stutter and her breath hitch. "No problem, beautiful."

The rest of the drive was quiet, and they reached the hospital in an hour including the make-out session pit stop. Her muscles tensed as Blake came around her side after parking and helped her out, his body blocking her from anyone wanting to take a shot at her. Once inside the glass doors of the reception area, he held tight to her hand as he found out what floor her father was on.

Pax felt sick as they took the elevator to the second floor where the cardiothoracic theatre was.

Blake lifted her hand as the door stopped and kissed her knuckles. "Ready?"

Pax looked at him and nodded then faced the doors as they opened. She was ready and she could do this. Together they walked out onto the floor to meet whatever came her way. She had a wonderful man beside her. She knew he was on her side no matter what.

CHAPTER EIGHTEEN

BLAKE WAS GRIPPING on tight to Pax as they rounded the corner of the hospital corridor and saw the nurse's station where they stopped, and he asked about Robert Paxton. The nurse pointed in the direction and they walked through a set of double doors and saw Pete and Eddie hovering outside a relative's room.

Seeing them, he wanted nothing more than to turn and run and take her away from the people he knew had hurt her, scarred her, and not cared. He killed the impulse knowing deep down that for them to have the future he now wanted with her—meaning everything from marriage and kids, to retiring on a beach where she could wear a bikini all day—he needed her whole. He had to help her find peace one way or another and the only way to do that was for her to face her pain and for him to find the truth.

It was the only thing she needed right now; the rest would come later.

Pete nodded when they approached. "Hi, Miss Paxton," he said, his tone gentle.

Blake got a sense that these men were not out to harm Grace. There seemed a genuine affection for her when they greeted her.

"Hi, Pete, Eddie. Is my mom in there?" She sounded anxious and he felt the tension running through her.

"Yes, she is," Pete responded opening the door for them to enter.

Henrietta Paxton looked up as the door opened. Her eyes were red from crying, her make-up had run, and she had been dabbing at it with a tissue that was now scrunched up in her hand. Her clothes were couture and expensive but seemed to hang off her as her shoulders slumped. She looked grief-stricken and Blake was shocked.

"Mom," Pax said and let his hand go to move to her mother.

"Grace, oh, Grace," she said on a broken sob as Pax sat beside her and took her mother into her arms to cradle her.

Blake gritted his jaw not ready to forgive the woman for what she had done to her daughter for so many years. But Pax didn't have it in her to turn away when her mother was in pain and needed her. He watched for a second as Pax rocked her mother as if she was a child before he turned to the door and opened to speak to Pete or Eddie.

"Can you ask the doctor or someone to come and fill us in. We can't get much out of Mrs Paxton."

Pete frowned and looked at Henrietta, his face softening as he did. So it was like that—Pete was in love with Henrietta. But did she feel the same? Maybe they should look closer at that.

"Mrs Paxton is distraught. Let me find someone."

He turned to Eddie and said a few low words before Blake shut the door and moved to sit opposite Pax and her mom, giving them some space. A few moments later a knock on the door proceeded an older man who was wearing a white coat and green scrubs. His face was leathery, and he clearly liked the golf course, but Blake didn't judge.

"Miss Paxton," he said holding out a hand to Pax who had stood when she heard him enter.

Blake had done the same, moving closer to Pax in case she needed him. Her hand shook the doctor's hand firmly and then instantly grabbed his own holding it like a vice as she waited for news on her father, the man she'd adored her entire childhood and hated her whole adulthood.

"How is my father?"

The doctor tilted his head and pursed his lips and Blake stepped closer to Pax bracing for the bad news. "Your father is in surgery now. He's had a severe heart attack and we're performing a triple heart bypass. The surgery should take around six hours or so, but we'll keep you updated as and when we can. Rest assured Dr Elliot, who is operating on him, is the top doctor in this field."

"Thank you, doctor—" She paused searching for his name and locating it on his badge continued. "Dr Frackle. I appreciate you taking the time to talk to me."

The doctor nodded. "Of course. If you need anything, please ask one of the nurses at the station."

The doctor left the room and Pax's eyes came to his for a moment, the depth of understanding and fear for her father mixed with relief that he was still holding on. Blake pulled her close and held her for a minute hoping to give her some strength. Her body relaxed into him and he kissed her temple, the scent of her hair tickling his nose.

"You okay?" He kept his voice low, so her mother didn't hear. Pax nodded and gave him a tentative smile. He released her and she moved to her mother who looked ashen.

"How you doing, Mom?" she asked touching her arm gently making her jump. The woman was away with the fairies.

Henrietta looked up at her daughter and then across to him before back to Pax. "I..." She stopped and cleared her throat. "I need some air."

She stood and moved to the door, but it opened before she could touch it. A tall imposing man with salt and pepper hair, tan skin, and the bearing of someone who was used to people doing what he said walked in. Blake was on his feet as he stepped inside the room making Henrietta step back and the colour drained even more from her face.

"Daddy! What are you doing here?"

The man looked at Henrietta, his face harsh before he looked to Pax and smiled softly. Ignoring Henrietta, he took Pax's hands in his. "Grace, my darling. How are you?" His voice was smooth and bellied his age. Blake guessed he was in his late seventies.

"Grandfather," Pax said kissing his cheek lightly. Blake could see she was somewhat reserved with him though. She also didn't answer his question which the man didn't miss. He also didn't react to the fading bruises which Blake found interesting.

"And who might this be?" her grandfather asked turning his full gaze to Blake.

The man had wise and cunning eyes and Blake would bet his last penny that this man had a cupboard full of skeletons just waiting to be dug into. He guarded his reaction and smiled instead, stepping forward and offering his hand to the man who he hoped one day to be related to. Not because he had a burning need to be part of this fucked up family but because he was falling in love with Grace.

"Calvin Blake. Nice to meet you. Sorry it is under these circumstances."

The man shook his hand in a firm grip slowly taking his measure before he nodded. "Albert Lawrence. Very nice to meet you, Calvin. I assume you are with my granddaughter?"

"Yes, I am," he said as Pax slid her arm through his and around his back making it very clear where things were with them.

The man nodded slowly. "Very good. You will come to dinner while you are here." He stated it as an order, and nobody argued, not even him. Dinner would be the perfect chance to find out more about Sana.

"We would love that, sir," Blake replied.

The man turned away from him and Pax and his gaze landed on Henrietta who had moved back into the corner like a mouse hiding from a tiger. She looked nothing like the woman who had propositioned him earlier. Visibly shrunken and almost meek. Blake felt a sudden pang of sympathy for her.

"Henrietta, please go and clean yourself up. You look like a disgrace. At least have some standards," he barked at her making her jump.

"Yes, Daddy." She jumped from her seat and scurried to the door in relief.

"Henri?" he called as he reached the door.

She turned to him. "Yes?"

"Clark is outside. Have him escort you."

Henrietta's shoulders sagged low as if beaten. "Thank you."

The words sounded hollow and Blake was keen to get some answers on this family.

He felt Pax bristle beside him and gave her a squeeze of reassurance. She could feel it too and he wondered if things had always been this way or if the strain was starting to make masks fall. Albert sat where Henrietta had been and crossed his legs, resting his hand on his knee, a large gold pinkie ring with a diamond flashing there. The cream slacks and navy shirt and blazer were probably as relaxed as this man got and Blake wondered if that was where Pax had learned to use clothes as armour.

He didn't ask about Robert and Blake assumed he had spoken to the doctor on his way in.

"You're British? What is it you do?" Albert asked.

"I was a PPO for the London Met." He left out the part about working for the Royals.

"Very impressive and what is it you do now?"

"I work for a private security company," he said giving him the same story as he'd given Pax's parents.

"How did you two kids meet?"

Pax answered this one as she leaned into him. "Blake was working security at the gallery I work for. We had some high-value artwork come in and the client wanted some increased protection, so he hired Blake. We hit it off and the rest is history." She smiled and leaned her head up to catch his eyes. Her smile was genuine as she looked at him even if the story was bullshit.

"You make a lovely couple, my dear."

His affection for Pax was as evident as his disdain for his daughter. It confused Blake. He showed no reaction to the bruises but seemed to care for Pax. He had contempt for his own child and yet had financed her husband's business. Things were not adding up. He needed to call Waggs or Decker.

"You want to grab a coffee, Gracie?" he asked, and she seemed to catch his mood.

"Definitely." She turned to her grandfather who was regarding them openly. "Would you like us to bring you anything back?"

"No, thank you, dear. Clark will get me something."

"Okay. We won't be long."

"Take your time. I won't be going anywhere until we hear about Robert."

Pax nodded as Blake opened the door and stepped out first checking the hallway was clear. Eddie was standing beside the door, but Pete had disappeared. Perhaps he was looking out for Henrietta and this Clark who seemed to make her shoulders slump in defeat. He walked with Pax's hand in his as they followed the signs for the cafeteria.

Even though it was the middle of the night, the coffee shop was open and had a few people inside. They got in line as he grabbed a couple of muffins and some fruit for them both.

Blake angled his head to Pax and spoke, "Do you want to go sit down?"

Pax didn't answer and he noticed she was looking across the room at something. He followed her line of sight and saw Henrietta having a heated discussion with a man of a similar age to herself. It wasn't Pete, he was nowhere in sight. The man was tall, around six foot two, with a slender frame, blond hair which he thought looked dyed, and a black pinstriped suit. Henrietta was pointing at him and clearly upset but had lost the fear from her eyes now. The mouse was gone, and she was holding her own. The man shook his head angrily and moved to grab Henrietta Paxton's arm, but she shook it off.

Blake felt Pax move but stopped her. "Wait," he said softly still watching.

Grace went still but did as he said. The man looked furious now as they exchanged more words Blake couldn't hear before Henrietta walked away. The man looked up, his face red with fury as he watched her leave before moving after her slowly. Pete stepped out from a pillar and came between the man and Henrietta, a warning in his stance as he slipped his hand into his inside pocket.

Fuck, the last thing we need is a public shoot out.

The man obviously thought so too because he backed up hands out. Pete walked after Henrietta and the unknown man walked in the opposite direction.

Pax made to move again but he stopped her. "Blake," she gritted out in irritation.

"Let's get coffee," he said.

They had reached the front of the line and he quickly ordered their usual and paid for them and some snacks. Pax was silent as she followed him to a table in the corner away from prying ears.

When he had taken a sip of coffee, he looked at her. "Do you know who that man was?"

Pax nodded her eyes on her coffee. "Yes, that was Clark Baker. He and my mom go way back. They went to college together and their families were friends. He's the VP of finance for Sana."

"They didn't seem very friendly now."

"It's always been cool but polite between them. I have no idea what that could be about."

She sounded tired and he took her hand in his across the table. "You want to stick around?"

Her eyes came to his. "Yes, just until we know how the surgery went. Is that okay?"

"Babe, of course it is. You're in charge, just let me know. I'll need to make a quick call to Waggs though."

"Okay, thank you."

Her face brightened a little and he smiled back. She was so beautiful it made his teeth hurt to look at her sometimes. He wanted to kiss her so damn badly it was an ache. He didn't though, he instead took out his phone and dialled Waggs. He stood as it rang and stepped into the corridor where he could talk in private and still keep an eye on Gracie. Her head was down as she texted on her phone. The phone went to voice mail, so Blake tried Decker who also went to voicemail. He left messages and then decided to call Reid and see if he could be reached. A tiny knot of apprehension unfurled in his belly.

Reid answered on the second ring. "Hey."

"Hey, Reid. I was trying to reach Waggs or Decker but they ain't answering. Can you add a name to the list of people who need looking into and push him to the top?"

"Yeah, sure." Blake heard some movement in the background before Reid said, "Shoot."

"Clark Baker. He's the Vice President of finance for Sana. He seems to have some history with Henrietta Paxton and he and her dad Albert Lawrence seem tight."

"Sure, I'll get on it." Blake heard Reid pause as if he wanted to say more but stopped.

"Thanks, and ask Waggs to call me, please."

"No problem. How is Pax's dad?" he asked sounding genuine and making Blake feel like a complete douche bag.

"He's in surgery now. They're performing a triple heart bypass on him. We should hear more in a few hours."

"Cool, look after her, man. I have a shitty feeling about all this."

"Yeah, me too, Reid. Me too."

Blake hung up feeling more confused than ever. He needed to start investigating but until Robert Paxton was out of surgery, they weren't going anywhere. Maybe he could use the time to check out the dynamic between Clark, Albert, Henrietta, and Pete because there was definitely something going on there and he would get to the bottom of it.

CHAPTER NINETEEN

PAX CRAWLED across the bed in the room they had rented just a mile away from the hospital and felt the energy leave her body in a sigh. The long emotional day yesterday coupled with the long and nerve-wracking night had wiped her out. Flopping down still dressed, she face-planted on the pillow and used her toes to kick her heels to the floor with a clunk.

She felt the bed dip beside her and then Blake's heat at her back and at her neck as he shifted her hair from her face. "You need to get out of those clothes, babe."

"Too tired," she replied with a muffled sleepy voice.

She heard the chuckle in his voice as he rubbed her back. "I know but you'll rest easier without jeans on. Let me help you."

Pax turned her head to face him and opened one eye to look at him. God, he really was gorgeous. He was the real deal and all hers for the taking. "Are you trying to get me naked?"

Blake laughed again his eyes crinkling at the corners. "Always, babe, but this time my intentions are to let you sleep when I do."

Pax wished she had the energy for more, but she was dead on her feet. "Fine."

She moved to sit up and Blake leaned in and kissed her softly. "Glad your dad's holding his own, Gracie."

"Me too." Her voice was quiet as her mind replayed the last few hours like a film.

Dr Frackle, who it turned out was the head of surgery, had come to tell them her dad had survived the surgery and was being moved to the ICU. Her grandfather had stayed with them until the doctor came, typing away on his phone and ignoring everyone mostly. Her mother had burst into tears when they got the news behaving almost like a different person. Someone Pax didn't recognise, and it irked her.

When they had left, Clark had been in the hallway using his phone while Pete glared at him from the door. She wondered why Clark hadn't come into the relative's room. He would have in the past. There were too many strands to untangle when her brain was shattered mush.

"Lift your arms," Blake urged, and she lifted them and let him pull the cream blouse over her head. He then pushed her back and undid the snap of her jeans and pulled them down, stopping to kiss her belly as he did.

She couldn't stop the shiver that coursed through her and the gruff sound he made in his throat made her panties wet. Pax closed her eyes wondering if he would continue his journey and found she was actually hoping he would, but he didn't. The next thing she felt was soft fabric being pulled over her body and she knew it was his tee.

It smelled of his laundry soap and him. Pax sighed as he rolled her and pulled the covers out before settling her under them. "You forgot my bra," she teased.

"I'm not a saint, Gracie," he said as she heard him shuck his jeans, climbing in behind her and tugging her into his arms.

She allowed herself a smile as a feeling of contentment rushed through her. Moving back, she snuggled close with her back to his front. Blake's heavy muscled arm draped across her middle as their legs tangled.

"Sleep, baby."

"Okay." Pax lay there for a few minutes letting Blake surround her, giving her the warmth her heart craved. Her feelings around her father were so fucked up. She thought her heart would break when she had seen him lying in the ICU with tubes everywhere. Only Blake at her back and his sold warmth had kept her from losing her feet. She wondered what she would have done without him there supporting her.

One thing she did know was that more was going on than she knew, and she had to find it out, regardless of what the answers might cost her. She couldn't live her life not knowing anymore and she wouldn't allow Blake to live under a cloud as she was. If she wanted to build a life with him as she thought he was suggesting, then she needed this over once and for all.

PAX WOKE FEELING MORE energised than she had in days. Looking at the clock she saw it was one in the afternoon. She reached back and found the bed behind her cold. Blake had obviously been up for a while.

She sat up and swung her legs out of bed, his tee hitting her mid-thigh. She padded to the bathroom and took a quick shower tying her hair up in a bun to keep it dry. She didn't have time to wash and blow it out so she would go for the messy look again today. Blake seemed to like it that way. *Blake seems to like it all ways.* She grinned to herself and rushed getting dressed in yesterday's clothes although she had clean underwear in her oversized bag thank goodness.

The bruises were barely visible now, so she lightened her make-up just using some tinted moisturiser and mascara with a slick of blush on her cheeks. She left her lips bare knowing—or rather hoping —Blake would kiss the gloss off anyway. She couldn't hear him in the other room, but she sensed him. It was as if she could feel the vibrations from him coming through the walls. She laughed at her fanciful thoughts silently and made sure everything was packed with nothing left behind. She doubted they would come back here. This had just been a place to allow them to get some sleep.

Crossing to the door, she opened it and saw him working on his laptop which he must have collected from the car earlier.

His head came up and those beautiful blue eyes moved over her with heat before settling on her face with a smile. "Morning, beautiful."

"Afternoon more like," she said as she slid her arms around his neck from behind and leaned in for a kiss which he happily obliged. It was a warm hungry kiss that hinted at so much more.

He pulled away with a growl and looked up at her. "That's how we should start every morning."

Pax smiled and looked around. "Any news?"

Blake stood and started packing his laptop away. "Your father had a good night and is stable. He came around briefly but is sleeping a lot. Your mum has gone home but is coming back later to be with him. Do you want to go and see him before we head back to the hotel?"

Pax frowned and pursed her lips as she contemplated that. "No. Let's get moving. I want to try and see Sally today."

Blake moved to the door, his arms rippling as he carried the bag in one hand and opened the door with the other, keeping his body in front of hers again, always protecting her.

Once in the car he drove to a coffee shop on the way back to the hotel and picked up a caramel latte and a pastry for her and an Americano with cream for him.

"Have you heard from the others?" she asked as she chewed the apricot pastry and ignored the fact it was probably going straight to her hips along with the muffin from last night.

He glanced across at her with a grin twitching his lips at the enjoyment on her face. "Yes, Waggs called me earlier. Decker has Lopez working on the background checks and he has an appointment with Clark Baker for the fake magazine article later today."

Pax looked at him as she brushed the crumbs from her legs. "Doesn't that seem odd to you? Him being so available at short notice."

"I thought so too, but Decker is damn good at what he does so we'll have to leave that to him. Waggs is working his angle too, so we've arranged to meet tonight after we get new accommodation. I don't want us going back to the hotel except to collect our stuff."

"Do you think they'll try again?" she asked a shiver going through her.

"I think they don't want us to find out something and will do anything to protect it," he said tone serious. "How do you want to play the meeting with Sally? Make an appointment or just turn up?"

Pax considered it for a moment as she watched people skating on the sidewalk. "Just turn up, I think. Catch her off guard. It might reveal more."

"Good call," he said with a slight nod of pride which made her happy inside.

Pax was quiet then as she considered things. Soon they reached the hotel's car park and Blake parked as close to the door as possible. He ushered her out and quickly moved to the lift that sped them to their floor where he proceeded to check out the room before letting her in to gather her things.

Pax shoved everything into a bag which didn't take long as she hadn't unpacked a lot. Once done, he did a final sweep of the room, his eyes locking on the glass that had the bullet crack in it and ushered her out.

Once back in the car she asked the question that had been playing on her mind. "How come nobody called the police when we were shot at? I mean, I understand why *we* didn't, but I would have thought someone would have called 911."

Blake's face was grim as it met hers. "Whoever was shooting knew enough to use a suppressor. There wouldn't have been that much noise."

"Oh! I guess I hadn't thought of that."

"It happened in a second, so you wouldn't have necessarily taken in the fact that it was quiet. The sound of the glass being hit would have been loud to us but not necessarily enough for anyone else to hear it."

The sun was shining bright and Pax was desperate to change into clean clothes, feeling dirty in the ones she had worn all night. "Will we go to the new place first or to Sally Nixon's home?"

"Let's get to the new digs so we can shower and change. My guess is Sally is at work, so we'll have more chance of catching her tonight when she gets home. I also have a few emails from Lopez I need to check, and I need to call Jack." He eyed her; his face gentle. "Have you told Evelyn or Roz about the attack or your father's heart attack?"

Pax shook her head. "No."

"You should, they would want to know. They care about you."

Pax sighed. "I know. I will later."

The truth was she didn't want to tell them. She already felt weak. Admitting to these strong women her family was trying to kill her, and she still gave a shit about them was embarrassing to say the least. She knew they would have cut Robert Paxton's head off rather than still care about him if they were the ones he had betrayed.

CHAPTER TWENTY

Just over an hour later they pulled up at a beautiful suburban home that looked like an advert for a modern-day '*Leave it to Beaver*' home. It was gorgeous and Pax instantly loved it.

"Where are we?" she asked turning to Blake.

She'd been too pre-occupied with the shit going on in her head to ask earlier. She saw a Ford truck and black SUV parked in the drive, neither of which she recognised.

"Reid's mum very kindly offered to let us all stay here."

Blake pointed at Reid who was walking towards them with his long, almost lazy prowl. That prowl, along with the sexy tattoos and gorgeous light blue eyes that seemed to see right through a person, combined into an amazing package. If Pax weren't wholly head over ass for Blake, she definitely would have found Reid attractive.

She was, however, madly in... She stopped her thought, not sure how to define how she felt for Blake. It was more than lust or like but was it love? She glanced at the handsome man beside her and felt her heart flip when he smiled at her and winked. Who was she kidding? She was madly in love with him. If she was honest with herself, she had been for a while. The instant she had seen him in Monaco she had been finished for other men. As she smiled and looked up at Reid, she realised she could admire him without guilt as he made her feel absolutely nothing except a natural admiration for a handsome man.

"Reid also has an update for us on Benny's real father," Blake said getting her attention.

They exited the car and she greeted Reid with a warm smile as he took her bags and led her and Blake up to the house.

The house was warm and welcoming as was Reid's mother who had to be in her late fifties but was still a beauty. With shoulder length brown hair and blue eyes like her son's, it was easy to see who he took after.

"Y'all come in and don't stand on ceremony." She ushered them in with a friendly smile. "Kirk, take the bags and put them in the spare room in the attic."

Hearing his first name sounded odd when she'd only ever heard him called Reid.

Reid grinned and kissed his mom's head. "Yes, ma'am."

Pax smiled at the sight of a man so dangerous and feared being such a sweetheart with his mom.

"It is so kind of you to put us up, Mrs Reid."

The woman took Blake's hands and nodded. "Any friend of Kirk's is a friend of ours. Unfortunately, I have to go to work. The girls are at school but shouldn't be back until after five. There's food in the fridge and a lasagne in the oven for you to warm if you get hungry."

The woman was a flurry of activity as she grabbed her bag off the small sideboard in the living room, smiled at them both and walked out the door. "See you later."

Mrs Reid waved as she walked down the road, her stride quick and no-nonsense.

Reid came down the stairs, eyes on the door, a frown on his face. Pax wondered what that was about but didn't ask. She was hardly in a position to discuss family dynamics.

"Shall we have a quick update before you guys get showered or whatever?" he asked with a quirk of his lips at them.

Blake tilted his head at her. "Want a quick update first?"

Pax nodded. "Yes, let's do that first. I feel like we're getting nowhere fast right now."

Reid led them from the front living room and into an open kitchen diner with a large wooden table. Pax took in the space, loving the fact the fridge was covered in papers and reminders of events with kitschy colourful magnets. He pulled down three mugs from a cupboard above his head and set about making them a coffee.

"So, Benny's father is Frank Castillo. He was serving fifteen for armed robbery at California State." Reid handed Blake and Pax a mug and pushed creamer and sugar towards them as he took a sip of his own before going on. "Castillo made parole about three months ago. I talked to his parole officer and he says Frank was a model citizen inside and even earned his qualification as a mechanic. He's working at a garage an hour north of Loma Linda and by all accounts, is a reformed character."

Blake took a long drink of the coffee and Pax noticed how tired he looked and wondered if he had gotten much sleep last night. "Do you believe the reformed character story?"

Reid shrugged at Blake's question. "Difficult to tell without meeting the guy. I can go pay him a visit if you like?"

Blake shook his head. "Nah, let's see if anything pops on the background checks first. No point going all that way until we know more, and we may need you here with everything else going on."

"You're the boss on this, Blake."

Blake snorted without humour. "Yeah, I'm the monkey in charge of this circus."

He sounded frustrated which was new for him. Usually Blake was calm, but something was getting to him. Probably exhaustion and pain from his knee which was swollen again.

"We should probably get showered and maybe you can rest that leg for an hour."

Blake looked at her and nodded. "Good idea." He looked to Reid. "Pax and I are going to visit Sally Nixon later. Can you see if Waggs needs help with the employees at Sana?"

Reid nodded slowly. "Sure, I'll call him now."

Blake nodded and then they followed as Reid led them to the attic room they would share. It was large with an en-suite that contained a shower, toilet, and sink. It also had a king-sized bed opposite a large Velux window.

Reid pointed at the bags by the chest of drawers. "I left your bags over there."

Pax smiled. "Thank you so much for this, Reid."

"My pleasure, ma'am," he said with a wink and Pax grinned wider as Blake rolled his eyes.

"Okay, enough flirting with my woman."

He pushed Reid to the door as Reid chuckled low. Pax walked to Blake as he stood by the bed. Placing her hands on his chest, his arms came around her lower back just above the curve of her ass. Her eyes searched his. She saw tiredness and pain but also desire and something else.

"You okay?" she asked knowing that for the most part he had been taking care of her and thought the scales needed balancing.

He smiled. "I am now."

"I think I can make it better," she purred as she stepped out of his arms and pushed him lightly until he was sitting on the edge of the bed.

Blake looked up at her his eyes stormy with need and interest. "Yeah, how so?"

Pax dropped to her knees in front of him and moved so she knelt between his spread muscular thighs. "Well, I hear there are ways of relieving pain by causing an endorphin rush."

Blake watched her as she moved her hands to the zip on his jeans and slowly lowered it. "Is that so?"

Pax saw the hardness of his dick against the denim fabric of his jeans. "Uh huh."

Her hand slipped in and grasped the hard cock in her hand and her body reacted to the sound of the hiss that came from his mouth at her touch. Blake sat back; his body propped on his elbows as he watched her stroke his cock.

Pax swiped a thumb over the slit as she bent to lick the bead of pre-cum from the head, her eyes never leaving his. Blake reached forward and wound her hair around his fist causing a tingle in her scalp to shoot straight to her clit.

Slowly she lowered her head until she took him into her mouth, the groan that reverberated up his chest and into her mouth heady and powerful. This man who had protected kings and queens, who was so self-assured and in control, was losing control because of her.

Her mouth worked his cock as he watched, his hips moving as he tried to hold back the desire to fuck her mouth. His eyes were crinkled, red slashes of desire across his cheekbones, jaw rigid. It made her want to make him lose it, so she doubled her efforts.

"Gracie, fuck," he rasped out.

Running her tongue over the head of his hardness, she reached up and cupped his balls, rolling them as he began to swell in her mouth, the breath coming from him harshly as he groaned.

"I'm gonna come," he moaned as he gripped her head.

Pax wanted him to come in her mouth, to taste him on her tongue and know that she made this man as weak as he did her. She didn't pull away but sucked harder, bobbing her head up and down his stiff cock. She felt him stiffen before his release filled her mouth.

"Gracie, Jesus Christ," he said letting go of her hair and falling back on the bed as she rose up to look at him. The tension was now gone as he looked at her with hooded eyes that had lost the weariness of earlier.

Blake reached for her and she crawled up the bed and into his arms, being careful of his injured knee. She nestled against him as he wrapped his arm around her and held her to him kissing her head.

"Give me a sec, babe, and I'll return the favour."

"No, you won't. That was for you. You've done nothing but take care of me for days now and it was my turn to look after you."

"I'm not keeping score, Gracie. Looking after you is entirely my pleasure. But if you feel the need to take away my pain, you can do that any time you want."

Pax chuckled and shook her head. "You're such a boy."

Blake rolled so that he was above her looking down and smiled. "I think you mean man, beautiful."

The smile on her face felt good as she replied, "Fine, *man* then."

"How about we get naked and I show you how much of a man?" He waggled his eyebrows adorably and nudged the soft curve of her tight pussy with his erection.

Pax raised her eyebrows in surprise. "Already?"

"It's all you, babe. All you." His head descended and he kissed her softly then showed her how much of a man he was which resulted in them falling asleep until a knock on their door woke them two hours later.

"Blake, not sure if you guys fell asleep but its five-fifteen and I know you wanted to see Sally Nixon," Reid called.

"*Shit!*" Blake exclaimed as he sat up. "Thanks, Reid, we'll be down in a sec."

"No problem. I'll see you before you head out."

Blake and Pax shared a shower which involved some making out but nothing else before they dressed. She changed into white jeans and a grey slouchy knit sweater that hung off her shoulder and grey stiletto ankle boots. She left her hair loose at her shoulders in waves.

"Do you have to look so fucking beautiful all the time? It's distracting," Blake said as he kissed her bare shoulder and strapped his shoulder harness over a white shirt before adding a leather jacket that made her want to strip him naked again.

Pax snorted. "Have you looked in the mirror?"

Blake smirked at that and winked. "Insatiable."

She rolled her eyes at him. "Come on, stud, let's go find out what happened with Sally Nixon."

Blake held the door for her to proceed him and followed her down the two sets of stairs. They came to the kitchen and heard two feminine voices along with Reid's deeper one. Moving inside, Pax was taken aback for a split second when she saw a girl of about nineteen or twenty sitting on a stool watching Reid chop veggies for a salad. She had a pale blue headscarf on her bald head, and was pale, but had the biggest blue eyes and widest smile as she watched Reid. She looked up at them and Reid's eyes followed.

"Hey."

"Oh, hi."

"I'm Nessa." She motioned to a girl behind her who was probably a couple of years younger and looked exactly like her siblings. "And this is my sister, Tori."

"I'm Grace and this is Blake." She turned and saw Blake was focused on Reid, his jaw hard, his expression severe, a frown marring his forehead. Pax elbowed him and he looked at her guiltily.

"Hey, nice to meet you both," he said to both girls as he reached out to shake their hands.

"You staying for dinner? Reid is warming mom's lasagne and making a salad."

Pax was about to say yes but Blake interrupted. "Unfortunately, we can't but thanks anyway."

"Your loss and more for me. Mom's lasagne is the best and now the chemo is finished for a while and I don't feel so sick anymore, I'm going to enjoy it while I can."

Pax nodded and smiled. "Good plan."

Reid laid the knife down and looked up. "Let me walk you out."

Reid walked them to the front door and pulled it closed behind him as he followed them out. "Nessa has Large B Cell Lymphoma. She's just finished her second round of chemo." His voice was monotone, but Pax could see it cost him.

"I'm so sorry, Reid," Blake said, and Pax could hear the regret in Blake's voice. "What's the prognosis?"

"Difficult to tell. We should know more with the next blood count, but we try not to speculate and live every day to the fullest."

"Yeah, I get that. If we can do anything, please let us know. We should probably get out of the way. Your mum has enough going on."

Reid shook his head. "No, she's loving the distraction of having everyone here."

Blake nodded. "Well, let us know if you change your mind. Does Jack know?"

"Nah. Didn't want to cause a fuss, and anyway, I can't do a lot."

"Well, we'll call when we finish with Sally. Did you get hold of Waggs?"

"Yeah, he has it handled so I'm going to help Lopez with the background checks."

Blake lifted his chin. "Good idea. Call if anything comes up."

Reid lifted his hand in salute. "Of course." He looked at Pax. "See you later, Pax."

"Yeah, see you later, Reid."

Pax followed Blake to the car and got in fastening her seat belt. She felt sad that Reid was shouldering things alone. So many good people around and yet hers were mostly bad. But she was lucky in some ways and seeing Nessa Reid and her stunning smile had given her a kick up the ass.

She spent way too much time feeling sorry for herself and that was going to stop right now.

CHAPTER TWENTY-ONE

Deep in thought Blake took the exit towards Loma Linda, the revelation about Nessa Reid worrying for more than one reason. He was gutted for Reid and he couldn't imagine how he would feel if it was one of his sisters. That aside, it also put Reid in the perfect position to be blackmailed.

As one of the names on the list, he had been watching Reid and had realised that on the mission where he had been injured, Reid hadn't been accounted for. Now with Nessa being ill he wondered if Reid had a weakness that someone was exploiting. He refused to believe that Reid had just gone bad.

The man loved his family though, and Blake wasn't sure there was anything he wouldn't do for them. He couldn't blame him as he would do anything for his. What he couldn't figure out was if Reid was the mole, why he hadn't gone to Jack. It also didn't explain the motive behind the attacks on Eidolon.

He felt Pax's hand on his thigh. "Blake?"

Blake tilted his head towards her. "Yes?"

"Are you all right?"

He nodded slowly. "Yes, just thinking about Reid." He didn't add that he wasn't thinking about Reid's situation—well, not only that.

"Are things okay between you and Reid? You two seem…" She paused as if seeking the right word. "Tense."

He nodded tightly. "Yes, all good."

He looked at her and saw the hurt cross her face. She knew he had just lied to her. He wanted to take it back and tell her what was going on with Eidolon and the mole, but he'd made a promise to Jack and he took that seriously. He kept quiet and slanted a glance at Pax who was watching the cars on the opposite side of the highway. Her jaw clenched, head tilted up with pride, he could practically feel the pissed off vibe fill the vehicle.

Blake sighed. "Listen, Grace," he started but she interrupted him holding up her hand.

"You don't have to explain it to me. I get it. We're not in that place yet. I am, but you obviously need more time." Her words were short and clipped with an underlying cadence of hurt.

He wanted to kick himself for that. "I am there." He took her hand firmly as she tried to resist. "Gracie, I am there but I can't tell you. It's Eidolon business and I made a promise."

Blake glanced at her as she turned slightly towards him, her posture less tense as he spoke. "If and when I can, I'll share but until then I ask you to give me this without reading something into it." He kissed her knuckles. "I love that you feel we're at the point where we share things like that. I'm definitely in that place. I wasn't lying when I said I wanted to build a life with you and that includes confidences, but I can't break this one. Even for you."

"I understand, Blake. I guess this is new for me and I already feel so vulnerable with my family that I reacted like a shrew."

"I would never hurt you deliberately, Grace."

"I know." She smiled but it didn't quite reach her eyes.

They remained silent as he drove the last five kilometres to Sally Nixon's home. He pulled up and parked on the road beside a single storey home with an attached garage and perfectly landscaped gardens. A new Lexus was parked in the drive. He knew from the information Lopez had sent him that it was Sally Nixon's car. He got out and moved to Pax who was already on the sidewalk.

The front door was open as they approached. Instantly, he got a bad feeling in his gut. He turned to Pax to tell her to go back to the car but that would also leave her exposed. "Stay behind me," he said voice low as he drew his weapon and watched as she did the same.

Pax was not a marksman, but she could handle a gun well enough. Nodding, she followed as he entered. The house was eerily silent—the type of quiet that was unsettling as if all signs of life were gone from the home. It caused a shiver to snake down his spine. On soundless feet he moved down the tiled floor of the hallway, past an empty study on the right, and towards the kitchen.

He entered and his eyes found the body of a woman. A low gasp behind him confirmed his fear. It was Sally Nixon, blood pooling around her from a bullet wound to the chest and one to the head. Eyes closed in death, her face a relaxed mask.

"I need to clear the rest of the house."

Blake felt Pax behind him as he moved from the kitchen to the bedroom wing of the property. The first two bedrooms were clear, both looked like they belonged to her younger sons. In the last bedroom he found the body of a man. He was around the same age as Sally Nixon and he presumed it was her husband.

"Marvin Nixon," Pax whispered into the quiet of the room.

Once he had finished clearing the rooms, Blake returned to the kitchen with Pax. He knelt down close to Sally to try and get a closer look for a clue of some sort but found nothing visible.

"We need to call the police, but we should try and keep you out of this."

Pax looked at him her head tilted in question. "Why?"

Blake stood and moved closer, until he was in her space. "If the press gets hold of this you won't be able to move."

He saw her think it over before she answered. "Maybe, but I owe it to Benny not to abandon his mom. I want to stay."

"Okay, Pax," he answered with a kiss to her forehead. "Let me have a quick look around for clues before you put in the call."

Pax nodded and again followed him as he moved through the rooms looking for anything that could tip them off as to who'd killed the Nixons. He felt an ache in his chest as he looked at the boy's rooms. Their lives were about to be ripped apart. He vowed to find out who killed Sally and Marvin Nixon if it was the last thing he did. Deciding there was nothing to be found without disturbing any evidence he and Pax walked back to the car and made the call to the LAPD.

It was a long three hours later after having given their statements to the homicide detective including his history in brief and Pax's reason for being there, that they got in the car and headed back to Reid's mom's. He glanced across at her as she gazed out the window. She looked tired. There was a sadness surrounding her that he wanted to take away.

Reaching out, he took her hand in his and rested them both on his thigh. She looked over and offered him a smile that filled his heart with so much feeling he didn't know where to put it all. His throat felt clogged as he tried to control his emotional response to the woman next to him. "How you doing?"

Pax shrugged. "I'm okay. I just feel sad that this has left those boys without parents and I can't help feeling responsible. This is tied to my family and Sana in some way. I just know it is, but I can't figure out how."

"This is in no way your fault, Gracie."

"I know, but it doesn't stop me feeling like I could have done more somehow."

Blake was quiet for a moment before he spoke. "When I was working as a PPO I worked for the royal family. My main duty was offering personal protection for Queen Lydia and her eldest daughter Penelope. What I'm about to tell you is something I've never told another living soul." He looked at her and she nodded, her attention focused on him as he spoke.

"Penelope was the first woman I ever loved." He heard a sharp inhale and kept his eyes on the road. "We had an affair. We were both young and single, and in hindsight I was very naive to think it would ever be anything else. I fell for her hook, line, and sinker, but she thought I was fun before she settled into life as a working royal. She was due to attend an opening at a new children's hospital and because my mind was so busy with her and not on what I was doing, the job I was paid for, I nearly missed a dangerous threat to her safety in the form of a small explosive device near the entrance." His heart pounded as he remembered finding it and realising how close he had come to getting her killed.

"Anyway, I broke it off and I was heartbroken. Completely blamed myself. I was ready to give up there and then. Then I got a call that Her Majesty wanted to see me. I thought for sure I was fired or worse, but do you know what? She was the one person who didn't blame me for what had nearly happened." Blake squeezed her hand gently as he slipped onto the highway.

"What did she say?"

Blake grinned at that. "She told me that I was young and stupid, and she knew I had learned a valuable lesson. She had known about Penelope and me and in another life, would have been honoured to have me as her son-in-law but that was not the life she and her family led. I was transferred to her personal protection duty that week and served as her PPO until I left. She trusted me with her life even when I didn't trust myself. She gave me back what I thought I had lost—my self-worth.

"So, you see, Gracie, we all do things we wish we could take back or have situations that change us but there is always someone there to show us we're not the sum of our mistakes. We are how we handle those mistakes."

"Why did you leave the service? It sounds like you loved it," Pax asked as she angled more in her seat to look at him.

"The powers that be decided they wanted to mix it up, so the PPO assigned changed regularly and I vehemently disagreed. I quit and my then boss, Commander Helen Pope put me onto Jack." The car was silent for a few minutes as Pax processed what he had said.

"Did you love her a lot?"

He could hear the slight tone of jealousy in her voice and his lips twitched as he tried to hide his joy at that. He looked at her and smiled. "I thought I did, then I met you and realised I had no clue what love was before a red headed goddess stole my heart from my chest and placed it in her own."

The smile that moved over her face was like the sunshine after a storm it was so pure and beautiful.

He watched her open her mouth, but the words were stolen as the windshield on the car splintered into a thousand pieces as a bullet flew past his ear.

CHAPTER TWENTY-TWO

A SCREAM ERUPTED from her mouth as the car swerved dangerously close to the central reservation before Blake righted it.

"Get down, Grace," he demanded on a bellow as another shot hit the hood of the car.

Pax did as she was told unclipping her seatbelt and sliding low knowing she wouldn't be of any help to him. Her ability with a handgun was passable on a stationary object but a moving one was impossible.

She watched with her body ducked low behind the dashboard as Blake returned fire. Peeking in the direction he'd fired she saw a black Ford truck speeding away from them like the hounds of hell were following.

They fell back as Blake slowed the car and she watched as the person driving the truck took the exit. She expected Blake to follow but was surprised when he pulled over to the side of the road. Putting the vehicle in park, he turned to her and hauled her to him. His hands ran over her face and body as he looked for an injury that wasn't there.

His movements were frantic and panicked until she cupped his face. "I'm okay, Cal." Her gentle tone seemed to get through to him as she saw a visible shudder of relief go through him.

He took her face in his hands and dropped his mouth to hers in a soft soul-crushingly tender kiss that made the breath leave her body. It felt as if he was pouring every ounce of his feelings into her body in that second.

His head lifted and she witnessed the anguish and residual fear in his eyes. "Don't know what I would do if something happened to you, Gracie."

Pulse-pounding in her ears she echoed the sentiment in her mind. This man was everything to her. "I love you, Cal. You can't get rid of me that easy." She offered a small grin with her words.

He was still holding her face in his hands as she rested hers against them, holding his wrists and feeling the pounding of his heart in his veins. This cool-under-fire man was shaken because she had been there when they were shot at—again. "You love me, huh?" His smirk was cheeky and sexy as hell as she rolled her eyes at him.

"Okay don't let it go to your head, stud."

"You love me and I'm a stud. Not sure there isn't an upside to being shot at."

Pax scowled at him but felt it fall when she saw the trickle of blood from his neck. "You're hurt," she said wiping the blood with her thumb.

He rubbed his neck and shrugged at the small cut. "It's nothing."

He pulled away after dropping a kiss on her lips that shot straight to her core. Pax re-clipped her seat belt as Blake put the car in gear. He hadn't returned her declaration of love per se, but she knew he cared for her. He had called her a red-haired goddess and said she'd stolen his heart so that was more than enough. She didn't need the actual words. He had poured his heart out to her and revealed things nobody else knew. If that wasn't an indication of how he felt, then what was?

"We need to get back and find out who the fuck is trying to kill us," he growled as he drove towards Reid's home.

"Us?"

"Well, those shots weren't actually aimed at the passenger side, babe."

Pax picked at her cuticle as he drove and mulled over what had happened in the last few hours. Finding Sally and Marvin dead would haunt her for the rest of her life. Not because seeing their dead bodies weren't horrific because it was, but it was the feeling of loss that she couldn't shake. The detective had called Marvin's family and CPS to deal with the boys and her heart broke for those kids. The young lives they had led were over and they had no support from the two people they needed most.

Getting shot at in the car was also playing on her mind as they drove. Something didn't fit and she couldn't figure out what it was.

Glancing at Blake she saw his jaw was tense and knew he was probably running all the scenarios in his head like she was. "Do you think this is all connected? I mean it must be, right? But I don't know."

He glanced over and his eyes were dark with buried anger. "What don't you know, Pax?"

Pax blew out a breath. "I not sure. In part I feel it all must be linked but something feels off. I can't help thinking the shots fired on the car weren't about Sana and my father. If whoever killed Sally and Marvin shot at us in the car and on the balcony, why did they miss?" She angled towards him as she spoke her voice becoming more animated. "I mean, they proved they're willing to kill so why only fire warning shots at us? That truck could easily have taken us off the road and killed us so why drive off..." Her voice trailed off as her brain whirred.

"Go on?" Blake prompted.

"I think they are separate incidents and whoever is shooting at us is just warning us."

"I agree."

Pax noticed the knuckles on his hands go white as he gripped the steering wheel. "Shit. So who and why?"

"That's the sixty-four-thousand-dollar question and one I'm going to find the answer to," he declared as they pulled into the drive of Mrs Reid's home.

"Reid must be out," she said noticing his car was gone.

Blake didn't reply, just mumbled something under his breath she didn't quite catch.

They approached the house and Waggs came out to meet them, his face grave. "Sorry about the Nixons," he said to Pax who nodded. He listened in silence as Blake updated him on the shots fired on them as they drove home. Waggs' look was hard as stone as his jaw seemed to seesaw in anger. "We're missing something."

"My thoughts exactly," Blake replied. "I have to make a call to Jack. Let me catch up with you in a sec."

Waggs nodded, and Blake moved into her body as they headed upstairs to the room they were using.

Pax sank her ass on the bed and Blake sat beside her. "Now what?" she asked as he turned into her body lifting his cocked knee to the mattress. Her head tilted slightly as his hand came up and tucked a stray strand of hair behind her ear.

"Now I make some calls and see if I can figure out what the fuck is going on."

She could feel the heat from his gaze as his eyes wandered over her mouth.

"What can I do to help?" Her voice was husky as his hand moved to the galloping heartbeat in her neck.

"You're doing it," he said softly as he traced the soft skin the heat from him making butterflies take flight in her tummy.

"I want to do more," she implored wanting to be his partner in every way she could and wipe the worry from his face.

"I know and when there is something, I'll ask. But for now, why don't you catch up with the hospital and check in with your mom?"

"Okay, honey," she replied wanting to give him what he needed. She tilted her head as he dropped a kiss in the spot where her shoulder met her neck.

She felt his lips pull into a smile at her words. "Like it when you call me that," he muttered.

"I like it when you do that," she replied as he nibbled the spot behind her ear.

"So fucking beautiful."

"Cal," she said his name as the heat from his sweet words hit her.

"Don't know what I did to deserve you, Gracie, but I won't ever let you go." The words were uttered against her open lips.

She chuckled. "That would sound like a creepy stalker threat from anyone else but from you it's all I want to hear."

"I love you, Gracie."

The words were simple—three little words that she had thought she didn't need but hearing them opened a floodgate of emotion in her that was almost overwhelming. This sweet sexy kind man loved her and for the first time ever she believed it. There was no doubt to poison or tarnish it. It was merely the most breath-taking feeling she had ever experienced.

"I love you too, honey."

The rest of her words were stolen by his mouth on hers, a soft drugging kiss that made the world recede until only they existed. His tongue coaxed and teased a million sensations from her body until all she wanted was him. He was everywhere, surrounding her in a net of safety and love, passion and joy that she never wanted to end.

Blake pulled away with a groan. "I need to go and make that call." He leaned his forehead against her shoulder as they both tried to calm their racing bodies. "Can't wait until this is over so I can spend a week in bed making love and fucking you until you can't see straight."

The words shot straight to her clit. Her nipples peaked and her body ached, forcing a moan from her. "You're killing me, Blake."

"Only what you do to me every time I look at you, Grace." Blake pushed off the bed and moved to the door as she sat still. She didn't trust herself not to drag him back to bed and climb him like a tree if she moved.

He stopped and turned. "Check in with your mom and I'll be back once I made this call, hopefully with a plan."

Pax watched the door close before lying back on the bed a goofy smile creasing her face. She was in love for probably the first time and it felt better than she had ever imagined. Even with everything that was happening she couldn't feel too sad. Maybe that made her selfish.

People had lost their lives, more were on the verge of being ruined if Sana and whoever was behind the criminal trials wasn't stopped, and that was without her family drama, but she didn't let it faze her. She knew if Calvin Blake was beside her, she could handle whatever she faced because he loved her. With that happy thought in her head she picked up her cell and called her mom.

CHAPTER TWENTY-THREE

HE FELT like a complete asshole as he left Pax in the room they were sharing. He had used his declaration of love to distract her from the course she was on. It didn't matter that he had meant every fucking word. He did love her more than he could have imagined possible, but he also knew the words would move her focus from the fact that a third party had entered the game.

A third party that was very likely his teammate. Never in his life had he treated a woman with such disrespect, and she had no clue he'd done it. If she ever figured it out, she would roast his balls on a BBQ, and he would deserve it. When this was over, he would make it up to her. Even if she didn't know what he had done, he would relive the first time he'd told the woman he wanted to spend his life with that he loved her and feel dirty.

He found Waggs in the garden with Decker talking to Mrs Reid.

The three looked up when he approached, Mrs Reid wearing a wide friendly smile. "Blake would you like something to eat?"

"No, thank you, Mrs Reid, but thanks for asking."

"What about that lovely girlfriend of yours?"

Blake considered saying no not wanting to burden the exhausted woman, but he wanted to talk to Waggs and Decker in private. "That would be great if it's not too much trouble?"

She stood with a radiant smile on her face. "Nonsense, it is no trouble at all."

He waited for the door to close before he turned back to the two men watching him. "Where's Reid?"

Neither man spoke for a second and Blake could feel Decker profiling him. "He went to meet a friend for a drink. Apparently, the guy wanted a favour. Why?"

"No reason," Blake hedged knowing that he wasn't fooling anyone with his reply.

"Any thoughts about Sally Nixon?" Decker asked.

Blake was surprised that he let the bullshit he was feeding them slide. "Somebody didn't want us talking to her about Sana is my guess, which tells us we're on the right path."

Waggs nodded. "Agreed."

"Anything from the employees?"

"A few rumours about financial problems but nothing that any other company doesn't deal with. One interesting thing though. One of the older lab assistants that used to work with Robert Paxton before he hung up his lab coat and became a suit, said that before Robert and Henrietta got engaged there was some big hoo-ha about her leaving another man at the altar. Care to guess who it was?" Waggs raised his eyebrows at Blake.

"Clark Baker by any chance?"

"Bingo! Apparently, it was a big society wedding, but Henrietta met Robert and called it off just weeks before. From what I can tell there was a huge fallout from it."

"Which begs the question. How did he end up on the board of Sana?" Decker asked.

"Can you do some more digging on that angle? I have to make a call." Blake stood and wanting complete privacy, walked to the car and waited impatiently for the call to connect and Jack to pick up.

"Good of you to call."

Blake ignored the sarcasm from his boss. "I need an update on the other two targets."

He heard Jack sigh and had a feeling he wasn't going to like what his boss had to say.

"I was going to call you after I got off the phone with Will. Gunner has requested leave for his aunt's funeral which has been confirmed as genuine by Will, but it means he's away for two days at least as it's happening on the Isle of Jersey. Mitch has gone completely dark. He left here last night after training and hasn't been located this morning. We've tried his cell and tracker, but both are switched off."

"Fan-fucking-tastic. So the three men suspected of being the mole are all unaccounted for at this point."

"Where's Reid?"

"He went to visit a friend which is convenient because Pax and I were just shot at on the highway and I don't think it has anything to do with this case."

"Things are moving fast and whoever it is feels cornered," Jack mused aloud.

"I agree, but who is it? Can you ask Will to check the CCTV on the I-10 close to Loma Linda? Also have him see if he can track Reid's movements for the past few hours?"

"You really think it's Reid?" Jack asked sounding deflated.

"I'm hard pushed to believe it's any of them. I just can't reconcile it with the men I know. But the fact is, we know it *is* one of them. With Reid's sister being so sick he's a prime target."

"I fucking hate this," Jack growled.

"Me too and I hate lying to Pax."

Silence met his words on the other end of the phone. "This can't get out until it's confirmed and then only to those that I deem necessary. Your girlfriend is not necessary, and might I remind you, she works for Zenobi."

Blake clenched his jaw. "No reminder necessary. I'll do my job and keep my secrets and for the record, Jack, if you ever infer that my loyalty is in question again then you can shove your job up your ass." With that he hung up knowing that if he stayed on the line any longer, he would say something he would regret to a man he respected.

Blake punched the steering wheel hard letting his frustration course through him. He was angry at Jack for questioning him and yet here he was questioning Reid, Mitch, and Gunner. Three fine men with impeccable records of service to their countries and Eidolon. He was a hypocrite—to them as well as Grace now.

His eyes moved to the entrance of the street and he watched through the shattered glass of the still intact windshield as Reid's truck pulled up in front of him. Blake watched Reid exit the vehicle and glance in his direction before giving the glass a hard stare. Blake tried to read the look on his face, but it was almost impossible. Reid, like the rest of the team, was a master at controlling his emotions.

Blake was unsure what to do. Did he confront his friend or wait for the call from Will? Assessing a threat was one of his skills and yet he was compromised in this instance by the fact he didn't want Reid to be a threat.

Blake stepped from the car deciding to play it by ear.

Reid eyed him as if picking up on the vibe he was giving off. He lifted his chin to Blake's car. "What the fuck happened?"

Blake moved towards him, making sure his gait was relaxed. "Some fucker shot at us on the way back from seeing Sally Nixon, and by seeing, I mean seeing her dead body on her kitchen floor."

Reid shook his head. "Fuck, man, this is getting serious. Do you have any leads?"

Blake shook his head. "Not really."

They remained silent as they walked towards the house when Reid stopped short and turned to him "We good man?"

Reid was a quick study and Blake wasn't surprised that he was feeling the vibe Blake was throwing off. Blake angled his head to look at the man. "Where you been?"

He saw Reid's shoulders lock, a muscle in his jaw ticking as he clenched it. "Am I a suspect?" he asked incredulously.

Blake stayed silent giving him some rope and seeing how he would react.

"You have to be fucking kidding me? I offer you my home, give you access to my family, and you think what? That I'm behind this shooting?"

Blake had to concede he did have a point. Why would the mole make himself so vulnerable? The answer was he wouldn't unless he was playing a colossal bluff. Blake dismissed that idea. Reid loved his sisters and mom. There was no way he would drag them into anything shady.

Blake sighed and shook his head. "No, but it would have been good if we'd able to contact you."

"I had a call from a friend who needs some help with something. I would have called but didn't think about it to be honest. We've never been a team that needed to account for our every movement." Reid was still suspicious and rightly so. Things were changing and not for the better.

"Just give me a heads up next time," Blake said and began to walk away but stopped when Reid called his name

"You never answered my question? We good?"

"Yeah, we're good," Blake lied again and wished he had never agreed to this. Jack should have gotten an outsider in to do this. They should not be investigating each other.

Exhaustion pulled at him, he needed to sleep and rest his aching leg but with people dying it was imperative they tie this up and soon. He entered the room he was sharing with Pax and heard the shower running. His body reacted instantly to the thought of Gracie naked with water running down her perfect silky skin.

Stripping off, he walked into the bathroom to find she was singing softly as she lifted her arms to her head and massaged the shampoo into her lush mountain of hair then rinsed it out. Her body arched against the glass was like an erotic fantasy come to life.

Wasting no more time, he opened the door a grin etched into his face as she squeaked and spun to him in surprise.

"*Shit*, you scared me. Don't you know it's bad manners to creep up on a girl?"

Blake hooked her around the waist with his arm and hauled her closer, so she was hip to toe with him his erection pressed against her belly. Her hands came to rest on his shoulders as her hard nipples grazed his chest. "Sorry."

"No, you're not."

"No, I'm not." His laugh echoed in the small space.

He raked his eyes over her face before allowing himself to look lower. She was perfect in every way. Even her stubborn streak was perfect. He needed to lose himself in her body and forget the shit-storm that raged outside this room. Forget about the case, her family, the mole. All of it.

"Blake?" she asked picking up on his feeling of discord. This was how he should have told her he loved her, not as a way to distract her.

"I love you so much, Gracie." He didn't let her respond but dipped his head taking her mouth in a possessive kiss. She immediately opened for him, her arms coming around his neck as she rubbed her body against him. He trailed hot open-mouthed kisses down her throat his hands going to the full curves of her ass. "Fucking perfection."

"I need you, Cal."

Blake loved it when she used his real name and he needed her as much as she needed him. He wanted to feel her skin-on-skin though, without the barrier of latex between them. He never went un-gloved but with Pax he wanted it all. He lifted her leg and wrapped it around his hip as she rubbed her pussy against his aching cock, the hot water adding the sensations he was feeling. "I'm clean, baby."

She seemed to know instantly what he was asking. "Me too. Roz insists we get medicals every six months."

Thank fucking Christ.

Wasting no time he slammed into her, the soft folds of her sweet pussy hugging him tightly. He closed his eyes as he let the feeling of being inside her with no barrier wash through him. The desire to fuck her hard and fast ripped at his control as he resisted the urge to slam into her again and again.

"Fuck me, Cal," she urged, her voice husky with need as he backed her up against the shower wall and did as she asked. He fucked her hard, driving them both higher and higher towards the pinnacle of release.

His mouth was on her everywhere as she arched herself into each thrust of his hips. His thumb pressed against her clit and it was enough to push her over the edge. He caught her scream of release with his mouth, swallowing the sound as he joined her shooting jets of come into her body as she spasmed around him, her walls draining the last of his release from him.

His eyes moved to hers and he could see the profound impact their lovemaking had on her. He knew, he had the same look in his eyes. He held her gaze, the green flecks in her hazel eyes flashing holding him transfixed.

"I fucking love you too, Cal," she whispered softly. He felt connected to her on a cellular level with his cock still inside her.

"I love you, Gracie," he said as he kissed her softly exploring her mouth slowly and feeling his dick twitch again. Not even soft and with his come dripping from her, he wanted her, and he knew he would never stop wanting this woman. She was the one he would grow old with, who would carry his babies one day.

He grinned against her lips as he withdrew and lowered her leg before reaching for the shampoo. "Let's get cleaned off and close this case. I'm ready for us to go home."

Pax nodded and then frowned. "Me too. I hope Evelyn is watering my garden. I don't want my hanging baskets to wilt."

Blake threw his head back and laughed as he rinsed the shampoo from his hair and watched her step out and throw him a mock scowl.

"What? I love my baskets."

"Only you would finish the most soul-altering lovemaking I've ever experienced in my life worrying about flowers and hanging baskets."

He saw her face soften at his words before she smiled. "Love you, baby."

Yes, that was how you told someone you loved them, and for the first time in the last twenty-four hours, Blake felt calm again.

CHAPTER TWENTY-FOUR

THE RINGING of her phone as she was drying her hair pulled Pax from the comfort and contentment that had wrapped around her since leaving Blake in the shower. What they had shared had been beyond anything she had ever felt in the past, like the last shred of doubt had been wiped from her mind. He was her future and she'd felt giddy when he'd said he wanted them to go home. She wanted that so badly. She couldn't wait to see what the future held for them both.

Picking up her phone she saw her mother's name on the screen. She had left a message earlier when she hadn't picked up and then called the hospital who'd said her father was doing well and recovering better than they had hoped. Relief had been swift, she had things she needed to say to her father and now she would have the opportunity.

"Hello, Mom."

"Hello, Grace."

"I called earlier to check on Dad and ended up calling the hospital when I couldn't get hold of you. They gave me an update."

"He's doing well. They think he'll be home in a week all being well."

Pax could hear the smile in her mom's voice and the sound made her melancholy. Her mother hadn't sounded that way since she was a young child and she hadn't realised until she heard the sound how much she missed it. "That's great news. Are you still at the hospital?"

"No. I came home to change and make sure the staff were organising the downstairs bedroom for your father. I'll go back in tomorrow now."

Pax hardly recognised this woman. She was showing an interest in her father she had thought long forgotten and it made her happy. "Okay, Mom. Well, I might see you tomorrow then."

"Yes, okay, dear."

Pax hung up with a smile on her lips just as Blake walked out the bathroom with a towel wrapped low on his hips. Pax let her eyes travel over his fine form.

"Hey, babe, my eyes are up here," he said, with a smirk as her eyes jumped to him with guilt. Pax squinted her eyes and poked out her tongue. "Who was on the phone?"

"My mom. She was returning my call."

Blake dragged the smaller towel from around his shoulders and roughly dried his hair as he asked, "Everything okay?"

"Yes, she was organising some stuff at home. My dad is doing well, and they expect to discharge him next week all being well." Something in the way Blake went still sent her Spidey senses going. "Blake?"

He sat down on the bed beside her. "Did you know your mum used to date Clark Baker?"

Pax cocked her head and thought for a second. "No, but it doesn't surprise me. Our families have known each other forever. He was like a son to my grandfather."

"It was more than date, babe. They were engaged and weeks away from being married when she called it off to marry Robert."

Pax felt shock trickle through her at the announcement. Nobody had ever said a word to her. But why would they? She had been a child. "Wow. I had no idea."

"I've asked Decker to look into Clark and Waggs is going to poke into his connection with Albert."

"Okay, honey, you do what you need to do." He waggled his eyebrows and she laughed. "Behave yourself for a minute." She was about to say more when Blake's phone rang. He stood and walked to the window.

"Hey, Will, how's it going?"

Pax pointed to the hairdryer and he nodded as he looked out over the garden. Pax couldn't hear the conversation from her end, but it seemed tense and was over quickly. Shutting off the dryer she looked at him as he dropped the towel and pulled on some dark wash jeans that hugged his sexy butt perfectly. Throwing a white tee over his head and hiding his magnificent chest was only acceptable because even clothed, her man was delicious.

"Everything okay?"

He smiled and nodded. "Yes, I just need to speak to Reid for a minute." He moved into a crouch in front of her, his hands on her bare thighs. "Why don't you get ready and we'll go for dinner—just the two of us."

The thought of her and Blake on a date was exciting and little butterflies took flight in her belly. "Really? Shouldn't we be helping?"

"It's all covered. We can't do anything until we hear from my police contact about any leads on Sally and Marvin Nixon. Your father's doctor hasn't cleared him for us to speak to him yet and I want to hear from him before we talk to your mum."

"Sounds good."

She watched Blake leave and instantly started tearing her suitcase apart for the perfect outfit. He hadn't said where they were going so it needed to be smart-casual to cover all bases. Tagging on a black halter neck jumpsuit which was slashed to mid-thigh on either side, she looked for her nude pumps.

Perfect. Especially with her hair down around her shoulders.

This would be her first date with Blake. It was funny to think they had done it backwards, professions of love before the dating, but they were not an average couple.

Her heart jumped as she thought back to the shower when he'd told her he loved her while their bodies were still connected in the most primal way. It had been perfect and allowed her to see the man who had stolen her heart in Monaco just as surely as she had handed hers over to him. She finished getting ready with a smile on her face.

———

THE CALL from Will had Blake taking the stairs two at a time looking for Reid. He poked his head into the lounge and saw Tori Reid reading a book. She looked up as he entered and blushed when she saw him watching her. The girl was painfully shy by the looks of things.

"Have you seen Reid?" She frowned and he amended himself. "Kirk?"

"He was in the garage earlier working on his bike."

"Thanks."

The girl nodded and dropped her head back into her book.

Blake headed for the garage and found Reid working on a black Harley with a red skull motif on the front. He stepped inside and saw Reid's head come up. He looked at him cautiously and Blake knew Reid was still pissed about earlier. He didn't have time to smooth his ruffled feathers now though.

"We need to talk."

Blake crossed over to him, passing the bike and the selection of tools at his feet, noting the wrench in Reid's hand.

Reid eyed him before going back to work on his motorcycle. "What about?"

"I think you know what about." Blake skimmed closer, keeping his eye on the door and Reid.

Anger made his voice gravelly. "I have no fucking clue."

Blake knew this conversation could go south fast and he had to protect Grace. "Come on, Reid, don't play games."

He stood to his full height and faced Blake, anger emanating from him. "Only fucker here playing games is you."

Blake blew out a breath. He had been glad to get the call from Will but now he wasn't so sure he should share what he had to. With a deep breath and prayer that Reid wouldn't react badly with his family in the house he blurted it out. "We have a mole at Eidolon."

Reid went stock still, his body freezing in place as the shock hit him before realisation filtered through. "And you thought it was me?"

Blake couldn't ignore the hurt in his friend's voice. "You were one of three people who was suspected."

"Were?" Reid asked tightly.

Blake pushed his fingers through his hair as Reid dropped the wrench and leaned back against the workbench. "Yeah. Will just cleared you. He and Jack gave me permission to share with you, but it's not common knowledge, obviously."

"I can't believe you thought I would betray the team."

His voice was tortured, and Blake felt like a total prick for doubting him, but he felt the same way about the other two still under suspicion. "I didn't believe it. I find it difficult to believe the other two would either, but the evidence Will and Jack have is overwhelming."

"Who are the others?"

Blake wasn't sure if he should say but seeing the look on Reid's face, made a judgement call. "Gunner and Mitch."

"Fuck. I can't see either of them being a traitor."

"Me either, man. I didn't think you were any more than I think they are. Hence my fucked up part in this."

"Why you?"

"I had been cleared and with my background, I guess I was the perfect choice to investigate."

"How does being over here help you find the traitor?"

"Well, I'm pretty sure that was who shot at me on the balcony and then in the car. They leave no evidence and seem to be firing warning shots as none were close enough to injure us."

"So they followed us? Surely that's easy to check. Just see who's out of the country."

"Yeah, except Gunner is at his aunt's funeral in Jersey, which is confirmed as real, but his attendance is not, and Mitch has gone dark."

"*Jesus H Christ*. What a fucked upped situation. I guess with Nessa being ill I was a prime candidate. We're up to our necks in debt and mom won't let me help her out more than giving her the odd hundred here or there."

"I had no clue about your sister being sick." He stopped and decided honesty was best. "But yes, it did make you a more likely candidate than the other two so far."

"So what now?"

"Now we clear this case and then find the fucking traitor. I could do with some help on this if you're willing?"

Reid nodded and moved closer until he was toe to toe with Blake. "Of course, brother."

He stuck out his hand and Blake shook it. And just like that all was forgiven. It was one of the best things about Reid, he was reliable, logical, and a fucking grade A operator. Blake felt shame for ever doubting the man.

"I'm going to take Pax out tonight to give her some downtime. Could you go and look into her mum a bit more? I think she's hiding something. That woman blows hot and fucking cold."

Reid smirked as he nodded. "You are so gone for her."

"Guilty as charged. She is the piece that was missing all this time and I didn't even know it."

"Pleased for you, man." Reid was a good guy and Blake was as relieved as fuck he wasn't the traitor.

"I really am sorry, man," Blake said with sincerity.

"Forget it. You were doing your job and much as I hate it, I understand. The fucker to blame is the person betraying us and he won't be forgiven quite so fucking easily."

Blake had no doubt that when the mole was identified, his life would be over because he would have every last man at Eidolon out for his blood. He just hated it was a man he had considered a good friend—whoever it turned out to be.

CHAPTER TWENTY-FIVE

AFTER SCOPING out the local restaurants Blake had decided on a bar and grill with live music. It was somewhat dressy but casual enough that they could kick back and relax for a few hours.

When he had walked into the bedroom and seen Grace dressed in that sexy as fuck jumpsuit with all that hair around her shoulders, and the fuck-me-heels she wore everywhere, it had taken every ounce of self-control not to strip her naked and drag her back to bed. The excitement on her face as she'd asked where they were going had convinced him she needed this, and he always wanted to give her what she needed.

He stepped out of Reid's truck which he had loaned him, saying it was safer than his mom's Prius before shaking his head and walking away. The fact that Reid had forgiven so easily, and accepted things was a testament to the man he was.

Crossing to the front, he scanned the parking lot of Bert's Bar and Grill and noted the cars and motorcycles parked near the door. He wasn't overly concerned, just mildly interested as he made sure there were no immediate threats to Grace. The fire exit was at the side of the building beside the dumpsters, with a door onto a street behind.

He had done a quick check of the map to familiarise himself with all the available escape routes. Reid had confirmed the bar was a favourite hangout with an excellent reputation for food and music but warned him that the beer was not like he was used to back home. The warning had made him smile. With nothing to suggest trouble he had been happy it was a good place to go for a meal. He for one could murder a big, fat juicy burger with fries and onion rings.

His belly rumbled reminding him he hadn't eaten since lunch. Grace smiled as she stepped from the car, her hand in his and he walked with her to the door. He kept his body covering hers as he held tight to her. In part because it was his nature and was ingrained in him and partly because who wouldn't want to hold the hand of this woman and stake a claim on her for all the men in the room to see? She was his and off limits. The knowledge made him grin.

The interior of the place was as he'd expected. A long, dark wood bar ran along the side with stools in front filled with customers. Tables and booths littered the sides with a large stage and dance floor in the middle. A piano was in the left corner of the stage by a pretty woman in full cowgirl outfit including denim skirt, boots, check shirt, and cowboy hat while a man with a full grey beard played the guitar. A couple that made the chemistry between Lady Gaga and Bradley Cooper look tepid, sang 'Shallow' at the mic.

They followed the hostess as she led them to a corner booth against the wall and nearest to the fire exit at his request. From here they could get out either side and had visual on the entire area. Blake took a seat next to Pax, not wanting to be out of touching distance. The waitress handed them both menus and took their drinks order. He ordered a beer and Pax decided on a gin and tonic. He looked up and caught the secret smile on her face that he loved so much. It was probably the first thing he'd fallen in love with and would always be his favourite look on her.

"What's the smile for?"

She looked up and angled her head the thick hair falling over her shoulder as she regarded him. "Just feeling happy, I guess. Despite the drama going on around us, I feel content and free." She reached over and grabbed his hand in hers. "That's your doing. You make me feel safer and happier than I can remember. I haven't thanked you for that."

"Baby," he said her words hitting him right in the heart.

"It's true. You barged into my life and made me see the mistakes I was making and how I allowed the fear of failing to rule me. You made me brave."

He swallowed past the lump of emotion in his throat at her heart-felt words. Grace had the power to wash away everything he had ever believed he'd felt for a spoiled princess. He had thought he knew pain and love but losing Grace would not just wound him, it would kill him. His love for her was nothing he had ever felt, and Blake realised it was exactly what his parents had. He had found the other half of his soul but knew it wasn't the time to share that with her.

"I think technically you barged into my life," he said trying to relieve their emotions and lighten things up again.

Pax scowled at him and then pinched his thigh. "That was rude," she said with a flip of her hair.

He grabbed the hand she was using to torture him with a chuckle and brought it to his lips kissing it. "Babe, you gave me no choice. Any more from you and I'll drag you to the ladies' room and show you exactly what you mean to me, and I know you're excited about this meal so cut me some slack."

Her smile was back in place as her eyes softened. "Well, when you put it like that."

Blake chuckled again, giving her hand one last squeeze before letting go.

They both ordered burgers. His had extra bacon, onion rings, and fries and Pax decided to add grilled halloumi and avocado to hers. He loved that she dove in, getting her hands around the burger. His eyes caught on a group of eight men who walked in probably on a stag do if their drunken state were anything to go by. They took a booth just behind them and were loud and obnoxious enough to irritate the shit out of him.

He was going to say something when Pax put a hand on his arm. "Leave it, Cal. They're just drunk."

He sat down with a growl of frustration and he and Pax chatted for a bit longer about her childhood and he told her more about his sisters and his adorable niece, who his sister was positive was going to be a hellion when she was a teen. He couldn't disagree with that, the kid had sass already and she was barely out of nappies. For some reason the thought of her raising hell made him smile and then his thoughts turned to him and Grace.

"You want kids, Gracie?"

She nodded, sucking on her bottom lip as if not wanting to admit it. "Yes, always have. I would love to have a couple of kids."

Blake sipped his beer and silently agreed; it wasn't what he was used to as he watched Pax. "I want four. Three boys and a girl."

Pax laughed. "Not sure I can manage four, Cal."

He leaned in closer his mouth almost touching hers. "Three?"

"Why don't we wait and see but three sounds acceptable." The words were cut short as a burly man from the table beside them fell into Pax as he walked past, his hand going to her breast as he tried to stand.

Blake saw red and immediately pushed the man off as he stood and moved between her and the table of drunks.

"Watch what the fuck you're doing," he snarled.

The man weaved on his feet for a minute before glaring at him. "You can go fuck yourself," he said as his friends joined in, crowding them.

Blake could easily take these pricks but had no intention of doing so with Pax in the firing line. He caught the eye of a bouncer who came over quickly and with the help of a colleague, escorted the clearly pissed off men from the bar.

"Sorry about that." The bald bearded security guy nodded and left.

Blake glanced at Pax with a worried frown. "You okay?"

She smiled. "Contrary to common belief, I'm not a delicate wall-flower." Her head tilted as the band started playing Billy Joel's 'Uptown Girl'. "I love this song." She grabbed his hand and started pulling him towards the dance floor. "Dance with me."

Blake resisted. "Babe, I don't dance." The pout on her full lips made his own tip up as he quickly conceded. "Fine, but no laughing," he said as he followed her to the floor and took her in his arms.

He danced with her through that one and when Joe Cocker's 'You are so beautiful' came on, he held her tight against him his lips at her ear as he swayed with her and sang every word to her. The soft look in her eyes when he pulled away nearly pierced his heart it was so beautiful.

"Wanna get out of here?" he asked her, and she nodded. Not letting go of her hand he paid the bill and pulled her through the door with his arm around her, not wanting to let go for even a second.

The moment they hit the parking lot his senses went on alert as five men stepped from the shadows.

"Well, well. If it isn't the Brit and his pretty little girlfriend."

It was the man who had fallen into Pax. He felt her stiffen in his arms but remained still as he assessed the situation. Five against one wasn't great but then he wasn't worried about himself. It was Pax he was concerned about. He moved sideways, his head down, fear on his face as the men followed him in a semi-circle formation until he had Pax between him and the car.

"Go to the car and lock the doors," he said low as he shoved the keys in her hand.

"But..."

"Go. Now."

He felt her move away from him. He kept his breathing calm despite the helpless vibe he was showing the men who were still clearly quite drunk.

"Listen, I don't want any trouble from you drunk pussies. I just want to go home with my girl. Not pansy around with you assholes."

The words had the desired effect as the large man with short blonde hair and the Tweedy-Pie build of weightlifter stepped forward, anger on his face.

"What the fuck did you just say?"

Blake now had the pecking order sorted and would take this fucker out first. Not many people realised that when Jack took his men on, he had them all do a four-week course in the Russian Martial Art known as Systema, with the top instructor and a personal friend of his. The man had looked unassuming with a quiet calm about him that had fooled them all until one by one he had taken out every member of Jack's team as Jack had stood back with a shit eating grin on his face.

It had been the best training he had ever had and at this second, he was more than grateful. Staring down the leader he straightened his stance but still maintaining a non-threatening pose and kept the other men in his peripheral. The carpark was relatively empty with no immediate weapons they could use, although he easily identified plenty of things he could use.

The leader moved, aiming a kick to his groin. Blake avoided it with a sidestep then caught the man's leg, extending the movement and unbalancing his attacker who fell to the ground with ease. Needing to make sure he stayed there, Blake stomped on his jaw, feeling the bone break and the man pass out.

He turned and the second attacker moved in with a haymaker punch which Blake stopped at a distance with a brutal straight jab with his foot to the area between his foreleg and hip, shattering the neck of his femur as the man went down screaming in agony.

Arms came around his neck in an Indian Death Lock from behind. Blake immediately dropped and threw his attacker over his head, his elbow shattering as it hit the hard surface of the carpark. With only two men left, Blake sized them up. One stood in front and one behind him. Trying to keep moving, he let the man behind him think he had the upper hand by putting him in a shoulder lock and bending him over. Blake executed a forward roll bringing his legs into contact and knocking the attacker face down into the tarmac before neatly rolling to his feet.

The fifth and last man standing tried to run but Blake wasted no time and stalked him like a predatory cat and pinned him down and restrained him using the man's shoelaces on his feet and thumbs. The entire encounter had taken less than twenty seconds, but it always felt more protracted in the slow moments as he assessed each attack.

With a last look to the drunken men sprawled on the ground around him, he withdrew his phone and put in an anonymous call to the police and then one to Will to get the CCTV cleared from the bar. He headed to the car to see Pax with her mouth slightly open in shock watching him. He tapped on the window to get her to unlock the car as she just stared at him. With a shake of her head she seemed to snap out of the fog she was in and opened the door allowing to climb in.

"You okay, Gracie?" he asked softly taking in her shocked expression as she seemed to look at him like she hadn't seen him before.

"How did you...? Where did you...? Can you teach me?" she asked jumbling the three questions into one on top of the next.

He chuckled as he turned the ignition on and leaned over to fix her seatbelt then his own. "Systema. Hereford, and yes, I can," he said answering her questions. He shifted his head to her from the road and she was watching him again. Her eyes dark glassy pools, her face flushed. His body reacted to her unhidden desire, his dick twitching from being close to her, dancing with her, and now the leftover adrenalin.

"You keep looking at me like that and we won't make it home."

She blushed red even in the darkness of the cab he could see it. "That was so fucking hot."

So was her dirty fucking mouth.

Blake pressed the pedal on the accelerator and drove faster wanting to be inside this woman more than his next breath.

CHAPTER TWENTY-SIX

As THEY DROVE to the hospital the next morning to see her father and try and get some answers from him, Pax kept sneaking glances at Blake. Seeing him take care of those five men on his own as if they were no more than flies to be swatted was something else. She had known he was skilled but had no idea he was that highly trained.

He had been like a machine, an action hero like she had seen in movies not the sweet, cheeky man she loved. It had been hot as hell and the sex after had her blushing as she remembered practically climbing him as he tried to get them upstairs without waking anyone.

Blake was an enigma in some ways. To look at him no one would ever know he could do the things he could, but she should have guessed Jack and Eidolon did not just take on men who were trained, they took on men who were exceptional at what they did. Each man had a skill set that was second to none and Blake's was close protection and protect he had—not even breaking a sweat or breathing hard.

He glanced across at her as she sighed in contentment. "Everything all right?"

Pax nodded as she smiled. "Just reliving last night. I still can't believe you took out five men like that."

Blake shrugged as if it was nothing and maybe to him it wasn't. "Just sorry it messed up our first date."

"Are you kidding? That was the best date ever."

Blake snorted. "I'm beginning to think you have a bloodthirsty streak."

"Yeah, maybe. Nothing like watching your man fight to the death protecting you to get the juices flowing," she teased back.

"It wasn't exactly to the death, Grace."

"Hush, you're spoiling it," she said making a silence motion with her hand but the smile on her face gave her away and made him shake his head on a laugh.

"Right, woman, back to business. We need to find out if your father has any idea where Clark Baker might be. The prints from the Nixons are his and from what I can get from chatter Will is collecting, and what our guys have seen, he's in the wind."

Pax glanced at him. "When did you hear that?"

"Will sent me the results through a few minutes ago."

"I'm not sure Dad will be much help," she replied sobering at the thought Clark was out there, and they had no idea where.

The rest of the drive was quiet, and they pulled into the hospital car park before taking the elevator to the fifth floor where her father was now recovering well. They approached the room and saw Eddie seated outside.

"Hey, Eddie," she greeted him with a smile.

Pete and Eddie had always been kind and loyal. When Blake had called Pete earlier with news of Clark being a suspect and unreachable, he had immediately agreed to make sure Henrietta and Robert were covered at all times.

Her grandfather had not been so easily convinced and dismissed the idea until she asked him to be careful for her sake. Not able to resist his granddaughter's pleas, he had agreed to have his security team look into things.

"Hey, Miss Grace," he said and nodded at Blake.

"He awake?" she asked motioning to her father's room as sudden butterflies took flight in her tummy. She hadn't spoken to him since the argument at his place and things had been said that couldn't be taken back. He'd still been unconscious when she'd seen him just after his surgery.

"I'll say. He's chomping at the bit to get home already."

Pax let a laugh escape at the idea of her dad driving the staff crazy. Opening the door she saw him propped up in bed. A giant grin lit his face at the sight of her and she had to fight the urge to run to him as she had when she was a girl. Blake at her back kept her grounded as she noticed the monitors.

"Gracie," he exclaimed with a welcoming smile.

She moved to stand beside the bed, and he reached for her hand. She let him take it and tried not to let tears show. "How do you feel?"

"Like I got charged by a bull elephant but other than that good." His face had some colour, but he still looked weaker than she could ever remember seeing him.

"Do feel up to answering some questions?"

He looked at her with sadness. "Of course. I'll do whatever I can to help."

She and Blake took a seat beside him.

"Robert, can you tell us how you met Henrietta?" Blake was taking the lead knowing some of the questions might be difficult for her to ask.

A smile crossed her father's face that she had never seen before as he began to speak. "She was the most beautiful woman I'd ever met. Long red hair, pale skin, and a smile that lit the whole room. I was gone for her the second we met, and to my utter amazement she felt the same. I was working as a scientist for Collatech and she was visiting with her father."

"Wasn't Collatech owned by Lance Baker?" Blake interrupted.

Her dad nodded. "Yes, and from what I know it was sinking. Albert was going to invest money in the company as soon as Clark and Henri married but then we met, and she couldn't go through with it. I know it was wrong—we both did—but we were in love. I never knew it could feel like that. She broke off the engagement and Albert was furious, but he wanted the world to see how much he supported his family, so he had the idea to start Sana with me as the lead scientist and MD."

"How did Clark end up on the board?" Pax asked learning more than she ever had.

"Albert said he owed him after what we had done, and his appointment appeased Lance Baker, Clark's dad, who was his best friend. We didn't care as long as we were together. Everything was great. We had a beautiful daughter who was the light of our lives. Henrietta would spend hours just holding you in her arms gazing at you."

"What happened?"

He shook his head as if confused. "I'm not sure. When you were around thirteen, she started to withdraw and began cheating on me."

"You knew?" Blake asked as Pax swallowed.

"Of course I did but I love her. She is still my Henri and I know she got lonely when I was building the business."

"Tell me about Sally Nixon and the drug trial you offered them." Blake had finally asked the question they most needed the answer to.

Robert looked confused. "I didn't offer them a trial. I sent your mother to offer to pay the medical bills. I know how much that boy meant to you, Gracie, and we wanted to help."

Pax shook her head as she stood and paced to the window. "No, Momma told me you offered them an illegal trial of a drug you knew was dangerous."

"Never," he exclaimed looking angry. "I would never do such a thing. I am many things, Grace, but I would never harm a child or perform illegal trials. I thought you were lashing out because I hadn't invented a drug that could help him."

Pax saw the truth in his face all these years she had believed him a monster when it was all a lie. "Why did she lie to me?"

"Jealousy," Blake said beside her.

She turned to look at him. "Jealousy?"

"She was jealous of you, Grace. You said yourself you were the apple of your father's eye as she had been. I thought it before but now I'm convinced that's the case."

"So who offered the Nixons the trial?" Robert asked not wanting to acknowledge his wife's lies to his daughter. Pax took her dad's hand, guilt flooding her at the way she had believed her mother and subsequently treated her father.

"My guess is Clark Baker, but I need to make some calls and have a few things checked out." Blake stood and squeezed her shoulder. "You okay here for a bit? I'll just be in the hall."

"Yes, go. I'll wait." Pax watched Blake leave but not before flashing her a wink that made her heart jump in her throat.

"He loves you," her father said quietly.

"I love him too."

"I know you do, my sweet girl. I can see it in your face. You look at him like Henri used to look at me."

"I'm so sorry, Daddy," she said as a sob pushed through her voice.

"Nonsense."

Her father opened his arms and she flew into them, careful not to disturb the monitors. The familiar feeling of her daddy's arms around her opened a flood gate of emotion that had backed up for years. Her father held her tight making her feel like a little girl again. Not wanting to put too much strain on him she pulled herself together and pushed the emotion down to be dealt with later.

Wiping her eyes and nose on a tissue he handed her from the box beside the bed she smiled at him. "I really am sorry. I should never have believed her."

"Why wouldn't you? She's your mother and as far as you knew, she had no reason to lie to you. I'm just sorry it came to this."

"I guess we all have a lot of talking to do when everything is sorted."

He took her hand and squeezed. "I'd like that. What I still can't understand is how your mother knew about the trial if I didn't?"

"Would grandfather have told her?"

Her father shook his head. "No. He and Henri weren't close after she married me. Another thing I blame myself for."

"I think I know," Blake said as he stepped back into the room. "Eddie told me that on the day he drove your mother to see Sally Nixon about paying the hospital bills she saw Clark leaving the house. She had been standing at the front door for a few moments when she rushed back to the car without knocking and got in. She asked him to wait around the corner and twenty minutes or so later Clark came out."

"So, Mom knew all along and never said anything?" Pax felt hurt squeeze her chest.

"If that's the case, she's in danger too. A lab tech that worked on the trial has just been found dead in her home. A single gunshot to the head. It seems Clark is killing everyone who had information about the trial."

"Does he know she saw him?" Robert asked clearly distressed now.

Pax rubbed her father's arm. "It's okay, Dad. We'll go over now and make sure mom is safe." She looked at Blake who nodded.

"Okay good. She isn't a bad person, Grace."

"I know," she responded but wasn't entirely sure what she believed any more. With a kiss to her father's cheek she slid her hand into Blake's and turned for the door.

"Blake?" her father called.

"Yes?"

"Take care of my girl—please."

"With my life, sir."

The words reverberated around her causing a sick feeling to lurch in her tummy. Part love that he would do that for her and part fear that he would do that for her.

CHAPTER TWENTY-SEVEN

BLAKE WAS on the phone to Reid, Waggs, and Decker as soon as he hit the car. He needed eyes on Clark. The feeling of urgency swirled through him at the thought of him killing Henrietta and what that might do to Grace.

"Reid," he said as soon as the man picked up. "I need you to go to Henrietta Paxton's home and make sure she's safe. Pax and I are on our way there now, but it looks like she had knowledge of the trial. We don't know if Clark knows so she could be in danger."

"Shit. Okay, on my way now. Will update as soon as I get eyes on her." He hung up and Blake quickly dialled Waggs and confirmed he hadn't seen Clark either. Blake told him to get inside his house and see if he could find any evidence that included the trial or his possible whereabouts. Blake knew he was blurring the lines of legality, but he didn't care, they could deal with that later. Right now he needed information fast.

The last call was to Decker. "Decker, please tell me you have eyes on Clark?"

"No, I haven't had eyes on him since before the Nixon shooting. He must be holed up somewhere, but I've got a lead on a fishing cabin in San Bernardino that his sister owns with her husband. I'm going to check it out."

"Okay, check in as soon as you know anything and be careful. This asshole has already killed three people in cold blood."

"Relax, Blake, I know what I'm doing."

Blake hung up and looked at Pax who had been quiet since they'd left the hospital. "How you doing?"

She shrugged. "Not sure. I feel a little numb. I'm relieved my dad didn't do those things, but it's tempered with guilt that I believed my mom. Then there's the fact she lied to me and hurt me. I guess I'm confused and need more answers."

Blake took her hand and kissed the knuckles. "We'll get them." They were halfway to her home when Reid called.

He answered with the hands-free. "Reid you're on speaker."

Reid paused and Blake knew the news wasn't good.

"Tell me," Pax demanded.

"I'm at your parent's place and it looks trashed. Your mom is gone, and Pete is dead." Reid delivered the news clinically and concisely. Blake heard Pax suck in a breath at the words, but she remained calm.

"Shit. Any leads?" Blake asked.

"Nothing but someone is injured as there's blood in the hallway that can't belong to Pete."

"Okay, I'm calling Decker. Stay off your phone. I'll call you straight back." Blake hung up and called Decker and explained. "The cabin is our best lead. Send me the address and wait for us to get there before you approach."

He called Waggs to re-route him to the cabin and then did the same with Reid. The drive was tense as they were lost in their own thoughts. He couldn't do the thing he wanted most—which was to drop Grace somewhere safe and go find Clark. He respected her, and she would never allow it.

They were met by Decker and Waggs on the road about a mile out from the cabin, the two men looking every inch the operators they were. Both dressed in black combat pants, black long sleeved shirts, and black military boots. Only their faces were visible along with the diver's watches they wore.

"We have eyes on them?" Blake said as he got out of the car.

"Yes, we have eyes on Clark and Henrietta. He's injured. Looks like a gunshot to the thigh, probably from Pete," Decker replied calmly.

"And my mom?"

"She's fine but looks shaken."

"Where's Reid?"

"He's watching the cabin from higher up the ridge. He's scoping out the best points of access for a rescue."

Twenty minutes later Reid had joined them again. Blake looked at his teammates and Pax. "Okay. Let's discuss a plan." Ten minutes later the plan was set, all they needed was the darkness of night to fall.

As they waited, Blake changed into the same clothes as the other men and they checked and re-checked the weapons Waggs had provided for them.

"Will you be okay staying in the car alone?"

Pax rolled her lips in as she nodded. "Yes, I'd rather be there, but I know I'd get in the way. Plus, I have a gun and the comms you gave me."

Not willing to be totally out of the loop Pax had demanded a comms so she could listen in. Blake hadn't liked it, but Reid had convinced him it was a good idea for peace of mind for him and her. The birds began to quiet as the dusk settled around them, blanketing the secluded cabin in darkness.

"Time to go," he said sliding his hand into Pax's hair and cupping her head so he could kiss her.

The kiss was over before he wanted but going to rescue her mother with an erection was not part of the plan. He watched Pax lock the car's doors and put her gun on her lap before he gave a short wave and walked away. He hated leaving her, but he had no choice.

Pulling his night vision goggles into place he and his team headed towards the cabin. With the Silverwood lake to the east of the cabin and the ridge behind it, the best penetration point was to get Waggs up on the hill and Decker covering the lakeside. He and Reid would move in from either side and breach the cabin through the back door.

The cabin itself was a single storey and made of logs with a wrap-around porch at the front and sides. From what they could tell, the main floor was a combined kitchen living space with a hallway that led to the bedrooms and bathroom at the back. Two bedrooms looked to the ridgeline and a smaller bedroom and bathroom were on the south side.

Reid had used a high powered zoom to determine Henrietta was being held in the main room with Clark.

On silent feet, Blake approached the bedroom window on the southside and waited for the team to be in place. When low murmurs came over the comms saying they were ready, Blake waited for Reid to give the go order. As the hostage rescue specialist, Blake had him take the lead.

"Go, go, go," Reid whispered.

Immediately Blake moved towards the window and breached it with no sound. Climbing through he caught movement as Reid slithered through the bathroom window. He kept his rifle on his shoulder as he listened to see if Clark had heard them. The silence was deafening.

Creeping down the hallway, he checked each room making sure it was clear before poking his head around the corner into the main room. Clark was facing away until Henrietta looked up. Something on her face must have alerted him and he turned, weapon up, and fired at them.

He was never going to be fast enough though and Blake shot him in the shoulder throwing the gun from his hand. Before Clark could move and go for the gun again, Blake was on him pinning him to the ground as the man wailed and shrieked in pain.

Leaving Reid to restrain him, Blake moved to Henrietta and crouched low to speak to her. "Are you hurt?"

She shook her head, her face streaked with tears. "No, he didn't hurt me." Her voice trembled as she spoke.

The usually put-together woman was anything but that now with her clothes torn, make-up running, and hair dishevelled. Gently he helped her to stand as Decker and Waggs moved Clark to a sitting position.

"You're too late," the man laughed. His face held the maniacal expression of someone who was becoming unhinged.

Cold lumps of ice settled in Blake's gut when he heard the woman he loved scream over the comms before the connection went dead.

———

Pax listened as Blake spoke to her mother, her heart in her mouth until she heard her mom's voice say she was unhurt. The relief was immeasurable, the weight lifted from her as she let out an audible breath in the darkness of the car. Dropping her head she almost jumped out of her skin when a knock on the window had her looking up, a smile half-formed on her face, thinking it was one of the guys.

It fell from her lips when she saw Eddie standing there with a gun pointed at her father's head. A scream fell from her lips before he shook his head and motioned for her to open the door. Cautiously, she took a deep breath and opened the door, hoping the team could hear what was going on through her comms unit. She hadn't asked if it was two way and if they could hear her too. Another rookie error that might cost her dearly.

"Eddie, what's going on?" she asked as she kept her voice calm and her hands up where he could see them.

The glance she cast at her father showed the pale waxiness of his skin which worried her greatly. He was recovering from major surgery and looked unwell to say the least.

"Move over there, Miss Grace." The tone of his voice was the same as it had always been—kind and gentle. She needed to appeal to his better nature.

"Why are you doing this, Eddie? My father is sick. He should be in the hospital."

Her father was gagged but at the sight of his daughter in front of a gun, began to squirm and fight. He was no match for Eddie who had been their security for years and was still a fit man. He hit her father on his head with the back of the gun, and she watched in horror as he fell to the ground.

With no care for herself or the gun trained on her, she fell to her father's side and cradled his head in her hands as tears fell down her cheeks.

She looked up at the man who had pushed her on the swing and driven her to her first dance and cried. "Why?" she screamed at him anger replacing the fear.

He looked haggard and tired but remained resolute. "I'm getting old, Miss Grace and Clark Baker offered me enough money to start a new life away from here with untold luxury."

"Money? You're betraying my family for money?" she asked incredulously.

"Easy to dismiss when you have it, Grace, but not when you don't."

"Did you kill Sally and Marvin Nixon too?"

"They were going to spill their guts about Clark, and he wanted them taken care of. Stupid fucker decided to watch and left his prints behind. I should have gotten out then, but I always see things through. I have some honour left."

"Honour? You helped him take my mom and you're here with my father. I guess the plan is that we all die?"

Eddie nodded. "Clark has transferred ten million dollars to my account for offing you and your father. That's a lot of money, girlie. Much as I like you, and I do, I really do, I can use that money for my own kids, and I love them more."

"Please, don't do this," she begged, tears streaming now as she looked him in the eye.

"I'm sorry, Grace," he said and lifted the gun to her head.

In that second all she wanted was to tell Blake she loved him and to tell her mom she forgave her. Closing her eyes she heard the explosion of a gunshot and waited for the pain.

It never arrived and she opened her eyes to see Eddie collapse to the ground from a shot to the head. She looked around and didn't see anyone. She turned back to her father and dragged the cloth from his mouth. Pax stroked his face as she spoke to her unconscious father and begged him not to leave her.

A few minutes later she heard the sound of feet running before Blake rounded the vehicle and fell to his knees in front of her. He hauled her into his arms as she held on to him and her dad and cried.

"Jesus, Gracie, you scared the crap out of me." He pulled away and ran his hands over her "Thought I'd lost you." His voice sounded choked as he kissed her quickly and then tore her away as Waggs worked on her dad.

She shivered in Blake's arms as he held her tight not once letting go. Not when the police turned up, not when the EMTs arrived and loaded her father who was still unconscious into an ambulance, and not even when her mother put her arms around her, and they cried together.

Blake was her rock and she never wanted to be away from him again. She would follow this man to the ends of the earth but as she watched her mother climb into the back of the ambulance beside her father, she couldn't help but feel fear. They had been in love like she and Blake were and look how that turned out.

CHAPTER TWENTY-EIGHT

THEY WERE MET at the hospital by Albert and two detectives who wanted statements from them, not to mention a district attorney who wanted them charged with impeding an investigation. Blake couldn't find it in him to care at that moment. All he wanted was Grace checked over and her parents to be given the all clear.

Lucky for him, Albert had not arrived alone. He had his lawyer with him who quickly interceded and bought them some time. He sat with Grace in the waiting room after she was checked and cleared at his insistence, her head on his shoulder. Henrietta was beside Albert who had rushed to his daughter and folded her into his arms, the fear and affection he had hidden thus far clearly evident. To be fair, the man had not left her side as they waited for word on Robert who had been rushed back into the ICU.

Waggs, Reid, and Decker had given their statements to the police and had been told to stick around until the detectives could verify who they were. The three men were sitting on the opposite side of the waiting room giving them space but offering silent support. With Grace nestled into his body, her heat warming his side and knowing she was safe, he allowed his brain to go over the events of the last few days.

Pax had repeated what Eddie said to her and having heard things only from her side before, things became more apparent. What he still didn't know was if Clark had known Henrietta had seen him that day when he'd offered the trial to the Nixons and why she had lied to Grace about it. Those he could find the answers too and hopefully he'd also get answers to the more important question of who'd shot Eddie.

None of his team had and nobody had been seen near the cabin. It left a loose end that made him feel edgy. As if everything wasn't entirely done with.

"You want me to grab you some coffee?" he asked Pax who raised her tired eyes to him.

"Please."

"I'll come with you," Henrietta said.

Blake stiffened slightly but kept quiet as Albert moved beside Grace and put his arm around her shoulders and kissed her head. The man was like a different person. With a nod to Reid to keep an eye on them, he walked down the hall towards the vending machines with a quiet Henrietta beside him.

They stopped and got coffee before she spoke. "I feel I owe you an apology and an explanation."

"Not me, but to Grace you do," he said tightly.

"I know." She wrung her hands and he felt a modicum of sympathy for her.

"Have a seat," he offered, pointing to the seats behind them.

With a grateful smile she sat and faced him and for the first time he noticed the grit behind the woman. "I was like Grace growing up. I adored my father and he adored me. When my mom died it was just us and we were close. I was the good girl, never gave him a moment of trouble. Clark and I had always been friends, but I never loved him like that." She looked away as if composing her thoughts. "When my father proposed the marriage, I went along with it and let it happen. I wanted to please him. Then I met Robert and it was love at first sight." She looked embarrassed as she spoke but went on. "I know it's a cliché but it's true. I didn't know how to tell my father and let things get out of hand until I had to say something or risk losing the man I loved. My father was furious and never really forgave me for the public outrage I caused."

Henrietta took a sip of the coffee as Blake stayed silent letting her purge her guilt. "Publicly he backed Robert and me, but in private he was cold. I didn't care. I had Robert and then we had Grace. She was such a beautiful child and became a clever and stunning woman. Robert adored her and she adored him. I saw my previous relationship with my father in them. My husband worked long hours and when he was home, he only seemed to make time for Grace and I'm afraid I handled things badly. I looked for affection elsewhere. Even though I loved my husband and daughter, I was jealous."

"Why lie about Robert being the one to offer the trial?" he asked not willing to let her off the hook just yet.

"Clark came to me and told me he knew I'd seen him and if said anything, he would hurt Grace."

"So you decided to say nothing?" Blake stated as he sat forward.

"By that time I had isolated myself. Grace tolerated me, and Robert would have been gung-ho trying to protect us and would have gotten himself hurt. I figured if I drove a wedge between them then it would keep her safe." She held up her hand to stop him as he went to speak. "I know now it was wrong and I caused a lot of hurt I can never take back. But whether you believe me or not, I love my daughter and husband and would do it again if I thought it would keep them safe. I know it didn't but that is my guilt to carry for the rest of my life."

"I think you need to be honest with Robert and Grace. Grace is an amazing woman with a lot of love in her heart and despite everything you've put her through, she loves you." Henrietta went to speak but this time he stopped her. "But make no mistake, if you hurt her again it won't be her that puts distance between you. It will be me. I love her and I'll not see her ground into dust by jealousy or bitterness. Do you get me?"

Henrietta nodded. "Yes, I understand."

Blake nodded once and stood, giving the woman his arm as a peace offering. She took it and together they carried coffee back to the waiting room. Grace looked up and a slight frown marred her eyes before he smiled and let go of Henrietta when the doctor came in.

"Mrs Paxton?"

"Yes, that's me," Henrietta said as she reached her hands out to Grace and Albert, seeking their support.

Blake moved in behind Grace and slipped his hand around her waist from behind as she relaxed into his body wanting his strength.

"Your husband is a very resilient man and only received a minor concussion. He is, however, going to need to be monitored more closely because of the recent surgery and heart attack but as it stands, I can cautiously say he will make a full recovery."

"Oh, thank God." Henrietta seemed to sag against her father, and he felt Pax lean into him as the adrenalin that had been keeping her awake seemed to leave her as relief hit.

"Can we see him?"

"Yes, but two at a time and no excitement," the doctor warned with a stern frown.

Blake waited with Albert as Grace and her mother were led back to the ICU and then headed over to Reid and Decker. "Where did Waggs go?"

Decker motioned towards the door. "He went for some air."

"Any word from Jack?"

"He wants you to call him but said someone will call as soon as Clark says anything of interest."

It always amazed Blake that Jack seemed to have contacts everywhere willing to help him out or give him information. It made him wonder why Grace, who seemed to have informants coming out of every nook in Europe, had never mentioned any in the US.

"Okay. I'll call him now while Pax is with her dad."

He went to walk away but Reid stopped him. "Any idea who the shooter was?"

Blake swung back and shook his head. "No, but I want answers on that too."

Moving into the relative privacy of the hospital's spiritual garden, Blake called Jack. "Any news," he asked when Jack answered. A pause on the line made him tense. "Tell me, Jack."

"I'm waiting for confirmation, but Clark is saying he was contacted by a British agent offering assistance with taking down Robert Paxton. He also says this man ordered the attack on Pax in the UK."

"I'm gonna kill him when I find out who it is," Blake gritted out, feeling fury pump his veins with blood.

"Yeah, well, we might have an answer on that soon. Mitch and Gunner are still MIA, but Will is trying to clean up an image of someone leaving the area shortly after Eddie was killed."

"You think that our mole killed Eddie? That makes no sense. Why have Pax beaten and betray us, and then save her life?"

"I don't know yet, but we're getting closer. I can feel it."

"Fine, call me when you have news." Blake rubbed his head and hung up.

The lines were starting to blur between the two cases, and he wondered if the attack on Pax that started his involvement was a ruse to split the Eidolon team. A shadow fell across him and he glanced up seeing Waggs walking towards him.

"Hey, how she doing?" Waggs asked as he sat down with a tired sigh.

Blake looked at his friend and noticed the tiredness he knew was mirrored in him. "Okay, I think. She and her parents have a lot to figure out but now that Clark is in custody she can move forward."

"She's a tough cookie."

Blake smiled. "She sure is but then she works for Roz, so that's a given. My balls shrivel when I think about working for that woman."

Waggs chuckled and they sat in comfortable silence for a beat. "You gonna stick around and see your family or fly back with us?"

Waggs hadn't had time to see his family while he was Stateside, and Blake knew he missed them. "Not sure. Depends on Jack."

Blake nodded. Eidolon came first with all of them or it had. Now Grace was front and centre in his thoughts nearly all the time. "I better get back in," he said standing.

"Make sure you rest that knee," Waggs said when he groaned at the stiff joint.

"Yes, Mother."

"Fuck off, asshole," Waggs called making Blake laugh.

When he reached the ICU, he saw Grace and her mum walking out, arms around each other, heads together. He moved to them and Grace released her mum and slid into his embrace, planting her head on his chest.

He stroked her hair as he held her tight. "Tired, beautiful?"

She nodded against his chest. "Yep."

"Let's get a hotel close so we can be here for your dad." He saw Henrietta walk away, head down and alone and called out to her. "Henrietta, would you like to come with us? I can get a room for you as well."

Pax lifted her head and he caught the soft tender look she gave him in his toes.

Henrietta looked at him hopefully before turning to Grace as if asking for permission.

"Come on, Mom, come with us and then we can visit Dad together tomorrow." She held her hand out for her mom, who took it, and they walked to the car for some much-needed sleep.

It was cut short when his phone rang, and Jack was displayed on the screen.

"Sorry, give me a sec," he said holding his finger up and stepping away. "Jack?"

"We found Mitch. He's been roughed up and locked in a shed at his place. He confirms it was Gunner who attacked him."

"So, you're absolutely sure?" Blake asked not wanting to believe it.

"I have a confirmed sighting of him in the US two days ago and the image Will is cleaning up places him at the cabin when Eddie was shot."

"So he shot Eddie? That makes no sense. Is he out to finish Eidolon or protect us?"

"At this point we don't know but it seems he's working against us. It's possible he's being forced into it, and that would explain why he's still protecting certain people."

"Fuck, this is so twisted. I really hoped we were wrong."

"Me too," Jack added quietly.

"When are we telling the others?"

"Day after you get back. That gives us time to make sure we've not made a horrible mistake."

"Do you think that's possible?" Blake asked still hopeful.

"No, I don't." Jack said tiredly.

Blake knew this would be taking a huge toll on his boss as it would them all. Blake hung up after a few more seconds and shook his head trying to make sense of it. He couldn't and he knew he never would.

———

HE WATCHED Blake and Pax leave the hospital with a heavy weight on his chest. He had killed Eddie when he'd seen him lift the gun to Pax. Whether Blake would ever know or believe it now or not, he considered him a friend and he would never allow her to be taken from him if he could help it. The attack he had orchestrated on Pax had been the single lowest point of his life. He didn't believe women were the weaker sex but two against one, and one who had no skill to fight was despicable. He was vile. He thought about the woman who had been on his mind since the Christmas Eve wedding of a good friend.

She had been beautiful and resilient and so fucking proud. He had been bowled over by her. But much as she had shown an interest, he would not touch her. He would not drag a woman like her into the underbelly of society where he now resided. He had betrayed his friends and teammates and it didn't matter that his reasons for doing so were pure.

He was a traitor and he knew it was only a matter of time before Jack and the others identified him. He was done with Eidolon and the knowledge made him want to vomit on his shoes. It had been the greatest honour of his life serving with those men, but his life was leading him on a different path now.

He could no longer protect his friends from inside their missions, he would just have to try and do so from afar. Turning, he walked away and prayed that when this job was done, and the man he was protecting was exonerated, he would be left alone. Maybe they would put a bullet in him and end his sorry ass. It was no more than he deserved and quite honestly, his life meant nothing to him now.

Yet the image of Lacey filled his vision and he wished things had been different. That he could be the man to help her heal from the trauma she had gone through. A man worthy of a woman like her. One that was filled with light when his own world was now filled with nothing but darkness and death.

CHAPTER TWENTY-NINE

THEY HAD BEEN BACK in the UK for three days now and Blake was on his way to a meeting at Eidolon. He knew Jack would be telling the other men about the traitor and his identity. He felt bile fill his stomach at the thought that his friend could do this to them. Mitch had been told to keep quiet until Jack could break to news and had reluctantly agreed.

Clark Baker had admitted ordering the deaths of Sally and Marvin Nixon and the lab tech. He had also admitted his involvement with the illegal drug trial years ago and the plan for the one involving the Princess and was being charged with conspiracy to commit murder, kidnap, and a whole host of other charges relating to fraud. He had not named the British operative he'd first talked about saying he had no name and they had not met.

Baker was a classic example of a broken heart that had festered into a poisonous disease and caused him to do stupid things to prove himself worthy of a woman that would never love him. Blake's thoughts moved to Princess Louisa. He had made some inquiries and heard that she was now involved in a perfectly legal trial in Switzerland. With luck it would be a success and she would recover. Blake knew that the road for her parents would be long and gruelling, with no guarantees. He wished he could do something but there was nothing to be done except pray it worked and put their trust in the doctors.

Stepping into the conference room he took the last seat as Jack nodded at him. It was time for the rest of the team to know the truth.

"Thank you for coming in on a Sunday," Jack began as Will sat beside him, his face stony and angrier than Blake had ever seen. Blake could feel the tension coming from the men around him—they knew something was up. "I called you here because earlier this year we discovered there was a traitor sabotaging missions inside the team." A hushed whisper moved through the men as they looked at the others and around the room. One seat was obviously empty. The atmosphere could be cut with a knife as the tension went sky high.

"We have now identified and confirmed the traitor."

Blake flexed his jaw the fury at finding out Pax had been hurt because of his teammate was still a bitter pill to swallow.

Jack gave a tight nod to Will who brought an image on the screen with a few clicks of his fingers. An audible gasp of disbelief filled the room as they saw the picture of a man they had considered a friend, but who had now turned against them.

"Gunner Ramberg is now considered an enemy of Eidolon. I know this is a hard thing to acknowledge but nevertheless, it's the case. We don't know why or who he's working with, but it seems the objective is to bring this team down." He nodded at Blake and Alex. "Blake and Alex have been working on some theories but if anyone has any information, no matter how small, we need to know. This is our primary focus now. I want Gunner found and brought to justice. Nobody betrays my team and gets away with it."

"So that's why we were all on lockdown?" Mitch asked.

His jaw was tight, and Blake could see the anger radiating through the usually calm man as he held Jack's eyes.

"Yes, my only priority was, and is, to protect the team. Sometimes that means pissing off an individual." Jack held up his hand to calm the immediate angry response from the team. "I understand it's not nice to be kept out of the loop or come under a microscope. However, there were no obvious weaknesses in this team. Each one of you was chosen by me for your individual skill set and integrity, so to have to worm out a traitor was not an easy task."

Lopez looked at Blake and then Jack. "How come Blake was brought in on it? Why not Decker as he's the profiler?"

Jack was a fair and formidable leader, but he would not take kindly to being questioned in this way, so Blake, braced.

"I am not going to give you an answer to that, Lopez. What I will say is I had my reasons and you either accept that or you don't. If any of you feel you can no longer trust my judgement or leadership then you are free to walk away. Make no mistake, I will be sorry to see you go, but I cannot run this team without full trust in my abilities and I will not be questioned over my decisions."

Blake glanced around the room waiting to see if anyone walked. He would be shocked if they did but people reacted in different ways to betrayal.

"Anyone?" Jack waited a full minute, and no one moved. "Good. Now, let's get down to the business of tracking this target."

The rest of the meeting was loud and angry as the others tried to make sense of the situation they now found themselves in. Gunner had been a good man, an excellent operator, and friend to them all. None of them could understand what had caused him to turn on them. Blake had no doubt they would find him, and they would get answers one way or another.

Whether Gunner lived through that was not definite. Eidolon did not take something as serious as this lightly and as the men around him fizzed with fury. He knew it depended on which team member found him first whether Gunner kept his life or not.

When the meeting wound up two hours later there was still no set plan in place. They had agreed to meet Monday morning and review the last eight missions to see where Gunner may have been involved.

Now he just wanted to get home, pick up Grace, and take her for lunch. The last week with her parents had been emotional for her. Henrietta had been true to her word and admitted to Grace what she'd told him, doing so in front of her husband. There would be a long road ahead of them to get back to a place where they were a real family again, but they had made a start and despite his initial thoughts he knew they would make it.

Grace had so much love in her and she would be the glue that fixed that family.

He pulled into her drive and jogged to the door using his key to get in. He found the living room empty and called out to her. "Grace?"

"Out here," she called, and he felt the smile tip his lips up. He moved through the kitchen to the back garden of her house and found her doing stretches with Evelyn.

"What you girls up to?" he asked as he sat in the rattan chair. He was enjoying the sight of Grace in the skin-tight athletic shorts and bra top as she bent over to stretch her thigh muscles.

She laughed catching sight of him watching. "Stop perving, Cal."

He threw his hands up. "What? I can't help it. I'm only human."

"Well, go be human someplace else until I've finished this training session with Siren."

True to her word Roz had every member of the Zenobi team working with Pax to get her up to speed with hand to hand and firearms. This was her second training session and from what he'd seen from her first, she was picking things up without any problems.

"How about I finish moving my stuff in here and then we go for a late lunch?"

Pax stood up and faced him giving him her full attention. "I say it's a good plan." She smiled before going up on tiptoes for a sweet kiss that made his dick twitch.

His hand on her hip he growled. "Minx."

"What? I'm only human." She laughed as he swatted her ass and chuckled.

"You are so gonna pay for that," he replied with a stern look which only made her worse.

"Promises, promises."

"Okay, enough you two. Let's get the training done so I can go feel up my own man," Evelyn said.

Blake drove back to his place and finished packing his shit in record time before going home to Pax so he could take his woman out for lunch then spend the night making love to her.

EPILOGUE

Five Years Later

"We need to go get the kids."

Blake rolled over pinning his wife to the bed with his body. "Or we could stay here and let your parents have them for a bit longer." He nudged her thigh with his heavy cock. The husky whimper that came from her throat made him throb.

"That sounds like a plan. They do love having the girls and we do only have four more days here in L.A," she agreed as he kissed his way down her neck before sucking the hard nub of her perfect nipples into his mouth swirling his tongue and nipping the tender skin. Her back arched into him and he slid his hands around her back cupping her ass in his hands.

He missed his Grace sleeping naked, but since the girls had been born, she liked to have something on when she got up in the night.

Ariella and Matilda were three and one respectively. Both girls had their mother's red hair, but Ariella had his blue eyes and Matilda had inherited her mother's hazel ones. Ariella was sweet with a gentle nature always wanting to please people and toe the line. Matilda was the complete opposite—she was full of life and always looking for mischief.

He adored them both with every bone in his body. He had never known a feeling like it until he held Ariella in his arms. It had only made what he felt for Grace so much stronger and he hadn't been sure that was possible.

Moving so he was entirely on top of her he felt the slick moisture of her desire as he moved his cock through the wetness teasing her clit.

"Oh, God. That feels so good."

He smiled against her lips before he kissed her. Grace was always so responsive to him, so ready for his touch even with two young kids and lives that were busier than ever.

She grabbed his ass and tried to guide him where she wanted him most and he chuckled as he pulled away from her kiss. "So impatient."

"Just fuck me, Cal."

The heat in her eyes her rosy cheeks plump soft lips and the nipples rubbing against him were more than he could take. He slid into her slowly, relishing every second of the tight heat. Her legs came around his waist as he rocked into her slowly building their climax as his pelvis grazed her clit on the upward stroke.

"I love you, Mrs Blake."

"I love you too, honey."

He felt her tense as her climax washed through her tightening her pussy around him like a vice, her legs shaking as she moaned his name. He stepped up the pace not letting her come down and felt her body begin to milk his cock again as the second climax hit and he came hard, his cock pulsing his release into her.

He groaned as he sagged his weight onto her, and she wrapped him up in her beauty. "Fuck, Grace, you are so beautiful."

"Thank you for giving me a beautiful life, Cal. Without you I wouldn't have my parents back or our girls."

Every time he thought he couldn't love her more she proved him wrong with a look or word or even her secret smile. The song they had danced to at their wedding played in his head. 'Secret Smile' by Semisonic. He had known when he met her, he wanted that smile for himself and now it was—forever.

"Baby, I didn't do that, you did. But I do know this. Every single thing we have, we built together, and it's the honour of my life to always call you mine, baby."

"Always, Cal."

BOOK 3 SNEAK PEAK

Reid: An Eidolon Black Ops Novel Book 3

PROLOGUE

"Move to secure the hostages, I'm going back for the girl."

"That's a negative, Alpha One. Secure the HVT and move to the exfil now."

Reid could hear his commander loud and clear but as he looked at the burning building, he couldn't just walk away and let a young girl, with her entire life ahead of her, die of smoke asphyxiation. He turned to his teammate, Holler, who was looking at him and waiting for the order.

As team leader it was his job to secure his men's safety and the safest option was to secure the HVT and get out of there. But with the image of his sisters Nessa and Tori in his mind, he couldn't walk away and let a child die.

"Secure the HVT and head for the exfil." He turned to Skinner. "You're with me. I'm not leaving that girl to die."

His teammates nodded and they took off towards the burning building, their bodies low as the sound of gunfire from down the street hit their ears.

This should have been an easy mission, but the intelligence they had was off. The terrorists had hit the building before they could get

Senator Reece and his family out. The objective had been to secure the Senator first. His bill to introduce new legislation regarding the unification of gun control throughout the States was high profile and receiving mixed responses.

He personally didn't give a fuck. He just wanted to do his job, and although technically the first objective was to secure the Senator and his family, when the building had blown his orders were changed to secure Reece and exfil.

He'd thought the girl had been off-site—had been assured she was off-site—but the Senator had been screaming for his daughter as they'd dragged him out the building. The soul-deep desperation as he begged them to save her had been something he couldn't and wouldn't walk away from.

Now as they entered the building and made their way over the burning beam that hung down from the floor above, he knew that it was very likely not all of them would walk out of the building alive. He turned to Skinner who was wearing the same expression. "You can—" Reid started.

"Shut your Southern trap. I ain't going nowhere."

Skinner was a damn good agent. Loyal and a brilliant tactician. Reid nodded and moved forward, ascending the stairs. Smoke was billowing around him, making visibility poor as he rounded the first set of stairs in the grand old building. With eight bedrooms, the place was like a maze in the daylight but at night with smoke and fire—not to mention the added threat that they had two armed terrorists still at large—it was a fucking quagmire of shit.

With his Heckler and Koch HK416 at his shoulder, Reid advanced down the second-floor landing towards the bedrooms. A wall of fire blocked his path as smoke burned his throat. "We need to find another way."

Skinner nodded and they backtracked into one of the first rooms at the top of the stairs to see if they could move through the rooms. He knew from the plans that the office to their left had a balcony. If they could get past that, he had a chance of getting in through the window.

"Alpha One, this is Tack. Please be advised that the HVT is secure. We have more heat headed our way and our window for exfil is closing."

"Good copy. We are closing in on the target now."

"Good copy. Tack out."

Reid knew his boss was pissed but he also knew he was a good man. As he'd expected, the balcony gave them access to the daughter's bedroom window. He and Skinner made their way over the ledge as another explosion rocked them, causing him to lose his footing on the ledge and have to grab for the windowsill. Using all his strength, he hauled himself up and used the butt of his gun to smash through the glass.

Pulling himself up and through, he hit the ground and came up to see one of the men they had been searching for standing over the form of the half-naked teen, his pants around his knees as he attempted to rape her.

Time stood still as he took in the scene, and watched the man grab for his gun. Reid reacted and fired, unflinching as the man fell dead on top of the girl he had been about to rape. On his feet again, he heard Skinner curse behind him as he came through the window.

He ignored his teammate as he approached the girl and dragged the dead man off her prone body. Relief hit him as he saw the man had not accomplished his heinous and depraved mission. He caught the terrified look in her eyes and held his hand up as if he was calming a skittish animal. Her wild eyes went between him and Skinner.

"Rachel, my name is Special Agent Reid. We're with the FBI. I need to know if you can walk?" He watched as she nodded. "Good, we're going to have to go out the window and descend using ropes. I'm going to need to secure you to a harness. Okay?"

Again she nodded, but this time moved to stand. He saw the blood and bruises on her face and felt his blood boil. Pushing back his anger, he moved to her and quickly secured her to a harness attached to Skinner.

"Alpha One, this is Tack. Sitrep."

"Tack, this is Alpha One. We have secured the target and taken out one of the Tangos."

"Good copy. Please move to exfil. Helo is five mikes out."

"Good copy, Tack. Alpha One out."

The room was filling with smoke now, the roar of fire beneath them loud in his ears. The heat was all around them, causing sweat to pour from his body.

Skinner moved out first and Reid asked Rachel to swing her leg over the edge. The girl followed his lead as Reid began to cough on the smoke.

"Go, I'm right behind you."

Skinner nodded and began the climb down with the girl. Redi was about to swing his leg over when the floor beneath him gave way and he found himself falling through the floor into the large dining room.

The oak dining table broke his fall. The landing taking the breath from him as he felt a rib crack, sharp pain lanced through him as ash and fiery debris rained down on him. Rolling off the table he fell to the floor as the heat from the fire around him burned his skin. Glass smashing from the heat gave him a vague idea of where the window might be.

Limping, Reid moved in that direction when he felt someone plough into his body, knocking him to the floor. Twisting he fought with the man on top of him trying to loosen his attacker's hold as he tightened his forearm around his throat in a choke hold—the hold combined with the lack of air from the fire made his vision spotty.

Sliding his left arm up inside the choke hold, he pushed his attacker's face to the side and with his right arm locked his hands and applied quick pressure, making the tango release his hold. Rolling, Reid hit the man with a one-two punch, but the smoke was getting to him and he could feel himself weakening.

He needed to end this fight quickly but couldn't get to his gun. Applying the same choke the attacker had used on him, he used the last of his strength to choke the man out. He fell back on the ground as he heard voices from the window. As his vision began to blur, he saw the face of Clayton East, his oldest friend and FBI Medic leaning over him.

"Always getting yourself into shit and needing me to save your ass," Clay said with a grin as he lifted Reid and half dragged, half carried him to the window before pushing him into Holler's waiting arms.

As soon as the cold, fresh air hit his lungs he began to cough, hacking up the smoke from his lungs. "The girl?" he asked in between bouts of coughing.

"The girl is secure and on her way to Memorial Hospital. We need to exfil and get you to the same place.

The three of them jogged to the second exfil sight on the outer ridge of the property, close to a ravine. He ignored the pain in his ribs and throat and ran beside Clay and Holler. The helo was hovering above them as they moved to crouch behind the rocks. A sudden burst of bullets from a machine gun made them duck, and Reid watched in horror as Holler fell, his body riddled with bullets.

Noise and pain fell away as Reid collapsed to his knees beside his friend trying to find a way to save him, even though he knew it was too late. The responding fire from the helo made the night silent again.

"Reid, come on, we need to go," Clay called.

Reid nodded, his emotions in a fog as he acted on instinct. He pushed his arms under the knees of his friend and lifted him. Clay moved around and together they carried the body of their friend to the helo that would take them to safety.

His eyes never left Holler as Clay shoved an oxygen mask over his face and Reid let him. This mission was fucked-up from beginning to end. Lack of reliable intelligence had put them all at risk. He went over and over in his mind what he could have done differently. Trying to see if he could have saved Holler.

The three of them—him, Holler and Clay had gone through HRT training together. Had been as thick as thieves and now Holler was gone. They all knew the risks but like so many, they thought they were invincible. Reid knew there would be an investigation into why he'd disobeyed a direct order.

He would do it again though, because that girl had not deserved to die for her father's mistakes. It was a feeling he knew all too well.

REID WALKED out of the office of the Director of the FBI offices at Quantico and felt the sun on his face. He was now officially a civilian. His superiors, although understanding of his decision to go back inside, could not ignore the fact he had disobeyed a direct order.

The HRT only worked because the men were able to carry out missions without question, he had been told. Offered a desk job or the opportunity to resign, he had signed his resignation letter there and then.

His best friend was leaning against a black truck, his arms crossed when he left the building.

"You quit?" Clay's tone was more statement than question though, he knew him better than anyone, except perhaps his mom.

"No other choice. I won't spend the rest of my career sitting at a desk."

"What you gonna do now?"

Reid slid into the passenger seat beside his friend. "Not sure, but a buddy of mine from Delta said there's an opportunity he's been offered in the private sector."

Clay angled his body in the seat to look at him, raising his brow. "And?" Clay knew him too well and knew there was more.

"It's in the UK."

Clay's eyebrows shot up and he drew in a breath. "Wow, you considering it?"

That was the sixty-four-thousand-dollar question. Was he considering it? All his life he had stayed close to his mom, helping out with the girls since his dad had left when he was ten. She didn't need him as much now Nessa and Tori were older and finding their own lives.

"Yeah, I think so. The guy heading this new team has a stellar reputation and the team he's putting together is in a class of its own."

"What they want with you then?" Clay joked as he started the car.

Reid laughed. "Yeah, good point."

They drove in silence for a bit towards the local bar they had been frequenting since they were old enough to drink before Clay finally spoke. "Seriously, Reid, you should take the job. It sounds like an amazing opportunity."

"Yeah, but mom..."

"Stop. You can't put your life on hold forever because your dad was a deadbeat asshole who left your mom high and dry. She and the girls will be fine, and I'll keep an eye on them for you."

"You could come with me," Reid suggested.

"Na, not me. I need to be stateside."

Reid understood. Clay was close to his family too and travelled upstate to see his younger sister every weekend.

"I guess I'm going to the UK then."

"Guess so, but before you do, you're buying."

"Will you really keep an eye on Mom and the girls for me?"

"Sure, but you owe me."

Reid laughed knowing that watching over two teenage girls wasn't his friend's idea of fun anymore than it was his. "I'll owe you."

"Yes, you will."

BOOKS BY MADDIE WADE

Healing Danger

Stolen Dreams

Love Divided

Secret Redemption

Broken Butterfly

Arctic Fire

Phoenix Rising

Nate & Skye Wedding Novella

Digital Desire

Paradise Ties: A Fortis Wedding Novella (Coming Soon)

Alex

Blake

Reid (Coming Soon)

Deadly Alliance

Knight Watch (Coming Soon)

Tightrope One

Tightrope Two

CONTACT ME

If stalking an author is your thing and I sure hope it is then here are the links to my social media pages. If you prefer your stalking to be more intimate, then my group Maddie's Minxes will welcome you with open arms.

General Email: info.maddiewade@gmail.com
    Email: maddie@maddiewadeauthor.co.uk
    Website: http://www.maddiewadeauthor.co.uk
    Facebook page: https://www.facebook.com/maddieuk/
    Facebook group: https://www.facebook.com/groups/546325035557882/
    Amazon Author page: amazon.com/author/maddiewade
    Goodreads: https://www.goodreads.com/author/show/14854265.Maddie_Wade
    Bookbub: https://partners.bookbub.com/authors/3711690/edit
    Twitter: @mwadeauthor
    Pinterest: @maddie_wade
    Instagram: Maddie Author

Printed in Great Britain
by Amazon

40187128R00139